# A Little Bird

CW00432915

OCTOBER

ISBN: 9798701953589

# A Little Birdie Told Me…

This book is set in the 1980s, so some expressions may appear odd to the modern reader. Of course every family is different but, during my childhood, first names were out of bounds when talking to most older people, unless they were close family friends.

In this book, the work undertaken by the staff at Rockbeare is based on my experiences while employed at two care homes. Each home had vastly different routines and methods of operation. One expected the young – and untrained – staff to undertake the personal care of the residents, while the other offered excellent care with trained nursing staff. This home asked the residential workers to serve and eat with the residents, which sounds lovely, but it could be frustrating for those trying to watch their weight. However, Rockbeare is entirely fictional.

I hope you enjoy this novel. For those who lived through the eighties, it may bring back some nostalgic memories. For those born later, it gives a glimpse into an era just before the birth of internet, while mobile phones were in their infancy. It was also a time of fun music and 'interesting' fashion although, by 1988, the zany colours of the early eighties had (thankfully for my teenage self) become more muted.

# Chapter 1

On the patio outside, two women tussled over my hoover. One gripped the handle, while the other clung to the sucking end, or whatever it was called. I'd abandoned it in the lounge to answer the door, not expecting to come back to find it the centrepiece in a tug of war. I mean, who would? It made a strange whirring noise, as if overheating, so I pulled the plug out of the socket. The noise died and was replaced by angry voices.

"I'm sick and tired of your racket," the taller woman snarled. "I'm trying to read. And you're vacuuming up all those poor ants."

"All I'm trying to do is to tidy it." The other one jabbed a gnarled finger in my direction. "*They* don't bother."

"Get a broom, like most normal people."

"They won't give me one."

Worried, I glanced around, hoping to spot another member of staff. A man snored in a chair beside the patio doors, his head tilted back, mouth open, hands clasped in his lap. How could he sleep through the din? Others sat nearby, some nudging one another and chuckling. This was anything but funny. I hesitated, unsure whether to search for help or intervene. I settled on the latter. The hoover might not survive the two women wrenching it back and forth.

"Er, excuse me."

They ignored me, leaving me floundering. I didn't like

to raise my voice to older people. When I'd taken this job, Gran had told me I had to respect the elderly residents. They'd gone through hardships I'd never know. Then she'd regaled me with another story from the war about having to eat bread and dripping because they had little else. It was lucky that I found her tales interesting, since she told enough of them, starting from when she'd left domestic service to become a land girl. She blamed the outside lifestyle for her weathered face and roughened hands, but I had joined the dots to her later years, when the war came to an end and she took in other people's laundry. The steam and chemicals couldn't have been great for her skin. Stress must have been a factor too. Not helped by being sent home during the war from the farm she worked on with a surprise. My mum!

I'd rather work in an old folks' home – or a residential home, as we were told to call it – any day than do what she'd had to do to make ends meet. Not that my wage would be much better. When my friend Tracey got me this job, she'd warned me that working six days a week, four days split shifts, would be hard. And the pay wouldn't make up for it either. "Expect a thin envelope" was all she'd said. I could do with her advice right now, but it was her day off.

I lifted my voice a notch. "Excuse me, ladies." But the tall woman's screech drowned my mouse-like squeak. I took a deep breath.

"Ladies!" I shouted.

That shut them up. They swung around, looking

surprised to see me.

I held out a tentative hand. "Please can I have it back?"

"Who are you?" The tall woman's eyes bored into mine.

"Belinda. I just started this morning and…" I glanced behind me to see if anyone was watching us, especially Gloria, the warden, who didn't seem to like me. "I'll be in trouble if I don't finish this by dinner-time."

"You mean lunch. You're not at school." The other woman spoke in clipped tones. "First, I need to clear this mess, then you may have it back."

Her gaze settled on the patio, littered with blossom from the tree above. Whatever kind of tree it was, it was pretty, with delicate pink flowers, although they didn't look so good crushed into the paving slabs. The area might need a good sweep, but were hoovers meant to be used outside? I frowned and glanced at the sky. Azure, like the sky in my aunt's photos of Benidorm, with a few puffs of cloud. At least these women wouldn't be electrocuted…

"Oh, give over, Alice. Just ask for a broom."

"I've seen one in the storage cupboard," I said. "I'll fetch it."

Swap made, I plugged in the hoover and rushed around, not caring that it bumped the legs of the few unoccupied chairs that lined the walls, but I made sure to slalom around the slippered feet of residents sleeping off their breakfast. Even though the fern pattern and swirls on the carpet made me dizzy, I managed to finish with minutes to spare. Sally, another worker, had promised to collect me but when the grandfather clock chimed noon I sniffed my way towards the kitchen, following the scent of liver.

Joe – another newbie who'd started the previous week but who acted like an old hand – helped me set the tables. Each staff member was assigned a table where we would eat with the residents. Would the old folk expect me to talk? I hoped not. I couldn't imagine they'd be interested in George Michael or the Pet Shop Boys, and I wasn't into Vera Lynn or my gran's great love, the Glenn Miller Band. At least Mum's taste was better: Gerry and the Pacemakers and the Beatles. I pitied the residents. They'd missed out on the best tunes.

Gloria strode in and glared at me. "Why have you put the brush outside?"

Flipping heck! I'd forgotten about that. "I-I…"

Before I managed to get a word out, she threw her hands into the air. "I bet you let Alice take it. Where's Sally? She's supposed to be keeping an eye on you." She clomped away, leaving me with burning cheeks. What harm could be done by giving Alice a broom?

Joe gave me a sympathetic shrug. He had kind eyes, startling in their blueness. "Don't worry about her."

"I didn't know what else to do. Those women were fighting over my hoover."

He shook his head. "My nan did weird stuff like that. She had dementia. My mum had a right time with her. It was pretty horrific."

Maybe that woman, Alice, was like his nan. I'd read about dementia, but none of my family or friends had any family members with it. At my interview, when Gloria had asked about my experience with older people, I'd told her about Gran and my neighbours, although they were all living in their own homes and didn't need extra support. Gloria had mentioned dementia too, so I'd told her how awful it was that people suffered such confusion. She'd been so busy ticking things off her sheet, she hadn't quizzed me further. If she had, she would have known that my knowledge came from reading a true-life article in Mum's *Woman's Own*.

I had no idea what else to say, so I gave Joe a banal but sympathetic, "That sounds horrible."

The residents filed in. Those who could walk unaided arrived first, followed by the ones with walking sticks, Zimmer frames and, finally, a lady in a wheelchair. It was parked to one side, while she was led to her seat. A woman curved low by a humped back shuffled over to my table, clonking a Zimmer frame which she placed by the wall. She twisted her head to give me a smile.

"You're the new girl."

Before I could answer, a scowling Alice appeared. "You gave me that broom and she's taken it." She pointed towards Gloria, who stood, arms folded, at the other side of the room. "You need to tell her that I didn't steal it."

I groaned. Please don't say she would be sitting with me. I'd assumed that I'd be surrounded by lovely old folk, just like the ones who used to ruffle my hair and offer me sweeties when I went shopping with Mum. When I became a teenager, they'd moved on to compliments about my gorgeous brown eyes. Pools of velvet chocolate, apparently. That's about the only thing they could admire. Not my puppy fat, overbite or ginger frizz, although a few did tell me they paid a fortune to get hair like mine. They had lied. Not one had chosen to dye their hair my colour, and they used rollers to tease their hair into manageable curls.

Alice glared at me, waiting for an answer. I decided to appease her, even though I'd only swapped the broom to get my stolen hoover back. "I'll tell her after din— lunch."

The woman with the hunched back clutched her arm. "Sit down, Alice, and leave the girl alone."

Opposite them, a man pulled out a chair. It juddered over the carpet. "You've picked the best table." He jerked his head towards Alice and winked. "But you'll need to eat quickly, or she'll pilfer your food from under your nose."

She had no chance of that. I'd started my shift at nine thirty after Gloria had said they had enough on their plate without dealing with me at breakfast. Worried about being late for my first shift, I'd left the house twenty minutes before the bus arrived, too nervous to eat. Now my stomach rumbled, even though I'd seen the unappetising slabs of liver and piles of mash the cook had splatted onto the plates. I hoped it tasted better than it looked.

Gloria caught my attention, jabbing her thumb towards the kitchen. I flushed and leapt up. I'd forgotten it was my job to bring the plates to our table. This job would give domestic service a run for its money, although at least I didn't have to traipse to the servants' quarters to eat. Although, seeing my table companions, maybe the old way was best…

Lunch went well, apart from all the old folk being curious about my life, my family and who I was 'courting'. Gran used that expression too.

I blushed and said, "No one," only to be told that a girl like me should have a man dangling from each finger. Some chance!

The lady with the hunchback introduced herself as Freda Purdy. She had a lovely smile and more laughter lines than I'd ever seen, but her mouth curved down at the edges, merging with deep grooves that ran to her chin. From stress or nature? She took the lead in the inquisition, the others leaning forward, adding relevant questions.

After we'd moved on to pudding – or dessert, as Alice insisted on calling it – Freda rested her spoon in a pool of custard. "What about your previous job, duck?"

Of all things to ask, it had to be that. The uncomfortable discussion about my boyfriends had been bad enough, but this question had turned this meal into a torture session.

I hid my fluster behind a shrug. "The usual."

She raised an eyebrow. "Well, I worked at a nursery school, Wilf over there was an architect, Ernest was an accountant, Arthur was a milkman and Al…" Her voice trailed off as Alice shot her a look of fury. "Well, returning to my point. What is the *usual*?"

"Yes, what is that?" Alice bestowed a smile on me, which transformed into a snarl when she met Freda's gaze.

"I… um…"

"It will be supper by the time you spit it out," Alice growled.

"Alice, Alice!" Wilf held up his hands. "Give the girl a break. You can see how embarrassed she is."

My cheeks burned hotter than the stove in the kitchen. One of my nicknames at polytechnic had been 'Ribena Bubble' after the TV adverts. Not accurate, as my face flamed a blotchy crimson, but it was a term my tormentor had loved.

"There's nothing wrong with asking what she did before she came here," Alice told Wilf.

"Well, you don't like personal questions!" Freda's hand flew to her mouth. "I'm sorry. That wasn't fair of me."

Intrigued, I leaned forward, hoping they'd spill more of Alice's story. They seemed oddly keen to dodge the subject of her previous work. It must be something shocking – maybe she'd been a go-go girl? But that would be exciting. I couldn't ask, though. It wasn't the done thing.

Alice ignored Freda and narrowed her eyes at me. She must have worked for MI5. Maybe that's why she wouldn't talk about her job. "So…?"

"I… I went to polytechnic for a year. To do sociology." My cheeks flamed. I dreaded to think what I looked like. "But it wasn't for me."

"Pah! Sociology." At the other end of the table, Arthur shook his head. "Not worth the paper it's written on."

My answer hadn't just disappointed him but, from their expressions, Alice and Freda too. I had a feeling they'd be upset for different reasons: Alice would be frustrated by my response, unable to tease any juicy gossip about a job gone wrong or something similar, while Freda would be sad. She'd been a teacher and would know the value of education. Unfortunately, while I'd been the first in my family to go on to higher education, I was also the first to be booted out. But I had no intention of telling the residents that. If they noticed I was older than the average poly student, I'd come up with an excuse. No amount of interrogation would reveal the truth. That was best left in the past. Along with my tutor.

# Chapter 2

On my first day I'd finished at two – a short shift but an exhausting one. Today I started at seven o'clock and, apart from three hours off in the afternoon, I'd be working until eight. To think I could be sitting in the polytechnic refectory, smoking and listening to the jukebox while waiting for my next lecture. I glanced at the clock and chuckled. I'd got that wrong. At seven in the morning, I'd be in bed.

Before I'd started at the home, Tracey had told me about the routine. The first job would be to knock on each resident's door to pour them a cup of tea or coffee and give them a biscuit. After that we'd serve and clear up breakfast, then clean the bedrooms, before going downstairs to tidy the lounge or help in the kitchen.

But today, Gloria pointed at a toilet. She checked her watch. "Sally will show you how to do them today, then you're on your own."

Sally scowled and marched off in the opposite direction to the toilet Gloria had pointed out. Confused, I looked at Gloria, but she shooed me away. I found Sally by the cleaning cupboard. In silence she stood by a sink filling a bucket with steaming water. She handed it to me, along with a mop.

"Tracey should be doing this. She's your mate. I'll show you one, then you do the rest."

"The rest? How many are there?"

"Seven around the building." Smirking, she lifted a basket filled with cloths and sprays. "After breakfast, it's the commodes."

I frowned as I waddled after her, the bubbly water slopping against the sides of the bucket. Commodes? Where had I heard that word before? It sounded like a cross between accommodation and abodes. Maybe that's what they called the bedrooms here.

When Sally had said she would show me what to do with the first toilet, she hadn't been joking. She pointed at the bowl, the handrails and the sink and gave me instructions on which cloths to use, before leaning against the wall, her arms folded. I didn't blame her. Now I could see why Gran called it the throne room. There was no way to clean it without kneeling on the tiled floor. Hesitating, I eyed the suspicious blotches that glistened beneath the strip light. Yuck! No way did I want to spend the day with that on my skirt. Perhaps I should wash the floor first, but then I'd get wet knees...

Yawning, Sally tapped her watch. "You've got forty minutes to do all seven. Not just one."

♦

Tracey agreed to meet me on the common. First, she wanted to go home to change her clothes. When I'd accepted the job, I'd been so chuffed to be working with my best mate that I hadn't thought about what I'd do for three hours each afternoon before the shorter evening shift began. I'd hoped we could go to her bedsit, but her landlady didn't want her to bring all and sundry around.

It was a good half hour before she arrived, dressed in jeans ripped at the knees, her white T-shirt tucked in, showing off her trim waistline. The way I hunched on the grass made me look like the Michelin Man, so I breathed in and sat upright.

She dropped down on the grass beside me, smelling of soap and fabric softener, whereas I'd had to spray half a can of Impulse over me to get rid of the stink of toilets and commodes.

"No offence," I said. "But you should be an estate agent."

"Should I? D'you reckon I'd be good at it?"

My sarcasm had bypassed her. "Fantastic! You told me I'd get to dole out tea and biscuits and stuff." Grimacing, I gazed at my skirt. Even though I'd wiped it half a dozen times, a splotch glistened like a slug's trail. "It's a shit job. Literally."

"Aw, don't worry, Bee." She used my family nick-name. Leaning back on her elbows, she stretched out, long and willowy, toeing off her shoes to reveal pale feet and maroon nails.

We fell into silence, until she gave me a sympathetic smile. "You won't be on toilet duty all the time."

"And commodes." I'd never forget what they were again. Or the smell of the slopping contents as I carried them to flush down the toilets I'd cleaned.

I leaned back, mirroring her. If I stretched out, my

bulges might flatten. "I don't think Gloria likes me. Or that Sally."

Squinting, she lowered her Ray-Bans from where she'd pushed them into her hair. I couldn't make out her eyes, but I could see the logo. Where had she got the money? She was meant to be skint. Unless she'd been to Bilton market.

She didn't spot my critical stare. "Glo's okay. But don't give Sally an inch. She's a lazy cow."

Still focused on her sunglasses, I said, "Are they real?"

"Nah. I'm not made of money." She ripped a buttercup from the grass and twirled it beneath her chin. "D'you remember doing this?"

A shadow crossed me and a lad stepped over my legs. He gave Tracey's foot a nudge and bent down, his knees cracking.

"All right, Trace. How's the old fogey?"

"Waiting for you to visit," she said.

"He can't have been waiting long, seeing as I saw him on Saturday."

The lad glanced at me, then turned back to Tracey. I didn't expect anything more. It meant I could watch their interaction. Of course he'd fancy Tracey. Who didn't? The question was, did she like him? It was hard to tell. If she'd been sixteen, she would have stuck out her boobs and pouted. But we'd come a long way since those days. Or, to be accurate, she had.

We'd left school at the same time, with Tracey determined to earn a crust. She'd found her first job in the local pork pie factory, before moving to the old people's home. She seemed pleased with her lot. In a way I envied her lack of ambition. I had higher hopes for myself to start with, but my BTEC course at college, which didn't work out, was followed by a year or so working on the tills in the local supermarket. Boredom had inspired me to attempt another dose of education. I came away with two A levels, which got me a position in a small office, where I spent the next few years listening to my boss talking about his boys, their university education and what he hoped they'd achieve in the future. Lawyer, doctor. He'd gazed at me over the rim of his glasses as he told me that a degree would be the key to my future. He'd even given me a bonus towards it.

Except it had led me here.

I hadn't mentioned my office job on my application for the residential home. For one thing, I was embarrassed that my ex-boss might find out. More importantly, he might mention that I'd left his company to go to polytechnic the previous year. That would raise questions. My mum told me not to be daft and to apply for other office jobs. If anyone asked, I could say I took a year out. But I didn't dare. My face would give me away. When Tracey said they were short of staff at her workplace, I'd leapt at the chance to redeem myself. The warden, Gloria, didn't ask too many questions about my missing years, while I didn't ask for enough detail about the job. Especially when Tracey had mis-sold it with Snow White-style tales of tea and biscuits, singing as she swept, and kindly residents who spent their days making her life a joy. She hadn't mentioned Alice, not so Wonderland.

"What are you doing Friday night?" The lad spoke to Tracey as if he didn't care, but his flushed cheeks gave him away.

Tracey shrugged. "Probs going down the George and Dragon." She turned to me. "You up for it?"

The lad's face fell. If I said yes, he wouldn't be able to ask her out, but if I said no, I'd be stuck in. Either way, I'd have to check my bank balance and the cost of a taxi back home before deciding.

"Maybe," I said, going for the compromise.

Wrong answer. They both frowned, while her admirer pursed his lips. I wouldn't let him know that money was the issue. It was none of his business.

"I'll think about it," I said.

Tracey sat up, brushing grass from each elbow. "Maybe we could make a foursome. What about Gary? Would he be up for it?"

*Did I have a say in this?* I didn't know Gary, but I could imagine his disappointment when he saw me. Most likely he'd sneer, like the last boy Tracey had tried to pair me up with had. That one had come up with an excuse and left early, leaving me a gooseberry with Tracey and her date.

The lad turned to look at my hair, my flushed cheeks. His gaze terminated at my stomach. Although I'd breathed in, my elusive hip bones hid under a thick blanket of flesh.

He shrugged. "I can ask."

But his tone warned Tracey not to get her hopes up.

# Chapter 3

By Thursday I'd found my stride. After arriving at seven o'clock, I'd spent an hour kneeling to worship the toilets before heading off to serve breakfast. It reminded me of an Enid Blyton book, with lashings of jam, thick slices of toast in toast racks, and real butter. There was also a choice of five cereals, plus bacon and eggs and fresh orange juice. A food lover's dream. My dream.

Having said that, this was the first morning I could face eating after 'throne' duty. I'd built up a good appetite while bringing everything to the table. This included honey donated by a local beekeeper which, he'd said, tasted like lavender. Imagine that! I could hardly contain my excitement. Until I caught Alice watching me rubbing my hands together.

"We don't do prayers here, but if you wish to lead us in one, we'll be quiet."

Freda grasped my arm with her crooked fingers, her nails the same pink as the Twilight Teaser lipstick I'd worn to under-eighteens discos years before. Her perm was working its way out; her grey tips gently curled below new growth that clung to her scalp. Her hunched back curved her low in her seat but her cheekbones were high and defined and her grey eyes sparkled beneath arched eyebrows.

"Ignore her, duck. She's only teasing you."

Smiling to herself, Alice scooped up a huge portion of

the honey, placing the laden spoon on the side of her plate. It seemed that I wasn't the only person looking forward to it. More than once, the word 'honey' rose above the hubbub. Whoever said older people had small appetites hadn't met these people (or my gran, for that matter). When the honey had made it around the table and my neighbour, Arthur, had helped himself to a large portion, a lump remained at the bottom. Just enough for me!

He held up the jar. "I've left a bit."

"Great. It looks scrummy." I held out my hand.

But he passed the jar across the table to Alice. Her talons curled around it. Humming to herself, she pilfered the dregs, scraping the side of the jar. She didn't look at me, even though I couldn't take my eyes from her toast moving into her gaping mouth.

Freda swallowed her piece of toast. Her lips glistened with honey. "What did you say, duck?"

I flushed. I didn't want to admit that I'd held out my hand for Arthur to pass it to me. It felt a bit like waving back to a person to find that they were greeting someone else.

"The jam." I picked up the blackcurrant jam, holding it as if I were selling its benefits in an advert. "I can't wait to try it."

Alice chuckled to herself and took a sip of her tea, her pinkie curled like a pig's stumpy tail. She knew that I'd been missed out. Tracey would have had another finger in mind for her, but I hated confrontation. Instead, I bit my lip and smeared blackcurrant jam across my toast. As I munched, I surveyed nearby tables in the vain hope there might be some leftover honey.

When we cleared away, I moaned about it to Joe, who grinned.

"If you're on Alice the gannet's table, you'll have to start thinking on your feet."

"I can't take the honey first." I'd found a pot with an inch of deliciousness at the bottom, so I was happy. "We have to wait until everyone has helped themselves."

"You're the server. If we get that honey again, sneak a bit out first. Plan ahead. The woman who used to work on your table had it sorted. Didn't you get warned about Alice?"

"I know not to give her the broom. And to address her as Miss Swann, not Mrs." I winced at the memory of her reprimand.

"Just be glad you're not on my table. I have Sir Bartholomew Hamilton, who insists on being called Sir Bartholomew.  It's a pain as I have a Mrs Bartholomew too. They're both half deaf. Sir Bartholomew tells me off for not speaking clearly, even when I'm talking to Mrs Bartholomew."

Joe spoke well, so the blame could only lie with Sir Bartholomew. Maybe I was better off with Alice, especially with mumbling being my speciality.

"Why is he here and not at the posh old people's home in Bilton?"

Joe shrugged. "This one's not too bad. Better than the other council-run one there." He glanced around as if to check we were alone. "Apparently, he loved poker, but it didn't like him."

"Cards?"

He rubbed his fingers together. "Lost the family fortune. That's why his son never comes to visit."

"I know someone else whose grandad is here."

Joe frowned. "Don't tell me. Aiden West." When I gave him a baffled look, he added, "He hangs around with Gary, Ben and that lot. I don't go near them. Aiden's got a thing about Tracey – that's the only reason he visits his grandad." He glanced at the clock. "We'd better get a move on."

Before I could question him further, he strode off with his tray. I sighed. We wouldn't get the chance to talk in the kitchen and Joe would be out of the door the minute the clock struck two. Now I wished I'd hadn't agreed to go out with Tracey on Friday night. I'd have to ask her more about Aiden and Gary when we met on the common later.

♦

I'd finished the commodes and had started cleaning downstairs when Sally strode past, arm outstretched, clutching a dinner knife. She didn't look my way, although she must have seen me. Puzzled, I watched as she headed down the corridor that led to Gloria's office. While her manner was unsettling, I didn't think she was about to kill our boss. For a start, she could have got a much sharper knife from the kitchen.

When she disappeared, I sprayed the grandfather clock and set to work with the duster. This was one job I didn't mind doing, although the hoovering wasn't too bad, especially when I could pretend to be the Shake 'n' Vac lady, whizzing around to put the freshness back. It was much needed, as the smell of cooked food seemed to stagnate in the air.

Gloria and Sally appeared, catching me sniffing the duster. This time Gloria brandished the knife. Her expression was easier to read. Murderous. I shuddered as she curled her finger to call me over. As I reached her, she pointed the knife at me. It looked like the ones used on the side plates at breakfast.

"How did this get into Alice Swann's room?"

I went to shrug but decided against it. "I-I have no idea."

"Belinda must have let her take it this morning," Sally said. "Or we'd have found it when we cleaned her room yesterday."

"Residents" – Gloria emphasised the word by rolling the 'r' – "should never have knives in their rooms. And I've already warned you about Alice Swann."

A rounded knife couldn't do much damage, so why was it an issue? The residents weren't children. Far from it. Most of them appeared a decade or more older than my gran. One had even mentioned that she'd been my age at the start of the Great War. Perhaps there was an age limit to knives, although the idea seemed ridiculous. Anyhow, asking older people's ages was off limits, unless they offered to tell me. That didn't happen until they were well into their eighties when, once again, age became something to celebrate. They were a bit like children in that respect.

Sally crossed her arms, gloating, forgetting she'd been assigned to train me.

I wilted under Gloria's glare. "I-I'm sorry. I-I didn't realise. No one's said why I should take extra care with Miss Swann."

Gloria handed the knife back to Sally. "I'll leave you to explain that. I have work to do."

Sally's face fell. Had she expected Gloria to punish me more? She rounded on me. "This is the second time you've been told. Don't let me find out about any more objects ending up with Alice, do you hear?"

Then she stormed off towards the lounge, before spinning around in exasperation and stomping past me. The kitchen door smashed shut, leaving me standing alone, bewildered.

If I'd hoped to be educated about Alice Swann, I was in for a wait.

# Chapter 4

Joe answered my question – or part of it, at least – when we were clearing up in the kitchen that evening. He couldn't tell me why Alice wasn't allowed a knife in her room but, thanks to a loose-lipped resident, he'd heard about her past.

"Her parents put her in a mental hospital. I don't know why. She's one of the savviest people here."

"But why a mental hospital? She's posh. Or she sounds it."

"Anyone could end up there back when she was young. Maybe she got pregnant or something."

"Pregnant? They'd put her in a mental hospital for that?" I gasped.

He shrugged. "They did back then to single mothers, women of supposedly immoral character, and for a whole host of ridiculous reasons. I was told they didn't release Alice until about ten years ago."

"What? In the 1970s they still kept people in those places?"

"People got institutionalised after they'd been there too long. They couldn't survive living alone outside. I've read up about it."

"What? When you went to poly?"

He shrugged. "I went to uni. But I didn't learn about it there."

Although I'd been doing a sociology degree, I hadn't

learned about institutions. Not that I'd had much time to learn anything but the basics of Maslow, Margaret Mead and a few other names that had stuck. No doubt Joe had failed to get his degree too. Why else would he be here? But I didn't say anything in case it led to a discussion about my time at poly, and how I'd thrown the opportunity away. Or, worse, in case the conversation moved on to my tutor.

I looked more closely at Joe. He was a little older than me. Perhaps twenty-seven, although it was hard to tell. When I'd worked at the supermarket, I'd had a terrible time trying to work out who was eighteen, unless I knew them. My ex-schoolfriends expected me to turn a blind eye to their bottle of Thunderbird or packet of B&H. Sometimes I had, just to keep the peace. Except when my old school bullies had come in. Then, I'd got sweet revenge.

But Joe wouldn't need to show his ID. By the end of the evening shift, he had a hint of stubble although, since he was fair, it didn't show much. His strong jawline was softened by his kind eyes. They were lovely. A striking blue.

He looked up and caught me scrutinising him. Blushing, I turned back to stack plates into the rack, but I couldn't help snatching another glance or two.

"What made you read up on mental institutions? Was it because of Alice?"

He shrugged. "I'm working here to gain more experience with older people, so I thought I'd learn more about the past. What they went through."

In a way, I hoped he'd ask why I was here. It might sound pretentious, but I wanted him to think I was more than just a toilet cleaner and server.

The kitchen door banged open and Gloria appeared, looking anxious. "Have either of you seen Mrs Irving's watch? She put it on her bedside table before going out with her family."

There wasn't a commode in Mrs Irving's room, so I hadn't been in there. But that didn't stop Gloria from giving me a hard look.

"I saw it when I was cleaning this morning," Joe said. "Was it there when she went back to her room this afternoon?"

"Her family collected her before lunch. She's been out all day. Are you sure you left it in her room?"

"I didn't touch it. I asked Sally what I should do. She said to leave it."

"Did she indeed?" Gloria glared at him. "She – and you – should know that residents' valuables go in the safe. Then I wouldn't be chasing my tail to find the damn thing."

I'd not heard Gloria use that tone with Joe. Usually she spoke in a motherly way to him, reserving tongue lashings for others. But Joe accepted the telling-off. If it had been the other way around, I would have blushed and stammered. He didn't even bat an eyelid when Sally stormed in a moment later.

"You told Gloria that I told you to leave the watch on

26

the side."

He frowned. "Of course I did. Would you rather I lied?"

She banged her fist on the counter, making me jump. "I do not expect my subordinates to contradict me."

Joe's expression was steely but calm. "So, you did expect me to lie." He kept his expression bland. "I'm never going to do that, Sally. No matter who I'm dealing with."

Hesitating, she looked from me to the worker on the other side of Joe, then back at Joe. Then she burst into forced laughter. "Who said anything about lying? I just wanted to ensure we were singing from the same hymn sheet. You know…"

Joe faced her, looking relaxed. Then he shook his head. "No, I don't."

She paled and spun around, slamming the kitchen door behind her.

When I gazed at Joe in admiration, he said, "I've probably gained a lifelong enemy there. But…" He grimaced. "Why does she need to lie about a misplaced watch?"

♦

The missing watch was the subject of much speculation at breakfast. Wilf Preston told me that Edith Irving was batty enough to have lost it, but he didn't have an answer when I said that Joe had seen it on her bedside table. Freda

Purdy wondered if it had fallen down the side of her bed. But we'd checked there, pulling off the bedding and emptying her bedside drawers. We'd looked everywhere, leaving the residents with only one conclusion. Someone had taken it.

"Sally's been telling everyone that I didn't ask her about the watch when we were in the room. That I lied," Joe whispered when the residents and staff had left the dining room.

My mouth fell open. "No!" After witnessing the scene in the kitchen, I couldn't believe Sally had the audacity to lie.

"But the other worker who was there…" I clicked my fingers. "Whatshername… She saw Sally trying to get you to change your story."

"I know, but I don't think Gloria knows who to believe. But why would I have said I'd seen the watch if I'd taken it?"

I couldn't imagine Joe would steal from anyone. Maybe Sally had taken the watch and was covering her tracks. But that seemed unlikely. She'd been here for years, with plenty of opportunity before now. More likely, she didn't want to get into trouble for telling Joe to leave it where it was. She preferred to point the finger of blame, and wasn't happy when it spun back around to her.

"That Sally is a right one," I said. "She dobbed on me about Alice having a knife in her room. I didn't know I was meant to count the cutlery each time I clear the table."

"Neither did I." Joe gazed down at his heaped tray.

"I'm in the wrong occupation. A prison guard might have been a better choice."

I decided to lighten the situation, to make Joe think of something other than the watch. "Now, would you be Mr Mackay or Mr Barrowclough? My mum loves *Porridge*. She's always on a look-out for the reruns. I think she fancies Richard Beckinsale, although he's been dead a while now."

Joe gamely responded. "I'd like to think I could be as tough as Mr Mackay, but I think Mr Barrowclough is more my style." He grimaced. "Although the chances are, if this watch isn't found, I could be banged up like Barker. That wasn't part of the plan."

What plan? Did he hope to take over from Gloria one day? No chance of that here – or anywhere – if he got labelled a thief. A bad reference would be the least of his worries. We fell silent. For a moment, I wondered whether to reassure him that references weren't the be all and end all, but I decided against it. My story wasn't one of hope and redemption, more like snakes and ladders, with my tutor being the snake. Thanks to him – not helped by my impulsive retaliation – I'd gone from an office job with good prospects to working in an old folks' 'jail'.

"It'll turn up." I meant it. It couldn't have gone far.

He gave me a wry smile. "I hope it does."

♦

I asked Tracey if she'd been there when Joe had spoken to

Sally, but she shook her head. Then she gave me a mischievous grin.

"Perhaps she nicked it and she's passing the blame."

So, it wasn't just me who had thought that. It gave me hope for Joe. "Do you think?"

"Nah!" She clipped my arm. "Don't be silly. I bet it's been picked up by accident and we'll find it in the laundry or kitchen." She tightened her hair band. "All set for later?" Without waiting for a response, she waltzed off with her hoover and cleaning bucket, her ponytail trailing down her back.

Pulling her hair back didn't work with her new style. She'd had the top section of her hair cut shorter – which she puffed up with tonnes of gel when going out – while the rest fell in sleek strands over her shoulders. When styled, it looked amazing. Sadly, there was little point teasing mine to look the same. I might as well stick my finger in the plug socket. It would have the same effect on my frizz.

I'd try to do something with it for tonight. My hair gel, make-up and outfit sat in a carrier bag in the staff cloakroom. I'd have to get changed in one of the loos while Tracey went to her bedsit to have a shower. I'd left my perfume at home, so I'd have to remind her to bring her Giorgio to mask the smell of stale food and goodness knows what else. Like this stench. I hitched my top over my nose before picking up the commode bowl. Holding it so the contents didn't slop over the edges, I made my way to the toilet opposite. Only another three to do, then I could douse myself in polish while cleaning the lounge and reception areas.

After we'd finished work for the afternoon, Tracey asked to see my outfit. I held out my baggy black top and leggings. I'd thought about jeans but settled on the gothic look favoured by my friends at poly. It hid my stomach, although the leggings added a few pounds elsewhere. After I'd been sitting down the material would sag, making it look as if I had a saggy bum and boobs on my knees.

"You're not wearing that!" She snatched the bag away, sounding like my mum, except there was nothing revealing about my top, which covered my chest and thighs.

So I arrived at the pub, arm in arm with Tracey – who had to push me through the door – wearing something that would have shot Mum's eyebrows into her hairline. The clothes didn't belong to Tracey. She'd begged them from a friend in a neighbouring bedsit, saying we were the same size. She'd got that wrong. I'd had to lie on the toilet floor after work and breathe in to do up the jeans. I couldn't see myself in the small mirror above the sink. Maybe that was a blessing. I didn't need a mirror to know that the borrowed shirt was my undoing. Literally. It stretched over my boobs, the buttons threatening to pop. The last thing I wanted was for anyone to see my mottled-grey bra – dyed by an errant black sock in the washing machine. At least my bra wouldn't turn illuminous under the strobe lights if we went on to a nightclub.

The pub was busy. I hugged myself as Tracey led me through the crowd. I'd been to the George and Dragon the year before, but it had been renovated since I'd left for polytechnic. Gone was the dark mahogany bar and dim candleholder wall lights. Spotlights glinted on the mirrored surround, which reflected an array of bottles and the heaving mass through which we pushed. The swirly carpet, which used to stink of beer, had been replaced by flagstone paving. But some things hadn't changed. Fag butts littered the floor and the pool tables still sat at the back by the toilets: a problem when you wanted to go to the Ladies' but had to excuse yourself to sidle through a mass of people.

Tracey's fingers cut into my arm – maybe she thought I was about to flee? – as she hauled me up a step and into what used to be the restaurant area. Beside two fruit machines, a jukebox blared in the corner, while drinkers packed the chairs and spilled around the tables.

She found the lad we'd met on the common – Joe had called him Aiden West – and tapped his back. He spun around, a grin widening on his face. When he put his arm around Tracey's shoulders, pulling her close, she released me.

"All right, Trace! Great to see you." He pointed to me. "Gary, mate! Here's your bird."

Bird? Was he from the 1960s? Next, he'd be calling me 'chick', but that suggested dainty.

Sniggers erupted from the lads at the table. Gary looked disgusted.

I knew why. He wasn't upset because Aiden had called me a bird, but because he'd been linked with me.

# Chapter 5

 "Good one, mate!" Gary chuckled.

He sat back to chat to his friend, leaving me to stand there, shamefaced. Did I look so terrible that he thought Aiden was joking?

Tracey nudged me and hissed, "Ignore him. He's a twat."

Again, I acted as gooseberry to Aiden and Tracey, like I had too often before. But at least most of them had something interesting to say. Aiden just puffed out his chest and told excruciating stories about pranks he'd played at work. Bored, I looked around. Aiden and his mates wore their hair in a fashionable flat-top style, while Gary – the one who'd ignored me – had a spiked quiff. There'd been a group of psychobillies at poly who'd played King Kurt and other stuff on the jukebox in the students' union bar. At poly, my 'cool' friends had liked the Smiths. My favourite A-ha and Whitney Houston cassettes had been left to fester at the back of my wardrobe.

Tracey tapped my arm. "Get us a drink, will you?"

She swung back to Aiden. Obviously, my round. Aiden had half a pint left, so I didn't offer to buy him one. I couldn't spend too much, not with the cost of the taxi home. At least I wouldn't need to worry about the price of a nightclub. No way would I last that long with this crowd.

More people had packed into the pub, cramming every

free space. It took ages to get served. Men thrust bough-like arms above my head, rustling notes as if they grew on trees. The bar staff didn't notice me, even though I tried to show them my money. But it was harder to do that with pound coins. I rifled in my handbag to retrieve the fiver I'd kept for the taxi. After a few waves of blue the barman spotted me.

It wasn't easy to make my way back through the crowd with a drink in each hand. When I finally reached Tracey, I steeled myself for more of Aiden's exploits. But they'd moved on to planning a future date.

Aiden tilted his head back to drain his pint. His Adam's apple stood like a mountain peak. "How about the flicks?"

"What's on?"

He hesitated. "*Predator's* still showing in Bilton."

"Nah! I'm not into aliens and stuff. How about *Three Men and a Baby*? I've heard that's fun."

I fancied seeing *Three Men and a Baby*. Steve Guttenberg was cute. But I couldn't imagine Tracey would want to see it twice. Maybe I should get hold of one of my old friends again. I hadn't seen any of them since I went to poly. But maybe not. While it might be nice to meet up, it would be odd suggesting meeting for a chat and then going to the cinema.

Clutching his empty glass, Aiden pointed at Tracey's drink. He had to shout above the racket. "Another one?"

"Yeah. What about you, Bee?"

His face fell.

I hadn't been included in his offer. Did I want to stay

for another drink? I glanced at my watch. We'd been here forty-five minutes. Could I bear another three hours here listening to his dull stories? The thought made me yawn.

"I'm knackered. I've got an early start."

"Are you sure?" Looking concerned, Tracey gazed at me. Beside her, Aiden brightened.

"Course she is. Look at her. Dead on her feet." He turned to me. "I'd give you a lift home but…" He jiggled his glass. "I've had a few."

I brushed him off. Lager may have been his get-out clause, but he wouldn't have offered me a lift even if he'd been drinking Coke. Goodbyes made, I turned to find a group of men blocking my path.

"Excuse me… excuse me." My voice didn't carry over the hubbub, but Aiden's did.

"Your mate's a laugh a minute."

Then Tracey. "Oh, give over. She's just shy."

A man staggered backwards, landing on my foot.

"Ouch!" I squealed.

He turned around, clasping my shoulder to stay upright. "Sorry, love. Hope I didn't hurt you," he slurred. His breath stank.

I gritted my teeth. "It's fine."

At least he'd made room for me to angle myself through the mass of bodies. Outside, the fresh air wafted away the heat of the pub and the smell of beer and cigarettes. I leaned against the brick wall to rub my foot. Couples passed arm in arm and groups of lads jostled through the narrow doorway. None of them noticed me.

Why would they? I eased my foot back into my shoe and hugged myself, feeling self-conscious in my too-tight top. Across the road, light glowed from the curved bay windows of the Ploughman. The last time I'd been there, there'd been a payphone just inside. I crossed the road, wincing with every other step.

Strains of 'La Isla Bonita' filtered outside, mingling with the low murmur of chatter when I stepped into the porch. Figures moved behind the patterned, swirled panes. I rummaged in my bag for change then picked up the receiver, dialling a taxi number shown on a business card pinned to the board.

"I thought it was you!" Joe stood by the door, smiling. "What are you doing here?"

I put the phone down. "Calling a taxi."

"Not going home already, surely?"

I flushed. Did I want to admit that my blind date had laughed at me?

Joe must have noticed my discomfort. "Have you got time for a drink? I'm playing gooseberry to Dan and Charlotte. They're at the cashpoint. They'll be along in a minute." He pushed open the door to the pub and jerked his head towards the bar. "My round."

Unable to believe my luck, I followed him through the low-ceilinged space. He ducked beneath a beam into a small area with a corner bar, pinball table and a cigarette vending machine. No more than a dozen people perched on stools or leaned against the bar.

"I prefer this side. The snug is a bit quaint for my tastes.

Also, Sir Bartholomew has been known to sneak out for a pint and find his way here. I don't think he's ever bought a drink – he always sparks up a conversation with someone who's about to order."

I gazed around. Above a corner table filled with laughing drinkers hung a familiar painting of a child with a tear rolling down his face. I grimaced.

"I thought they'd binned all those pictures a few years ago."

Joe chuckled. "*The Crying Boy*. This one survived the *Sun's* pyre."

A few years earlier, the *Sun* had encouraged its readers to send their prints in to be set alight on a bonfire after the print was reputed to be cursed.

"I'd forgotten that."

"Better than burning books, I guess. Do you read?"

I hadn't been asked that question for ages.

"Not for years, unless you count books at poly." I winced. It wasn't something I wanted to talk about in a pub – or at all. "I used to like James Herbert."

My deflection worked. Joe laughed. "*The Rats*! *The Crying Boy* has nothing on that for creepiness. I read it when I was twelve. My mum would've had kittens if she'd known."

Two people came to stand beside us and Joe introduced them as Charlotte and Dan. They gave me friendly smiles. They spoke well too, hinting at a classy upbringing. I noticed that Joe sounded different to how he spoke at work. Posher, somehow. Charlotte and Dan slipped off their jackets to reveal matching jeans teamed with white shirts cinched in at the waist. Both had dark hair – his swept back, hers in a long bob. She could have starred in a shampoo advert – which made me instinctively try to flatten my frizz. Why did I always end up next to perfect-looking people? Or pretty ones like Tracey? If I'd felt dowdy before, Charlotte made me feel plain ugly.

A diamond ring sparkled on her third finger. The few people I knew who had real diamond rings had ones where the silver had been designed to make the diamond look bigger, whereas fragile spikes of gold clawed around Charlotte's large stone. She noticed me admiring it and grinned, showing perfect white teeth.

"We got engaged last week. We haven't set a date yet, but it'll be next year. We've just put a deposit on a flat."

"Talking about being held to ransom." Dan laughed. "Joe says you work at the jail. He's been telling us some of the goings-on there."

"You mean about keeping stuff away from the residents?" I said.

Dan frowned. Perhaps he hadn't heard about Alice Swann. But I didn't get the chance to ask. Joe butted in. "What do you want to drink? We're still waiting."

Through an archway, the barman stood by the till in the snug. He gave a woman her change and headed towards us.

"Can I get my own?" I asked. "I'm just staying for the one and, well…" I blushed. "I can't afford rounds."

"I said I'll buy you a drink and I will," Joe said. "You

can return the favour another day."

Would I get the chance to go to the pub with Joe more than once? Just the thought made my cheeks flame. Not that I fancied him. What was the point? He was a league above me with his gorgeous eyes, slicked-back blond hair and slim build. But maybe he'd seen something in me. My sparkling personality and wit? I rolled my eyes. I took a sip of my drink and tried to think of something interesting to say.

"Do you come here often?" I flushed at my crass comment. "I mean, are you regulars?"

"Usually, we go to the Garden Gate in Bilton," Dan said. "But for some reason Joe convinced us to try this pub." He chuckled as he emphasised the words 'for some reason'. Did he not like it here? I could understand why if they frequented the Garden Gate. That was the preferred destination for the fashionable set, and out of my price range – a taxi home would cost a fortune, never mind the price of the drinks. Charlotte leaned over to hook her bag over the bar stool, revealing a Levi label on her jeans. Unlike Tracey, I couldn't imagine Charlotte buying knockoffs at the market. It disconcerted me that Joe had such well-to-do friends. At work he seemed on a par with us: an everyday bloke doing a menial job while trying to make ends meet.

The conversation flowed, led by Dan, who regaled us with a tale about a woman who'd bent over to pick up her shopping basket when her trouser seam had split.

"Ripped apart!" Laughing, he slapped his thigh. "The

poor thing. She went puce! The colour of her underwear. I lent her my jacket and walked her out to her car."

That reminded me. I crossed my arms. So far, the borrowed top had withstood the pressure of my boobs but, knowing my luck, they'd choose this moment to burst free.

I made my excuses and headed to the Ladies', down at the end of a tiled corridor. Pushing the creaking door open, I was confronted by a large mirror, showing me in glorious technicolour. My face was the same colour as the woman Dan had joked about, my hair was wild, my shirt gaped, revealing pale flesh and hints of a grey bra. Had I really gone out looking like this? What must Joe's friends think of me? Were they out there now, laughing at me, mocking me? I wouldn't blame them if they did.

I thought about Tracey's expression when she'd checked me over before we went out.

When I'd mirrored her uncertain look, she'd plastered on a smile. "You look fine." Then she'd put her hands on her hips, turning her head to one side. "Better! That look really suits you."

I hadn't felt comfortable. I knew I should have worn my own clothes. At least they fit me. But I'd believed Tracey had my best interests at heart. Now I wasn't so sure.

# Chapter 6

My pinny had finally arrived, emblazoned with the words 'Rockbeare Care Home'. They'd made a mistake; it was a residential home. Not that it mattered. At least I wouldn't have to worry about stains marking my blouse, although the pinny wasn't long enough to cover my skirt – or my knees – when I knelt beside the toilets or over the baths to scrub them.

I had also been promoted! My bubble of happiness lasted all of a minute, until Gloria pricked it with her pin-sharp words after spotting my jubilant smile.

"Just for four or five days, mind." She looked me up and down. "We've got a new staff member starting next week. Sally needs to show her the ropes and I want to test her mettle with the loos." She paused, then smiled. "You're so good at them. And Nancy looks more the part for greeting residents."

Ouch. That told me all I needed to know about why I'd been left with the toilets and commodes. My looks. Would my face frighten residents first thing in the morning, or was it my outfit?

When Gloria disappeared back into her office, I vowed to spend the afternoon looking around clothes shops – okay, charity shops – in town. I'd make an excuse to Tracey, knowing she'd ask to join me. I couldn't put my finger on why, but I didn't want her there.

At the charity shop, a friendly woman greeted me.

There were no other customers in sight, so she bustled around unhooking various garments from the rails. She had good taste in clothes. I put her at around forty-five to fifty years, but it was difficult to tell. Her smart crimson suit with its shoulder pads and matching court shoes looked out of place, but maybe these shops were going upmarket?

When I picked out a pair of black trousers and a white top she frowned, but ushered me through to the small changing room at the back. The waistband of the trousers cut into my stomach and when I tugged the top over my bust it cracked as if I'd split the seam. Flipping heck! I held my breath, hoping the woman hadn't heard. But she didn't poke her head through the curtain or call out to ask if everything was okay. I heaved a sigh of relief. Then I gazed at myself in the mirror. How I'd get it off in one piece, I had no idea. After checking that the top wasn't damaged, I came out, red-faced, my hair looking like an orangutan that had fought its way through a bramble bush.

"What do you think? Please be honest. I won't mind."

She narrowed her eyes. "Perhaps another size?"

"We're meant to wear black at work. You've only got this colour in this size. I'm going on a diet, so I was thinking they might fit in a few weeks."

The woman smiled. "My daughter tried the Cambridge diet. She lost weight but, it seemed to me, she paid a fortune not to eat. If you're looking for a quick loss, it might be an idea."

"I'm broke."

She crossed over to the counter and drew out a magazine from the shelf below. "Here – you can have this." Pulling a rueful face, she patted her stomach. "I *was* calorie counting, but I like baking cakes too much. There's good tips on recipes, though."

She handed me a copy of *Slimming* magazine. On the cover a woman stood, hands on hips, wearing a svelte dress, not an ounce of fat on her.

I sighed. "Oh, to look like that!"

"They've got success stories inside." The woman rubbed her chin. "Look, rather than going for those trousers, have you thought about buying clothes from a catalogue? You could pay in instalments."

I brightened. "That's a good idea. My neighbour's got one."

She rehung the trousers on the rail, out of my reach. "A pretty girl like you should be showing yourself off in lovely clothes."

Why did older people say I was nice-looking? At least she was younger than the typical person who made that comment.

She lifted my ponytail – rather apt, as it bushed out at the end, wiry like real horsehair.

"Your hair reminds me of Fergie."

I frowned.

"Sarah Ferguson!"

I'd never been compared to her before. "She's got curls. I've got frizz."

She laughed. "She just knows what to do with it.

44

Obviously, having money helps, but don't let that put you off. There's plenty of things you can do with little money."

"Really? I've tried yoghurt and cucumber on my face and tea to darken my hair, but—"

Her laughter cut me off. "We all did that at school. What products do you use?"

"My gran swears by Vosene. My mum likes Head & Shoulders."

Again, her laughter tinkled, not unkindly. "If you're not in a hurry, I can give you some ideas. My other daughter works on a beauty counter, so she's given me plenty of tips."

♦

The residents on my table seemed most put out by my refusal to have an extra slice of toast. Their concern inspired Alice to take an interest, rather than using it as an opportunity to squirrel the slice onto her own plate.

"But you've hardly eaten a thing!" Freda said. "You'll fade—"

"You haven't got that anorexia, have you?" Alice cut in.

"No!" I grabbed the roll of fat above my waistline, although she couldn't see from where she sat. "I just want to lose this."

She peered at me. "That's understandable. You've gone beyond the puppy fat years."

"That's a bit rude," Freda said. "Don't mind her, duck. But do have the last one."

The metal rack wobbled in her trembling hand.

Alice snatched the toast. "She's on a diet. We should respect her wishes."

"I was rather hoping that was mine," Wilf said. "You've already had three slices." Usually affable, Will had been quiet up to now, picking at his bacon and eggs. He'd taken so long, we'd moved on to the toast and jam – after asking his permission, of course.

"One learns that hope is for dreamers," Alice told him. "Anyhow, gentlemen wait for ladies."

"If I waited until you'd had your fill, I'd be a skeleton," he growled.

I'd started an argument. I pushed my chair back from the table. "I'll put more toast on for you."

He folded his arms and slumped back in his chair. "I'm not hungry."

"I thought not. That's why I had this slice." Alice bit into the toast. She reminded me of a hamster munching away, her little mouth working, her beady eyes bright with mischief.

Wilf muttered to himself, refusing to look at any of us. I didn't know what to do. Should I make him toast or not? Gloria would be annoyed if it was wasted, and I didn't want to eat it. Alice could, though. She might manage a fifth slice. But then Gloria might get mad because she'd eaten too much.

Alice swallowed and took a sip of tea. "Well, *someone*

woke up on the wrong side of the bed."

Wilf slammed his hands on the table, making the crockery chink. "I'm sick of you blasted women interfering all the time!"

As he strode from the room, I jumped up in dismay. Should I stay or follow him? But Gloria leapt from her seat, throwing a furious look in my direction as she hurried after him.

"Well!" Alice gasped, clutching her chest.

"Gordon Bennett!" Arthur said. "What was that in aid of?"

"Oi!" A woman at a neighbouring table jabbed her finger at Arthur. "Don't take my late husband's name in vain."

As a roomful of eyes turned our way, I sat back down. Freda rested her arthritic hand on my arm. "Don't worry yourself about him, duck. He's just upset. His daughter's cancelled taking him out."

"Where was he going?"

Joe stepped beside us. "Is everything okay?"

"Just men acting like children." Alice popped her crust into her mouth. At least with a full mouth, she couldn't speak.

Freda turned to him. "Nothing you can do, I'm afraid, duck. Wilf's daughter keeps letting him down. Last week it was an outing to the seaside, this week a trip to the cinema. She couldn't spare him three hours."

"I'm glad I don't have children to fuss about," Alice said.

"Neither do I," Freda said. "But at least those with children have something to do. That's if they keep their promises. The rest of us are stuck here, day in, day out, doing nothing."

I'd never heard Freda sound despondent before. Normally she was such a cheerful soul. Joe crouched down beside her.

"It would be nice for you *all* to do something. I'll have a word with Gloria."

Alice harrumphed. "She'll just say no. She always does."

# Chapter 7

The following days passed without incident. When Monday rolled around, I waltzed into work, looking forward to my short stint as a hostess. First, I dashed into the treatment room – a fancy name for a space with a bed, a table and a few bits of medical equipment. But it had weighing scales. In trepidation, I watched the dial whirring round until it settled on ten stone seven pounds. Three pounds lower than before. Just a stone and a half to go for my height, according to *Slimming* magazine.

Just? When I'd lined up the blocks of lard at the supermarket, I'd been shocked to see how much extra fat I had. At least I was two packs down. I breathed in. My new one-size-too-small clothes would be arriving on Thursday – my day off. I couldn't wait.

I found Joe in the kitchen. After stacking the trolley and filling the urns, I followed him to the lift, where we started on the first floor of the east wing. Giving out the morning tea wasn't as exciting as I'd hoped. We knocked on each door, greeted each resident with a tea or a coffee, and trundled on to the next. Instead of happiness, we were met with grumbles. No, they hadn't slept well. We should knock louder. Why was the heating off? When we reached room eight, Joe moved to the other side of the corridor. Curious, I pointed to a door that was usually closed, but which stood open today. I'd thought the corridor ended at this point, but I was surprised to see that another three rooms lay on either side, before the corridor finally terminated at a white door with a huge fire escape sign.

"What about those rooms?"

"We don't do those."

"Why not?"

"They're for residents with dementia or those who can't manage without help. They get looked after in their rooms."

I'd seen uniformed staff members heading off with trays, but I'd assumed they were for people in the ground-floor flats, where the more able residents and couples lived. I hadn't realised there were other residents secreted away.

"Don't they get out at all?"

He chuckled. "They're not chained up." Then his expression grew serious. "But I don't think it's great. They're looked after by dedicated nurses who spend time with them and take them to the garden or whatever, but they're kept away from the others. It's not one-to-one care either, so they're on their own a lot."

"Why?"

A reedy cry echoed through one of the doors which stood ajar, but I couldn't see more than the corner of a bed. "*No! No!* Where's Harold?"

Instinct made me head towards the noise. I found a spacious room, larger than the others, with a sink in the corner, an armchair opposite the bed and the usual commode chair, which smelled as if it was full. But I'd never been asked to empty it. A uniformed nurse knelt beside a woman who sat on the bed in a floral dressing gown, her bare feet dangling over the edge. The overhead light was off, but sunlight streamed in through the net curtains, revealing her glistening tear-streaked face.

"Mrs Calam! Will you please behave? I've told you countless times. Harold is dead."

The staff member turned, looking surprised to find me there. Unlike the grey pinnies we wore, she was dressed in a sky-blue uniform, like a nurse. "Do you mind? I'm trying to get her dressed."

She picked up a slipper but the elderly woman kicked out, knocking it from her hand.

"No! I want my Harold!" The woman attempted to shuffle off the bed, but the nurse clamped her thighs, pinning her in place.

"She doesn't like you being here. You're upsetting her," she said.

"I'm sorry." I stepped back into Joe, not realising he hovered behind me.

"Maybe she needs a bit of time to calm down before getting dressed," he said.

She glared at us. "Maybe you need to mind your own business. Haven't you got work to do? I'll be having a word with Gloria about this."

Subdued, we headed away. Behind us, the door clicked shut, muffling all but the shrillest cry. We moved down the dim corridor and Joe knocked on a resident's door.

"Morning, Mr Taylor," he called. "I'm the bearer of your brew."

He sounded jovial. How did he do it? I could barely raise a smile. My thoughts were still with the poor woman begging for her Harold. Was he her son or husband? Lost in thought, I poured tea from the urn and handed the cup to Joe, who popped it on a saucer along with a small biscuit and carried it into the room. The cup and saucer trembled in his hand. He *was* bothered by the scene we'd witnessed. I decided I'd speak to him later.

"Here you are." Joe placed the tea on Mr Taylor's bedside table. "Is there anything else I can get you?"

"Heating. It's ruddy freezing in here," the man grumbled. He pulled the net aside and gazed outside. Condensation beaded the lower part of the window. "There's frost on that there lawn. But I bet it's colder in here than out."

That wasn't the only frost of the morning. Gloria's expression when she caught up with us after breakfast was decidedly icy. She pursed her lips and curled her finger, indicating that we should follow her to her office. Great! I'd assumed the staff member's warning was a threat, not something she'd carry out. What was it with grassing on people around here? My heart thumped but Joe looked calm as we followed her down the tiled corridor, the clip of her heels echoing over the clatter from the kitchen.

She pushed through the door, not holding it open for us. But Joe reached over my head to stop the door as it rebounded. As we stood in front of her desk, it occurred to me that I'd not been treated like this since I'd been at school. No wonder they had staffing issues. Who wanted to go to work to be dealt with like a child? Perhaps infantilising the workers and residents made life easier. Now, more than ever, I longed for my cushy office job where my boss had talked to me as an equal. Well, almost. I'd had to call him Mr Clothier, whereas he'd referred to me as Belinda. Knowing the hierarchy they liked here, it was strange that Gloria allowed us to use her first name.

She stood, fingertips planted like roots on the wood, her expression fierce. Any moment she'd draw all her anger into a ball which she'd fire at us. Like now. She took a deep breath.

"So you think you know better than a nurse with twenty years' experience?" she hissed, but her next words moved up a decibel. "What the hell do you think you were doing? You have one job!" She prodded her desk. "*One!* If you've got enough time on your hands to snoop around, you're not doing it properly."

"We…" I was about to point out that we'd simply gone to investigate the noise and it had only taken a few minutes, but Joe gave my arm a warning squeeze.

"We're sorry," he said. "We won't do it again."

If he thought that would appease her, he was mistaken.

"Too right it won't." Her eyes locked on mine. "You're back on toilet duty. That should keep you out of trouble. And you!" She jabbed a finger at Joe. "If I ever catch you interfering again, that will be it. Now get on with your work."

Outside the door, we pulled sorrowful faces at each other. I didn't know what to do next. Sally and the new woman would be doing the commodes. I should be helping to clean the residents' rooms, but if I'd been moved back to my usual duties, should I relieve them? I half turned to go back into the office to ask, but Joe signalled for me to follow him.

"Come on. We've got to get the rooms done," he hissed.

"But she said I'm back on toilets."

"That's tomorrow."

As we fetched the cleaning materials from the cupboard, I spotted Nancy, arms outstretched, holding a commode bowl. She averted her face, grimacing as she walked over to the toilet she would have scrubbed earlier. That would be me tomorrow. Back to throne duties. And all because I'd been worried about a resident.

"Don't you think that was a bit over the top?" I asked Joe as he passed me the container holding the cleaning materials.

He shrugged. "Maybe they were worried about the resident's privacy."

"But I caught Mr Connor in the toilet the other day. That was a bit embarrassing, but he didn't rush off to complain."

*A bit?* It had been *really* embarrassing, with dozens of apologies on both sides. He hadn't locked the door, but I should have waited longer after knocking. I found him sitting, trousers round his ankles, reading a newspaper. If only that was all he'd been doing, but the stink told me otherwise. At least the newspaper had hidden his 'bits'.

"Mr Connor knows better. He should have locked the door." Joe hefted the hoover over the dirty mop and bucket that Sally had abandoned in the middle of the cupboard. "But the woman with dementia? Maybe we made things worse for her and that nurse by getting involved. Who knows what happened after we left?"

I mulled over his words. The resident had been agitated. I'd seen her kicking out, knocking her slipper across the floor. The staff member had held her down but, the more I thought about it, it had only been to protect them both.

He looked at me. "If you'd seen something that did look abusive, what would you do? Would you be prepared to lose your job over it?"

Instinctively, I went to say yes. But it would be another job lost without references. Another gap on my CV. But then I saw sense. Of course I would. I couldn't stand by and let people get hurt.

"If something bad happened, then yes. But it didn't. I'm still confused why Gloria was so OTT about it, though."

"Gloria was acting on what she'd been told. In my mind, if it doesn't feel right – and it can't be explained away – then the question should be: why did the nurse make such a big deal about us seeing her?"

# Chapter 8

That night Mum asked what I wanted for my birthday, which was the following week. Her eyebrows rose when I said I'd really like to have my hair done at Franco's in Bilton. I'd heard amazing things about it. The price was pretty special too. I didn't confess where I'd got the idea. The slimming magazine. As the featured slimmers lost weight, they had their hair done and bought new clothes to reward themselves. Mum wasn't a fan of my diet. Neither was Gran, who'd insisted on heaping chips onto my plate at the weekend. I imagined the lard congealing around the potatoes and in my stomach and had just picked at them, telling her I wasn't hungry.

I had a target. I had to double my two-pound weight loss by my birthday. Especially with my new clothes arriving soon.

"Ask the rest of the family if they want to contribute," Mum had said.

I couldn't pick up the phone fast enough. It might be embarrassing begging Auntie (my godmother, but she preferred to be called Auntie) and Gran for cash, but needs must. When Gran asked for a day to check her account, I felt bad. Had she already bought my present and wanted to see if she could return it? But when I told her not to worry, she wouldn't hear of it.

As agreed, when I had my mid-afternoon break from work the next day, I called her from the phone box in town, keeping the door ajar to let out the stench of urine and alcohol. An empty can of Special Brew had been left on the shelf, while someone had tippexed out the phone instructions – not that I needed them – and stuck chewing gum over the 10p slot. I had to use my coin to pick it away. Above the phone, a poster petitioned to keep this old red box with its crown above the door. It had been earmarked to become a card payment one. Whatever happened, it would be nice if it weren't a toilet for drunks when the pubs closed.

I slipped the handset between my chin and shoulder then dialled the number. It began to ring. I twirled the black cord around my fingers.

"Hi Gran," I said.

"Hello, dear." She said it as a question. Why was I calling her?

"I… um… I… You said to phone?"

I extracted my finger from its plastic bind and checked my waistband. I could get my fingers between it and my stomach without too much effort. But, while my trousers weren't exactly falling off, at least there was a gap, and the usual red weals where the material sliced into my skin weren't there.

"Yes." She fell silent.

Could she make this less painful? She can't have forgotten already.

Sighing, I said, "You know, when I asked about my birthday?"

Gran sounded surprised. After all, I'd never been

fussed about presents before, always smiling – or at least, not showing my thoughts – when she presented me with a purple cardigan or a frilly blouse from C&A.

"I can give you five pounds, love," she said.

Seriously? That was a huge amount for her. "I don't need that much."

"You have it. It'll do you good to have a nice hairdo. Live life while you can. Ooh, that reminds me, did you hear about Herb Whitmore?"

After telling me about her neighbour's sudden death – relayed with excitement rather than upset – beeps sounded down the line, and we said hasty goodbyes.

I phoned Franco's and checked if they had a slot free. They did. At four o'clock.

"Can I let you know for sure tomorrow?" I asked. Gloria had a half day, so I wouldn't be able to confirm the booking until then.

The woman sighed. "It's a cancellation, so you're lucky we can fit you in. We'll hold it until noon at the latest."

The next morning, I rushed into work, hoping my previous misdemeanour had been forgotten. I found Gloria at her desk, her head in her hands. Not a great start. She rolled her eyes when she noticed me hovering by her door, and again after I'd told her what I wanted.

"A day off?"

"I just want to swap my day."

"Tracey's already asked to switch hers to Friday."

My face fell. Why would Tracey do that? She knew

Friday was my birthday.

"I'll leave it for you two to sort out. I need someone to cover the morning and evening shifts. I don't care who it is. The new girl has just phoned to say she isn't coming back."

Once we'd cleared up after breakfast, I grabbed Tracey. Specks of mascara dotted the skin beneath her eyes. She gave me a walrus yawn, not bothering to cover her mouth.

"I've requested next Friday off, but Gloria says you've already asked."

"Oh yeah. That was meant to be a surprise, but she's wrecked it."

"What?"

She waved her hand in front of her face and stifled another yawn. "I thought a night out would be nice for you."

"But I'm working until eight."

She shrugged. "I know. I thought you'd like a night out at Blinkers. There's plenty of time. We won't get a taxi there until ten."

I gritted my teeth. For a start, I didn't fancy going to a nightclub. Scratch that. Usually, I'd love it, but the heat and sweat off the dance floor would wreck my new hairdo. Plus, I didn't fancy spending my birthday as a gooseberry. When I bumped into Joe by the cleaning cupboard, I couldn't help moaning to him.

"I've got a half day next Friday. I'll do your evening shift."

Really? I did a little happy dance. "That would be amazing." Then I groaned. "I have to let the hairdressers know by noon. I don't suppose you can talk to Gloria, distract her while I sneak into her office? She's in such a mood, she'd say no if I asked."

He scratched his chin. "Well, I could come up with a broken broom head or something. It is loose, and Sally's not here to sort it."

Beside us, the lift door whirred open. Gloria appeared, looking flustered. Joe dived into the cupboard and yanked off the broom head. When he held out both bits to Gloria, she sighed.

"Not another blasted thing. With Sally off sick and Nancy not coming back, I've got enough on my plate."

Then I realised she was wearing a pinny over her blouse. With us being so short-staffed, she must have come to help. At least with Gloria upstairs cleaning rooms, her office would be free for me to use her phone. Joe pushed the head back onto the broom and tightened it.

"I guess we'll manage with it like this for today," he said.

She frowned. "I don't know why you need it anyhow. Unless you were planning to sweep outside. Leave that until tomorrow."

I shot Joe an apologetic look. Thanks to me, he had another job. But my guilt didn't last long. After ensuring that Gloria saw me carting several commodes to the toilet, I rushed downstairs and made the call I hoped would change my life. An exaggeration, maybe, but at those prices I expected to leave with perfect waves like Princess Diana, although I was more likely to end up looking like Fergie. But I'd take her hairstyle over my current 'orphan Annie' look.

As expected, Gloria's door was closed but unlocked. I headed over to her desk. Next to a tiered tray filled with paperwork was a cream phone. Just my bad luck it was the old-style rotary dial, and not one of the new push-button phones like Mum owned. With the hairdresser's number having three eights and a nine, it would mean waiting for the dial to work its way back before I could dial another. I checked the corridor in case Gloria had followed me. She hadn't. I phoned the number. The receptionist at Franco's answered promptly, checking my appointment details in her brusque manner. As she spoke, I glanced down at a sheet on Gloria's desk and frowned. *Marten, Mattherson and Williams, Solicitors*. Maybe someone had left a bequest? After replacing the handset, I swivelled the letter around and scanned the first few lines. Then I gasped. The residential home was being sued. Wasn't that something that only happened in the US? But why?

A familiar sound stopped me in my tracks – the clatter of the morning tea trolley across the kitchen tiles. I put the letter back and darted to the doorway. As someone walked out of the kitchen, I slid behind the office door, pressing my back to the wall. The kitchen door banged open. Someone was coming out. Flaming heck! I'd be in for it if they caught me. The smell of baking wafted in the air as the trolley rattled closer, but it didn't move off down the corridor. I stiffened, hearing someone hum above the chink of crockery. Great! They'd only gone and brought the trolley into Gloria's office. I closed my eyes, tried to hush my breath, but my heart thumped like a drum and my legs quivered. The noise faded. Moments later the kitchen door shut. I peered around the door.

The tea trolley was by the wall, along with three cups and saucers, tea plates and slices of clingfilmed fruit cake, but no teapot or milk. They'd be back with those soon. I frowned. If Gloria was holding a meeting, why was she upstairs helping to clean the rooms?

I pulled her door shut, making sure to lever the handle so it didn't click, and hurried away. No wonder Gloria had been stressed this morning. It wasn't just about the lack of staff. Being sued was shocking. What could have happened? If only I'd had more time to read the letter.

When I reached the corridor, I found a pale-faced Gloria talking to the nurse who'd grassed on Joe and me after we'd seen her with the agitated resident. Gloria's hands shot to her face. Joe's solemn eyes met mine.

Had the nurse spotted me sneak into Gloria's office? But why would she? I'd never seen her downstairs.

"Please tell me this is some sort of joke," Gloria said. "Because he couldn't have chosen a worse day."

# Chapter 9

Mr Saunders had died. He was one of the home's 'hidden' dementia patients. It seemed strange that he'd lived and died yards from where I worked, yet I'd never met him. His death turned the residential home on its head. The nurse rushed off in the direction of her patients, while Gloria tore off her pinny and handed it to Joe.

"Get Belinda to help you with the rooms. The lounge can be left for today. We've got enough to do." She pointed her finger at us. "I do not want you gossiping with the residents about this. I mean it."

Puzzled, I waited until she'd gone before asking Joe, "Why can't the residents know? It's all so odd."

He shrugged. "They treat them like children most of the time, so why not now?" His words held a strange, bitter undertone, unlike his usual self. Catching my surprised look, he added, "They're from the generation where the professionals knew best. Doctors, institutions. They decided what they needed to know, and what they could and couldn't do."

What had got into him? Older people died. It was a fact of life, but his eyes glinted with fury. "These so-called professionals – they wielded power over people's lives, their jobs. I can't believe we're still doing it now. It might be in small ways, but it's still there. Look at Alice Swann and the butter knife. Has anyone given you a reason behind it? And us not being allowed to question that nurse's actions when Mrs Calam was upset. Who knows what else is going on?" He checked his watch and sighed. "We better get going. Sorry about letting rip like that."

"Talking about something else going on, I saw something interesting in Gloria's office."

But he hadn't heard me. He'd hefted his cleaning bucket and hoover, and started towards the next room.

I rushed after him. "I'll get on with the commodes and then help you."

"We'll do them while we clean. It's a stupid system, having one person doing the commodes and toilets when they could all be done together."

As we went from room to room, moving closer to the end of the corridor and the area we weren't allowed to see, I kept an eye on the open door in case they wheeled Mr Saunders past. But no one did. I'd assumed it would be like a scene from *Casualty*, with people racing down the corridor to wheel him away.

"I know it's strange to say this, but I've never seen a dead person before," I said.

"It's not that exciting. It depends how long they've been dead. Often they just look like they're asleep." He looked at me hovering by the door. "You won't get to see him. He'll be covered when they bring him out."

For the rest of the morning, I stole the occasional glance into the corridor until I tired of it and got on with the work in hand. By the time we had restocked the cleaning cupboard, no one had come to take poor Mr Saunders away. He lay alone, seemingly unwanted and unloved. Were his sobbing relatives downstairs? Did they want to see him first?

Alice Swann gave me the answer at lunch, having somehow discovered the news within thirty minutes of Gloria telling us to keep it quiet. The doctor had been to see Mr Saunders the week before and his death wasn't unexpected. The funeral directors would arrive in their own time.

"They don't rush here. No doubt he'll still be upstairs this afternoon, mouldering away in that bed."

She and Wilf Preston had been here when Mr Saunders had lived in the main part of the residential home before – as she put it – he'd lost his mind. She twirled her finger to the side of her head. "He started wandering around. He gave me such a fright. We found him in so many odd places."

Arthur chuckled. "Just like someone else we know." He jerked his head towards Alice and gave me a wink.

Ignoring him, Alice tapped Wilf's arm. "Do you remember when he wandered into Ethel's bedroom that night? She screamed the corridor down."

Wilf nodded but continued to butter his toast. If he didn't eat it, Alice would swipe it.

Alice frowned. "It must have contributed to her heart attack a few weeks later."

Freda sighed. "I wonder what's in store for us all."

The table fell silent. I gazed at them all. Were they thinking about their past lives or perhaps their future? How long did they have left? A month, a year or even a decade or two? It wasn't much of a life being stuck in here all day. They had lively minds and deserved more excitement than a colour TV in the residents' lounge. Had Joe spoken to Gloria about organising activities, as he'd promised? I hadn't thought to check. Neither had I told him about the letter I'd found. I glanced across to Tracey, who laughed with a woman on her table. She was my friend, so I should be telling her instead of him, but I knew what she was like. She'd have to tell just one other person, who'd tell another, then another and within hours Gloria would know that I'd been snooping around.

♦

Joe was sent home with a sickness bug the evening before my birthday. At first, Gloria cancelled my day off but, when I told her about my hairdo appointment, she made Tracey work the full day and gave me a half day. Talk about giving Tracey the hump. The next morning, she still didn't look happy when I passed her with the tea trolley while I was on my way to do the next toilet. Huffing loudly, she tapped on Arthur's door. Would she moan to him about being stuck here, like she'd done with Mrs Bartholomew? She knocked a second time. He didn't answer.

This time she hammered on the door and raised her voice. "Mr Birch, Mr Birch!"

Sally, who stood outside the neighbouring room, hushed her. Tracey gave an exasperated shrug and pushed her way inside. Curious, I paused to watch. The room lay in darkness but for a glimmer of light peeking through a chink in the curtains. A strange smell filtered into the corridor. She snapped on the light, then gasped. I put my mop and bucket down and headed inside, but she backed into me, her hand covering her mouth.

"Blimey! I think he's dead."

"Are you sure?"

She nodded, her face pale.

Sally barged between us, propelling me into the room. Arthur wasn't lying serenely on his back, as I'd expected. Instead, he hung off the bed, the blankets ruffled around his legs. His arm, which looked bruised, draped onto the carpet. Had he been trying to get out of bed? I couldn't see his face, just the wispy grey hair on the back of his head. On TV, grandparents died in their sleep in an armchair or in bed, hands clasped, their blue lips the only telltale sign. 'Is he dead?' the characters would ask, shaking them. There was no need for us to do this.

When I'd wondered what seeing a dead person would be like – guessing it would happen sooner or later in a residential home – I'd expected it to be a stranger. Like Mr Saunders had been. Not Arthur from my table, who'd worked as a milkman, had three children, seven grandchildren, and a wonderful sense of humour. A picture of him and his late wife sat next to his wallet on the bedside table, both smiling, his arm around her shoulder, his eyes twinkling like they always did. It looked like it was taken in the early 1970s, as she wore glasses with rims that curled up at the sides, while he had a full head of dark brown hair. Now they'd be together again.

Then a strange thought hit me. Today was my birthday. Today was also a date his family would mark forever, yet he would never know its significance.

Unsettled, I watched Sally kneel beside him and press her fingers to his neck. She turned to Tracey. "Get Gloria!" Then she signalled for me to help her. "Let's get him onto the bed. We can't leave him like this."

Thank goodness he wasn't a big man. We hefted his stiff body back onto the bed. I was surprised at its weight. Beside me, Sally mirrored the shock I'd seen on Tracey's face. Gone was her usual uppity sneer.

Panting, I asked her, "Do you get many people dying here?"

"Strangely, no. Most end up in the cottage hospital when they get sick. We've never had two in such a short time."

Grimacing, she gave Arthur a shove into the middle of the mattress. His body curved in a strange position, his arm splayed out. It felt so wrong. Intrusive. He wouldn't want me to see him like this. I didn't glance at his face, wanting to remember him as the smiling man he'd been.

Gloria bustled into the room, her expression grim. I moved aside to make space for her beside the bed.

"Get on with your work," she said. "We'll sort this."

I went back to finish cleaning the toilets. Images of Arthur rose in my head: stuffing toast into his mouth to get one over on Alice, muttering to himself when she'd said something that annoyed him, holding his belly as he laughed. My thoughts moved on to worries about Gran. Mum said you should bother with people now, as they might not be here tomorrow. She was right.

In the dining room, Arthur's chair might have been empty, but he was centre stage in our thoughts. We ate in silence. Gloria, who sat in Joe's place at the neighbouring table, stole glances in my direction that suggested I should chivvy everyone up. But I couldn't. I'd picked at my cereal that morning and now I moved a potato around my plate. Even Alice had lost her appetite. She pushed her plate away.

Tentatively I asked, to break the morose silence, "Will you go to the funeral?"

Alice's laugh tinkled in the air. "Goodness forbid that we'd be allowed out. Gloria will go and represent us all."

Freda used her napkin to dab a tear from her eye, then wiped a smear of gravy from her trembling lip. "Such a shame."

Alice glared across the table. "That chair is cursed. First Donald, then Hilda, now Arthur. I thought he'd be here longer than nine months, though."

"Alice!" Freda shook her head. "Not now."

Alice harrumphed. "This is a waiting room. A boring one, at that. At least before…" She hesitated. Was she going to mention her time in the institution? I put my knife and fork on either side of my plate, ready to listen. "Before, I was useful. Now we're just stuck here, wondering who will be next. Most likely the next person that sits on that chair."

"Don't be daft," Wilf said. "I'll sit there tomorrow if you're that worried."

"Please don't." Freda gave him a plaintive look. "Perhaps we should retire the chair?"

He laughed. "You women will be the death of me with your superstitions."

From her table, Gloria smiled at me. Obviously, she couldn't hear the thread of the conversation or she wouldn't be congratulating me on managing to get the residents to talk. As the occupants of my table returned to their thoughts, I flickered her a wan smile. I wouldn't be trying again.

It was only later that I recalled Sally saying that residents rarely died here. Yet three people who'd sat in that chair had died. But Arthur had been here almost nine months, so the others could have gone years before. How long did it take a residential home to fill a vacated room?

While I thought about it, Tracey headed over. She pulled off her hairband and shook her hair loose. The middle section bunched from where it had been tied.

"You're off now? Lucky thing!" She grinned. I must be forgiven for making her work the second shift. "Are you coming to the pub tonight? I'll shout you a birthday drink."

I shook my head. "I don't feel much like celebrating."

"Oh, come off it! Don't say this is about Arthur. He was well old. You won't get another twenty-fifth birthday again."

I smiled. "I know, but I really don't feel up to it. How about another day?"

She shrugged. "Your loss." Then she linked her arm through mine. "So, come on, tell me what hairstyle you're thinking of. Highlights might look good."

For once, she'd come up with a good idea. Highlights would be great. Except I didn't have the money. I'd just have my hair cut and blow-dried, then I'd go round to Gran's to show her my new style. She'd be surprised to see me, expecting me to be 'out on the town' as she put it. But, now more than ever, I wanted to see my family. If today had taught me one thing, it was to cherish them while I could.

# Chapter 10

Joe didn't return to work until Sunday. He hadn't even taken his coat off before Tracey tapped his shoulder and told him about the extra workload caused by his sickness. At first he seemed bemused, but when she told him about Arthur and how I'd been too upset to go out for my birthday, his face fell.

"It wasn't quite like that." I fired her an angry glare. It wasn't Joe's fault that Gloria had sent him home, worried that his bug might spread to the residents.

"I've just told him the facts. Arthur died and, because of that, you didn't come out. It's a shame. Gary might have liked your new hairdo."

Did I have a choice in the matter? Maybe she thought I should be flattered to think that my new wavy bob might win him over. But I didn't care for him. His spiky quiff could take someone's eye out and I couldn't imagine us having an interesting conversation. He was more the 'all right, love, fancy half a pint?' type.

Joe's concerned eyes met mine. "I am sorry. It must have been hard finding Arthur like that."

"*I* found him," Tracey said. "And, no, it flaming well wasn't nice."

She stormed off towards the kitchen, leaving Joe and me alone.

"Ignore her," I said. "She must have had a barney with Aiden or something. She wouldn't talk about it yesterday when I asked her how Friday night went. How are you feeling now?"

He shrugged. "Better. It was a short-lived thing, but Gloria wouldn't let me come back until today. I love your hair, by the way. It really suits you."

Thrilled, I patted my hair. No amount of toilet cleaning could dampen the spring in my step. Wow! Not just a like, but he *loved* my new hairdo.

It wasn't until we were clearing up after breakfast that Joe spoke to me again, placing his tray on my table and interrupting my cutlery count. I'd reached the spoons – all knives and forks were accounted for.

"Er…" He scratched his head. "You're a friend and I'm sorry that I let you down on your birthday, of all days. I'm having a party next Saturday." He chuckled. "At my parents' house. They're away but they're fine with me having a small gathering. It would be great if you could come."

My heart leapt. Even if he had asked as a friend, my hairstyle was paying off! Then I hesitated. If he'd invited me to the cinema, I'd have jumped at the chance. But a house party with people I didn't know? That didn't sound much fun.

"Charlotte and Dan will be there," he said, as if reading my thoughts. "I've only asked a dozen people. They're a nice bunch."

I didn't want to say no, but I didn't want to say yes either. We'd had parties at poly – loads of them. At first, we'd all been strangers, desperate to make friends, but it wasn't long before I'd got to know everyone. Partying with my mates was fun, but partying with people I didn't know? A shy person's nightmare. While I liked the idea of making new friends, I didn't like actually doing it. Maybe Charlotte and Dan wouldn't mind if I became a cling-on when Joe left me – which he'd have to, being the host.

"You won't be left alone," Joe said.

Flipping heck! Did he have ESP? My cheeks flamed. Was I really letting my shyness stop me from going out with him? I mean, who'd be stupid enough to turn down a chance to party with a gorgeous – if unattainable – man and his lovely friends?

Footsteps echoed nearby. Joe hefted up the tray as Sally strode into the dining room, huffing. Spotting us, she put her hands on her hips.

"What's keeping you two?" She clapped her hands. "Hurry up! We're paid to work, not chat."

She disappeared, leaving Joe and me to pull faces behind her back. Gloria's day off was always a nightmare with Sally being in charge. But Joe made it more bearable.

"Let me know later," he said.

"Yes," I said, surprising myself. "I'll come."

♦

The next day I sneaked into the treatment room to weigh myself. I'd shifted another two pounds since I'd last stepped on the scales. Seven pounds in total. It might even be more, as I hadn't time to check before breakfast. That slice of toast and cup of tea could have added another pound.

I'd been so thrilled to see the dial heading in the right direction that I'd forgotten to keep an eye out. When the door clicked open, I jumped in shock, clutching my chest.

"Flip…" My exclamation drained away, along with my excitement.

Frowning, Gloria clutched the door handle. "What are you doing?"

"J-just checking my weight."

"Do that in your own time. I want you in my office *now*."

I twisted my feet into my shoes and hurried after her. What had I done now? It couldn't be about weighing myself. She'd have given me what-for without needing to drag me away. Then it hit me. She must have found out that I'd been in her office, even though I'd only told Gran about the letter. We'd had fun speculating on the possible scenarios. She'd come up with some right corkers, widening the net to include Arthur being bumped off because he'd left the residential home money in his will. Her eyes had sparkled while we chatted. We'd had such fun laughing and joking – keeping ourselves rooted in the present, rather than the past – that I'd wondered why I didn't spend more time with her.

But this present wasn't so fun. Not when Gloria's angry face greeted me as I hesitated at her door. She pointed to the chair. The letter was nowhere to be seen.

"Sit down."

My heart thumped. I perched on the edge of the chair, my back straight, hands on my knees. Gloria pursed her lips and gazed out of the window to where the postman lugged a parcel from his van.

"You went into Mr Birch's room the day he died. Were you ever left alone there?"

Did she think he'd been murdered? She couldn't suspect me, surely? If that was the case, shouldn't the police be here?

My voice trembled. "Tracey knocked and I followed her in. He was already dead."

"Strange that you went into his room when you should have been cleaning the lavatories and bathrooms."

"I-I was passing."

The doorbell rang. She got to her feet, her heels clipping across the corridor to the kitchen. After asking the cook to deal with the postman, she came back, closing the door, then leaning against it. To my surprise, she sighed deeply and shook her head, before moving away to slump into her chair, head in her hands, her fringe a curtain over her fingertips. Perplexed, I sat in silence. What on earth had made her go from fiery to frazzled in a matter of minutes? Whatever the reason, it made me more worried than before.

I didn't dare move a muscle. Instead, I stared at her bowed head and the specks of dust dancing through the rays of sunlight until they drifted onto her bottle-blonde hair, betrayed by a hint of dark roots.

She lifted her head, meeting my gaze. "We've had another complaint."

The solicitor's letter? But if it was about that, why wasn't it in front of her? And how did it relate to Arthur? He'd been alive when I'd seen the letter. Then it clicked. She'd said 'another'.

"Mr Birch's daughter says he got his pension money the day before he died. She took him to the post office. But his wallet only contained two pounds. She – and I – want to know what happened to the other forty pounds."

"You think I took it?" I gasped.

Her composure had returned. Her steely grey eyes locked with mine. I couldn't look away in case it made me look guilty.

Her jawline hardened. "I don't know who, but someone did."

"Do you know that the money was there that morning? I mean…" Gran's devious speculation ran through my mind. Perhaps she hadn't been far off the mark. "Maybe he saw someone trying to steal it and had a heart attack or something?"

"Don't be daft," she snapped. "Mr Birch's wallet was found on his bedside table. It's most likely the money went missing after he died."

"Have you called the police?" I don't know why I asked. Curiosity? Or the fear that they'd want to interview me?

"We'll have to do so if the money isn't found. It won't look good. Not after…"

She fell silent. Had she been about to mention the reason for the solicitor's letter? Instead, she reached into her drawer and ripped a lined sheet of paper from a pad.

"I want you to write down everything you did here the evening Mr Birch died, including exactly what happened before and after he was discovered. Once you've done that, I'll accompany you while you take over from Tracey. She'll be next. You'll have to do the commodes and help with the rooms. Downstairs can wait." She pointed a finger at me. "If you mention one word of this to anyone – and by anyone, I mean exactly that – you'll be out on your ear."

# Chapter 11

The next few days were tense, even if Gloria acted as if nothing was wrong, while Sally was her usual annoying self. I got the impression she'd blamed me or Tracey because of the way she spoke to both of us, mimicking Gloria's imperious tone.

"You're not allowed in any of the residents' rooms unaccompanied," she'd said, clearly forgetting she was also on the list of suspects.

Tracey clenched her fists as if ready to swing for her. "Fine! So, who'll be making sure you don't, either? Cos you had more opportunity than me."

Sally paled and bent down, her nose inches from Tracey's. "How dare you," she hissed. "I'll make sure Gloria gets to hear about this."

"Go on!" Tracey's eyes glittered with fury. "I was in that room for two minutes before you sent me away. Bee was in there for a bit longer – but with you. What happened after we left? Did Gloria leave you alone when she went to call the doctor?"

I buried my face in my hands, wishing myself anywhere but here. I hated confrontation. When I peeked between my fingers, I found Sally glaring at me.

"I bet you two have been concocting some sort of scheme so you can make it look like it was me." She jabbed her finger at us. "I'll make damn sure you won't win."

With that, she'd declared war. While we were reasonably safe with Gloria in charge, her day off – Sunday – would roll around soon enough. Should I cancel going to Joe's party on Saturday night, in case I wasn't on form the next day? I worked hard to appease Sally, but nothing I did was good enough.

A few days later, she hoiked me out of Mr Hall's room, where I was trying to lever the brimming pan from his commode without spilling the contents, and led me to the toilet. She pointed to a skid mark in the bowl.

"You didn't do a very good job this morning."

I shrugged. "Sorry. I had a bit of hassle with Mrs Bartholomew's commode."

"You can clean that now."

"But Mr Hall's is full."

"Now!" She stormed out then paused and swung back around. "I'll be checking in five minutes."

Talk about stupid. Joe was right. It *was* daft to clean the toilets then do the commodes later. The rooms and commodes should be cleaned together, with the toilets left until last. But I wasn't going to be the one to tell her. If she wanted to duplicate work, that was fine by me.

But when Gloria came by fifteen minutes later and found me still doing the commodes, she looked furious.

Keen to placate her, I jumped in. "Sally told me to redo the toilets."

A sensible person would have kept their mouth shut, especially as I was supposed to be ingratiating myself with Sally.

From the way Gloria glowered, I hadn't managed that. "No doubt because you should have cleaned them properly."

"I did, but Mrs Bartholomew had a bit of an issue in her commode and it marked the toilet bowl."

Her clenched jaw told me I'd given the wrong answer. An apology would have been better. But it was too late. What was it with this place? The harder you tried, the worse you were treated. If only my old boss hadn't sold me tales of university life and the promise of a brighter road ahead. To think I could be back in an office, where the only 'cleaning' I'd done was to bin piles of paper when organising the filing cabinet.

I headed back to Mr Hall's room, then paused at the door. Sally had given strict instructions that we shouldn't enter rooms unless accompanied. But how could I do my job if I had to call someone over each time? I checked all around. A bedroom door stood ajar near the lift – Sally and Tracey must be in there. I darted in and out in seconds, then I wished I hadn't. Knowing my luck, something would go missing and the finger would point at me.

That thought niggled me all morning and throughout lunch. When I handed out the bowls of apple crumble, it stirred another memory. The one time in my life I'd stolen something was when I'd gone scrumping with Tracey and a few others. I hadn't really thought of it as theft, just as a free harvest, like conkers, although we didn't take the apples from the ground. My favourite tree had been a blood-apple one. It grew at an angle to the ground, so it was easy to clamber up. For some reason, my thoughts of the blood apples' crimson flesh made me think of Snow White being tempted by the witch's apple. Then a brief image of me being led by an apple on a stick stirred a strange feeling of betrayal. I had no idea why, but it made me feel discomforted.

Freda broke into my thoughts. "Aren't you feeling well, duck?"

My fork hovered above the apple chunks I'd been picking out. I'd read about the calories in the butter, which made the crumble a no-no. The sugar in the apple was okay, if I didn't eat too much.

Alice straightened up, narrowing her eyes. "There must be a man on the horizon. A change of hairstyle, weight loss, even new clothes, although…"

I stiffened, waiting for a rebuke about my choice of catalogue clothes, but Alice startled me with her response.

"She does look a bit peaky."

"That's what I thought." Freda pushed the custard jug towards me. "You need feeding up, duck."

"She doesn't quack." Alice rolled her eyes. "But at this rate, she might need one."

She must have told a joke, as Wilf laughed. Freda didn't get it either. She peered at me. If she'd been able to do so, I felt sure she'd check my temperature. If only Arthur was here. He would have deflected their attention by pointing out that Alice was stick-thin and could do with feeding up herself. Saying that, she ate for queen and country. So perhaps he wouldn't have encouraged her.

82

To prove my point, she nodded towards my bowl. "I could have eaten your crumble if you'd thought before you started. In future, let me know what items you don't intend to eat before you begin." She nudged Freda, throwing a knowing glance across to Joe. "It's obvious why she doesn't want it. Pass me the custard."

Indignant, I said, "My new look is for me. Us women don't have to run around after men nowadays." When Wilf frowned, I added, "No offence."

Alice harrumphed. "If that was the case, why didn't you bother before?"

I blushed at that. But she'd got it wrong. I'd made my decision after seeing Gary's expression at the pub. I hadn't realised that until later. But his dismissive laugh, combined with Tracey expecting me to fade into the background so she could bloom, had been the deciding factor. I'd wasted years doing just that. At school, I'd accepted my status as the ugly duckling. At poly, I didn't have to worry about it, as no one bothered about looks. I didn't know if I could turn into a swan, but I'd give it a try. Never again would someone like Gary snigger at the idea of being stuck with me.

At least, that was the plan.

# Chapter 12

We agreed that Joe would drive me to his house straight after work on Saturday evening. I could change there, stay over in one of the spare rooms – I decided I must have misheard that bit; everyone I knew only had one spare room – then he'd take me to work the following morning. It wouldn't be an all-night party. Not when we both had work.

I'd been embarrassed about stopping over at his. I mean, we hardly knew each other and, even though I was staying as a friend, it felt a bit odd. I'd never stopped over at a man's house before. I'd snogged a few lads in the past, but they'd been drunken fumbles, spent extracting wayward hands from my boobs in case the lad realised that the rolls of fat below weren't much smaller.

Dan, Charlotte and another of Joe's friends would also be staying rather than getting a taxi back to Bilton. How many rooms did he have? Or were a few of us destined to sleep on the settee? I didn't dare ask.

As he turned the car into Hummingbird Lane – the poshest road in Rocklington – I frowned. Surely he didn't live here? If so, why was he working at Rockbeare? It didn't make sense. When he turned towards a gated drive, I had to stop myself from gasping. I hadn't expected this. A black gate sat between brick pillars. Between it and a second set of gates, stretched a tall laurel hedge. An in-and-out drive! My mum would kill for that. In awe, I gazed at the mock Georgian frontage. Six columns lined the porch.

"My dad won the pools," Joe said.

I laughed at that.

"No, seriously. My dad won the pools doing the *Sun* Plan 40."

I knew about the *Sun* Plan 40. My gran used its formula when she did the pools. I couldn't explain why, but her favourite paper didn't seem to suit Joe – and, by extension, his family. I didn't have a problem with people reading it, although I wouldn't buy it myself – I didn't like page three. My gran liked the fact that the ink didn't come off on her fingers like some of the other papers.

Still, I couldn't connect the idea of Joe – or his father – having the *Sun* in their house. I'd always imagined that posh people only read huge broadsheets.

"Your dad read the *Sun*?"

"Back then he did. Quite a few things have changed since."

I gasped. "He got this with the pools!"

Joe's handbrake grated as he gave it a tug. How come he didn't have a pool winner's fancy car? Just a six-year-old Talbot Horizon in cherry red. He switched off the ignition and wound up his window.

"Well, not entirely. He got enough to buy out the manufacturing company he part-owned and it also meant he could expand it. This…" – he gazed at the impressive façade – "is the result of luck and a lot of hard work."

"Why…" I trailed off.

I wanted to ask why Joe did a mundane job at the residential home, but I couldn't find a polite way of doing so. But when he grinned, I realised that my face was like an open book.

"Why don't I work for my dad? Much as I love him, he lives for his job and expects family members to feel the same. He treats his workers well, but when I spent a few weeks at his place…" He chuckled and shook his head. "Let's just say, Gloria and Sally have nothing on him."

Outside one of the two garages sat a new E-reg Vauxhall Nova. The same colour as Joe's.

"Your family like red, then."

"That's Charlotte's," he said. "I told them to let themselves in."

As I followed him into his house, my shyness took hold. I'd met Charlotte and Dan before, so why did I feel so embarrassed? No matter how I'd tried to fight it – walking with a straight back, ignoring my burning cheeks – my body wouldn't behave. When I caught sight of my rosy face in the hallway mirror, I blushed even more.

From the spacious hallway, the size of a room, Joe led me up a staircase that swept around the wall and onto a landing that had a railing at one side, so I could see the hall below and out through the two arched windows to the front garden. White-panelled doors lined the corridor, but not like the ones at Rockbeare did. For a start, this corridor wasn't lit by strip lights. I couldn't wait until night fell and Joe could switch on the chandelier that hung near the stairwell.

He led me into a room – not as fancy as I'd expected – and told me to come downstairs when I was ready. I laid my Miss Selfridge carrier bag on the duvet – I'd lost the game of 'hunt the holdall' that morning, and had picked the poshest carrier bag I could find – and gazed outside, stunned to see a swimming pool with a blue cover. Beyond it, the lawn extended in perfect stripes to a hedgerow.

The room was fitted with a white-panelled integral wardrobe, a double bed, two bedside cabinets and a dressing table, beside which stood another door. As I reached out for the handle, I hesitated. What if it led to another room and I found Charlotte and Dan or someone else there? But curiosity got the better of me and I cracked it open an inch. I was stunned to find a whole bathroom there – okay, there wasn't a bath, but there was everything else. The white tiles and stainless-steel fittings gleamed as if they'd been buffed by someone in the army.

"Blimey!" I muttered, echoing one of my mum's expressions. If only she could see this. Gran too! We had one toilet, sink and bath in each of our houses. Gran thought that was fancy enough. She'd regaled me with tales of an outside lavvy shared with her neighbours and how she'd loved getting her prefab home with its own bathroom. Rockbeare had seven between the residents in the main block, but none were in the bedrooms. Some residents had sinks in their rooms, but I'd never seen a bedroom with its own toilet and shower. Joe's parents had even put out white towels. I brushed the fabric against my face. Soft and fluffy. It smelled gorgeous too.

I sank onto the bed and pulled out my clothes. Against the cotton duvet cover, my top looked cheap. It would have to do. No matter what the catalogue promised, its clothes were made for the lower end of the market. My end. At least I'd brought my old jeans, following Joe's suggestion when I'd asked him what I should wear. Not Levis like Charlotte's, but still a safe bet, even if I needed to pull my belt tight to hold them up. I slipped off my work trousers and assessed myself in the mirror. Disappointment showed in my face. Even when I breathed in, I couldn't see my hip bones. Perhaps mine were smaller than most, unlike Tracey's, whose jutted through her skin. I ran my hand along my collar bone, willing it to show. Maybe next week.

It took an age before I found the courage to step outside. I padded downstairs and into the hall, my nerves heightening with every step. Five doors led to different rooms, three of them ajar. Through one I glimpsed the lounge, where three cream sofas surrounded a coffee table. No TV to be seen. Perhaps it was hidden from view? I stepped inside, admiring the huge stone fireplace, quite unlike our tiled one with its inset gas fire. My feet sank into the piled carpet, the same shade as the hallway but thicker. Then I noticed the hoover streaks, now marked like pristine snow by my footprints. I scrubbed out each telltale print as I retreated.

I found Joe in a kitchen as big as the ground floor of my house. He stood beside a breakfast bar at which

Charlotte and Dan sat on tall chairs, holding what looked like glasses of lager. Charlotte beckoned me over.

"Joe's just telling us about his work."

Joe fired her an odd glance, then smiled. "We won't be boring and talk about that. Is your room okay?"

"Okay?" I whistled in amazement. "It's incredible."

Charlotte laughed. "You need to see their downstairs loo."

Joe rolled his eyes. "If you like kitsch, it's on the right in the hall. It was the only room where Dad allowed Mum to have full rein."

Charlotte chuckled. "Her taste is absolutely fine in comparison to Mummy's."

Mummy? Maybe that was someone's nickname, as I didn't know anyone over eight who called their parents anything other than Mum or Dad. She turned to me, lowering her voice to a whisper. "She came home with a doll dressed in a crocheted dress the other day. It was a loo roll cover!" Squealing, she put her hands to her eyes. "We were absolutely mortified! Daddy said she was showing her roots."

I had no idea what dyed hair had to do with loo roll covers. Until I realised that perhaps Charlotte meant the other kind of roots. The upbringing kind. Was there something wrong with Gran's toilet roll cover? I thought it sweet that she liked to dress her throne room with pink carpets on the toilet lid and around the base, with a matching one beside the bath. She'd even tied a ribbon on her toilet chain and hung frilly curtains at the window, which draped behind her potted cactus.

I wasn't offended by Charlotte's comment, just bemused. I didn't know a single adult who still called their father Daddy! I couldn't wait to tell Tracey. She'd laugh at that.

My shyness returned when Joe's friends began to arrive. Joe had made me a vodka and diet Coke, which magically refilled every time I turned back after being introduced to another group. New smells floated through the air. Aftershaves I recognised: Kouros, Jazz. Others I didn't. Everyone wore a uniform of belted jeans, so I fitted in, but they sounded like the newsreaders on TV, although friendlier. None of them raised an eyebrow at my catalogue top. I'd cut off the too-large shoulder pads, which had gone misshapen in the wash. Joe's friends oozed wealth but weren't snobby. Many of my poly friends had come from well-to-do families, so I wasn't out of my comfort zone in that respect. Just that I hated meeting new people. No matter where they came from.

The music started and Charlotte grabbed my hand. If I'd expected the Smiths, James or any of the other music that had played on a loop on the jukebox at poly (it had been fed with coins to stop it playing its default tune, Kylie Minogue's 'I Should Be So Lucky'), I was mistaken. Madonna, Bananarama, U2 and Rick Astley led the way until things descended into a spiral of alcohol and laughter, with 'Agadoo' and even 'The Birdie Song'.

The kitchen became stifling. My face prickled with heat. A lad on the improvised dance floor flapped his arms, showing sweat marks. Were mine like that too? Worried, I shot off to check. In the hallway the front door stood open, blowing a welcome breeze inside, along with the smell of tobacco smoke. Joe stood beside a group of lads, hands in his pockets. He turned and gave me a wave. "Are you okay?"

When I nodded and pointed towards the toilet, he chuckled. "Ignore the décor."

If he hadn't been watching me, I would have halted at the doorway, stunned by a room the size of our lounge. For some reason, there were two toilets. One of them looked strange. Perhaps it was for weeing only. They and the sink were patterned in blue, reminding me of Chinese plates. Even the toilet roll had printed flowers, while pristine towels were draped over stainless-steel rails. The white tiled floor and walls reflected in a huge mirror surrounded by lights. Flaming heck! Did people really live like this? It took me half a dozen steps to cross to the toilet.

When I caught sight of myself, I gasped. I looked like I'd run a marathon. Strands of hair clung to my forehead, and my cheeks were a blotchy red. I took some toilet paper and dribbled water over it. Then, sitting on the poshest toilet in the world, I held the cool tissue to my face, repeating each time my cheeks heated the paper.

A bang on the door interrupted me. I cringed to myself. They'd wonder what I was getting up to. After muttering an apology to the waiting girl, I hesitated in the hallway. The cool air beckoned me outside, but the porch lights that glared above the smokers would blaze on my puce cheeks.

Instead, I returned to the muggy heat of the thankfully dark kitchen.

Charlotte grabbed my wrist and pulled me into her huddle of friends. "'YMCA' is on after the next one," she hollered as she jigged, her voice blurred by alcohol. "My fave!"

I wished Tracey could see this. Then I thought again. She'd be standing on the edge of the dance floor, too cool to join in with the daft tunes. But this was more fun than I'd had in ages.

'Oops Upside Your Head' began to play and Charlotte dropped to the floor. As I went to sit in front of her, Joe dived in between us, laughing at my surprise. Although he'd waved at me several times, until now he'd spent the night moving between his friends, checking they had enough to drink or chatting.

He put his hands around my waist. Instinctively, I breathed in, hoping he didn't feel my spare tyres.

"I couldn't leave you all night," he shouted. The way he said it made me feel special. But he was just being his usual thoughtful self. As we leaned backwards and forwards, our bodies pressed together. I forgot to worry about my fat. Anyhow, the lad in front of me had a bigger belly than mine and he didn't seem to care. When we moved from side to side, Joe caught me when I leaned too far. He pulled me closer. The song came to an end and he hauled me to my feet, wrapping his arms around my waist. Not in a way someone would do with a mate, but…

My body tingled but my mind reeled. He could have

his pick of anyone here, so why me?

"Do you want to go outside?" he shouted above the opening beats of 'YMCA' and Charlotte's squeals.

I nodded, although I didn't fancy being under the spotlight in the porch. After pausing to chat to a friend, he took me in the opposite direction, through the gorgeous lounge where our shoes sank into the carpet. He unlatched the patio door and we stepped into the cool night. I burned with curiosity. Did he want to speak about work? I couldn't believe it would be anything else. In the past, I'd been asked to go outside at a pub, only to find my hoped-for admirer wanting advice on how he could get together with Tracey. But Joe had made his feelings clear about her. He wasn't interested. A good-looking man like him would be more suited to someone like Charlotte: well groomed, pretty and fun. Not like me.

We headed past the pool, where spotlights glowed against the aquamarine cover, to a set of wooden patio chairs beneath a Victorian-style streetlamp. When Joe sighed and shook his head, I turned, to see Charlotte cupping her hands against the kitchen window. He tapped his nose at her. In return, she stuck out her tongue and darted away, throwing her arms in the air as 'Superman' boomed out on the stereo.

I laughed. "I love your taste in bad music."

He chuckled. "There's no point being pretentious at a party but I promise, none of it will never make their way to the cassette collection in my car."

Then he frowned and leaned forward to pick something

from my face. His expression turned to bewilderment as he rolled it between his finger and thumb. I cringed, knowing full well what it was. When he tried again, I batted his hand away.

He burst out laughing. "You look like I do after I've been shaving."

"I was a bit hot."

His gorgeous blue eyes locked with mine. "Let me get that other piece off your face and then I'll leave you alone."

But after he picked away the fragment of tissue, he kept stroking my face. Was he drunk?

I hadn't allowed myself to think of him as anything but a friend. But in the warm fuzz of alcohol, anything seemed possible. He bent forward and his lips touched mine. Excitement fired through me. This was really happening! I only hoped he wouldn't regret it the next morning.

# Chapter 13

That night, Joe escorted me to my bedroom. Jitters had overcome me as we stood at the door. I didn't want to rush things. Being the perfect gentleman he was, he'd brushed his lips against mine before wishing me a good night, leaving me to hug the pillow in wonder. When I came down at six thirty the next morning, I found Charlotte sitting at a bar stool, eating cornflakes. I flushed under her scrutiny. Joe acted as nothing had happened, asking if I wanted a coffee. I didn't expect cereal to be on offer – we'd have breakfast with the residents – but his cool manner confirmed my suspicions. Last night had been a drunken mistake. I couldn't help feeling gutted. Hopefully we'd resume our friendship, though. I couldn't bear the thought of losing that. I loved our chats, his knowledge of the residents and his perspective on life in general.

But when we got into his car to set off for work, he put his hand on mine. Gently, like a father would do with a child.

"Last night…" He hesitated.

It had been a mistake. I understood. These things happened with drink. I hoped he'd ask if we could still be friends. That would be the least worst option.

"Do… Er, I…" He flushed.

I felt for him, but I couldn't make it easier. I had no idea what to say.

The words tumbled from his lips. "Did last night mean

the same to you?"

"You mean?" Now it was my turn to fumble for words. "You weren't drunk?"

He chuckled. "Absolutely sloshed. But it gave me Dutch courage."

I laughed. "Me too."

He squeezed my hand, looked towards the front door – no doubt to check if Charlotte was spying on us – and leaned over to kiss my cheek. "I'm so pleased." Grinning, he turned the key in the ignition and pulled away.

♦

We knew it would be frowned upon, so we didn't tell anyone at work about our relationship, not even Tracey. If we bumped into each other in the cleaning cupboard, Joe would squeeze my hand. When Sally found a soup spoon in Alice's room and Gloria came to castigate me, he shot me a look of empathy. Later we moaned and vowed to get Sally back one day.

I spent afternoons in the library, wandering around the shops, or meeting Tracey for an hour on the common. Joe had other things to do, which he seemed strangely evasive about, explaining that he wrote articles in his spare time. But he did find an hour to meet me in a café now and then and, after work, we'd go to the pub. There was no point going for a meal as we had to eat with the residents in the evening. We had different days off, which was a pain. But we made the most of the time we had.

A few days after the party, he discovered that the cinema in Bilton was still showing *Three Men and a Baby*, so I got my wish to see it. Later, he confessed that he'd seen it before, but he knew I hadn't. As we left, buzzing in the afterglow of a good film, he spotted me gazing at a poster about *Crocodile Dundee II.*

"We'll have to go when it's on," he said.

I shivered with excitement. Each day with him was an extra tick of happiness on the calendar. It would be weeks before the film would be showing at Bilton, which meant plenty more ticks ahead. Even now, I could hardly believe that Joe wanted to be with me, although Mum disagreed, saying I should be more confident and Joe was lucky to have a kind person like me. I could sort of see her point, but I couldn't bring myself to believe it. Mum hadn't been there when the kids had mocked me at school, calling me frizzy, chubby, ginger, goofy. Although braces had reduced my overbite, the taunts changed to 'metal mouth'. Their words left bruises hidden deep beneath my skin. Although I'd now lost eleven pounds and I had a lovely hairstyle – held fast with repeated applications of the ultra-hold hairspray Tracey had recommended – I still didn't feel good enough for Joe. Was that odd? It made sense to me.

Within a fortnight, I'd grown comfortable with our new routine. We spent Friday nights with Dan and Charlotte in their favourite pub, the Garden Gate. By the time we finished work and Joe drove there, it was after nine o'clock, which left a couple of hours for drinks. However, this week they wanted to go for a meal first as a new Indian restaurant had opened in Rocklington to rave reviews. They'd join us later in the Ploughman. I'd hadn't been there since I'd abandoned Gary and my disastrous blind date (if it could be called that) and bumped into Joe.

On the Thursday night, Joe drove me home from work. It was well out of his way, but he told me he'd rather drive than leave me at the bus stop. I didn't invite him in. He had work to do, and I wanted to get my clothes organised for the next day. When I walked into the kitchen, I found Mum huffing over the gas stove. A saucepan sat on the sideboard next to an opened tin of beans, a tub of marge and two slices of white bread on a plate. She wiped an arm over her reddened face.

"No matter what I do, the blooming thing won't light."

"I'm not hungry," I said.

"I am! I've been trying to light this blooming thing since I got in. I've even cleaned all the burners but I can't get it to work. I really fancy beans on toast."

"Are all the rings broken? Or just that one?"

She gave me one of her looks.

"What? I was only asking!"

"Do you think I was born yesterday? The ignition thingamajig must be broken."

"What about matches?"

She sighed. "I've been on my feet all day. Fancy a walk to the offy?"

Her pallid face and the grey smudges beneath her eyes spoke volumes about her hard day at the supermarket.

"Yeah, okay." I tried to sound enthusiastic.

"You don't have to if you don't want to," she said, unzipping her purse. As she stuffed a fiver into my hand, she yawned. "Get us a bottle of ginger beer and a box of Maltesers too. I fancy a treat."

When I returned from the off licence twenty minutes later, I found her on the settee. Yawning, she pushed herself up, but I waved her away.

"I'll sort your tea. You look knackered."

"I am." She curled back into the cushion, giving me a half smile. "Don't let me go to sleep. I want to stay up for the Wimbledon highlights."

In the kitchen, I opened my carrier bag to fetch the matches, which had wormed their way beneath the bottle of ginger beer.

"Love," she called. "Don't s'pose you fancy making me a ginger beer?"

I turned the gas back off, poured her the drink and took it through. She snuggled into the settee, giving me a warm smile. "Bless you."

Back at the cooker, I twisted the dial and went to pick up the matches. I gazed around. I'd seen them just a moment ago. But where? The carrier bag sat on the side, empty. After a quick search, I found them beside the kettle, where I'd been pouring Mum her drink. Without thinking, I bent to light the gas. Poof! A bright flame shot out, the heat searing my forehead. Something crackled and an acrid smell filled the air.

"Flaming 'eck!" I screeched and clutched my burning

skin. My fringe! It had gone.

Mum appeared, clutching the door frame. She clamped her hand to her mouth. "Oh blimey, love! Are you okay?" She grabbed the dishcloth and shook it free of crumbs before splashing it with cold water and plastering it to my forehead.

"My hair!" I wailed.

She grimaced. "I won't pretend that it's fine. I mean you'll find a mirror soon enough. But…" As my tears turned to howls, she patted my shoulder. "Don't worry, love. You know, where there's a will there's a way. We'll work something out."

# Chapter 14

Gloria pursed her lips when she spotted me the next morning. Before she could say anything, I hurried over and asked if I could have a word. Sally watched us curiously as we walked to Gloria's office.

"I'm wearing this band to cover what's left of my fringe. It's the only thing we could think to do to hide the damage."

While I'd cooked Mum her baked beans on toast at half past ten – midway through the Match of the Day special on the Wimbledon tennis – she'd found a solution. A cotton headscarf, which she'd made from an old black shirt. Mum had also used a red top to create another one for tonight, although I'd told her not to worry. But she waved me away, even though it was after midnight by then.

"A bad haircut is your problem," Gloria said.

"Oh no! It wasn't just the haircut. I got burned."

I lifted the headscarf to reveal a glimpse of plaster. Mum had insisted on covering my scorched patch with the largest one she could find, on the off chance that Gloria needed evidence. Mum reasoned that Gloria would be unlikely to tear off my plaster.

She was right. Gloria's expression turned to sympathy. I hoped she wouldn't ask to see my injuries – apart from a slight reddened patch, my skin had got away lightly.

I stifled a yawn. "It wasn't a terrible burn, just a bit

sore, but Mum and I were up for ages making a headscarf so I didn't scare the residents."

"I don't want you bending over the toilets and baths if you're in that state. Tell Tracey she can take over from you and you can do her tea rounds. She'll have to do the commodes too and then come to help you. We'll reorganise the rota to give you lighter duties."

"It's not so bad," I said, but Gloria was resolute. No more discussion; her decision had been made. Tracey would kill me! She'd come in wearing a new skirt, unprepared for a morning kneeling at thrones.

In the event, Tracey was more concerned with finding out what had happened to me. Though she changed her tune when she passed Sally and me as we doled out tea and morning greetings to the residents. A strange mark glistened on the front of her skirt.

I pointed to the stain. "What's that?"

"Ugh! Don't ask!" She looked up and down the empty corridor. "Blimming residents!"

"Tracey!" Sally warned.

"Well! You should have seen the state of that blinking toilet. Talk about disgusting."

She stormed off with her bucket while Sally pushed the trolley to the next room. Even she'd put me on light duties, refusing to let me push it. We bypassed Arthur's room, which had been empty since his death. Since his chair had been moved aside, he was rarely mentioned in the dining room, and all had gone quiet about his missing money too. I wondered if Gloria had come up with the 'lost' amount rather than involving the police, as they hadn't wanted to speak to me, even though I'd written out the statement Gloria had asked me to.

Joe's theory was that Rockdeane wouldn't want to bring more attention to itself. When questioned, he'd shrugged, saying that most residential homes would feel the same. Negative publicity might put off potential residents.

After handing Sally a cup of tea, I dug my fingers into my headscarf to scratch an infuriating itch. I couldn't rub too hard in case I loosened the scarf. Mum had sewn in a line of elastic to ensure it didn't slip off, but I didn't want to risk it. Anyhow, I had more pressing concerns. It was Joe's day off so he hadn't seen my wrecked hair. I could imagine his shock later. Hopefully, he wouldn't be too embarrassed to be seen with me.

At breakfast the residents commented on my new look. Alice peered at me through her glasses, her beady eyes narrowing. "How come you were so close to the flame?"

I reddened. "Daft, I know, but I left the gas running before I lit it."

Freda patted my hand. "You poor duck."

Alice sighed. "For pity's sake, Freda. How many times do I have to tell you? Belinda is a woman, not a bird."

Wilf glared at Alice. "Talking about birds, it seems we have the magpie back again." He turned to the others. "I put my pen down for one minute and someone squirrelled it away. Luckily, Gloria retrieved it."

"As I said, I found it on the lounge table and I was

going in search of you."

"It sat next to my crossword. You must have known I would return, so why did you take it?"

"That I have also explained." Alice flushed, her eyes glittering with anger. "I couldn't find you."

At the end of the table, Ernest kept his head down as he cut his bacon. I wished I had something on my plate to focus on.

Beside me, Freda's reedy voice pleaded, "Let's leave it be for today. Thanks to all the fuss, I missed *Coronation Street* last night."

But Wilf didn't hear her. He jabbed his finger at Alice. "Is nothing sacred around here? It's ridiculous that I should have to take everything with me each time nature calls." He pushed his chair back. "I've had enough to eat. Will you all excuse me?"

He strode past Ernest, who continued to saw at his bacon. At this rate, he'd go through the plate.

"I can't believe you did that," Freda's voice quivered. "You must have known it was the last gift his wife gave him. And he was only in the lounge because his daughter cancelled again."

From where she sat at a nearby table, Gloria glared at me. This was the second time Wilf had stormed from my table. No doubt she'd tell me that if I knew what was good for me, there wouldn't be a third time. But what could I do? I was between a rock and a hard place. They might be residents, but they were older and I had to respect them.

Alice's pink-varnished nail prodded the tablecloth. Her

tone was brittle. "As I said, I went to give it back to him, thinking he had left." She sank back into her chair. "I didn't know it was his wife's. I'll apologise to him later."

The three of us gawped. I'd never heard Alice offer an apology before. Like the prime minister, she was usually a lady not for turning.

"That would be nice," Freda whispered, but Ernest drowned her voice out by clattering his cutlery onto his plate. "I've had enough." He sat back into his chair and folded his arms.

The half full toast rack sat in the centre of the table, untouched by everyone but Alice.

"Don't you want your toast?" I pleaded. He'd need more than two rashers of bacon and an egg for breakfast.

"Thank you, Belinda. But I'll leave it for today." He stood and nodded to Freda. Then, ignoring Alice, he tramped away, his gait stiff.

Freda clutched my hand. "Don't mind us, dear. We're all a bit out of sorts with cabin fever. The weather doesn't help. It's all so changeable."

I cursed myself. Joe and I had talked about asking Gloria to organise activities for the residents. While it had crossed my mind a few times, I hadn't done a thing about it. I glanced across to the neighbouring table. Gloria's stony expression told me there would be no point in asking today.

"I'm so sorry," I said. "I wish I could do something."

She gave my hand a squeeze. "There's no need to worry about us oldies. We've had our fun."

If Freda heard Alice mutter under her breath, "Well, some of *you* have," she didn't show it.

Even though Alice could be infuriating, I felt for her. It must be hard to look ahead to a future stuck in a boring residential home. At least most of the residents had positive memories over which to reminisce. Alice's past was hidden beneath a flint shell which covered an impenetrable core of steel.

♦

That night I spoke to Joe as we stood by the bar at the Ploughman waiting for our drinks. He hung his arm around my shoulder, something I didn't mind when we went to the Garden Gate, but one of the workers from the residential home could spot us here. I didn't disentangle myself, though. I liked being close to him.

When he'd picked me up, I'd promised to tell him about the reason for my new look – but only once we'd got to the pub and as I didn't want him taking his eyes off the road. Now that time had come. I took a deep breath and blurted out the whole sorry saga.

He roared with laughter. "Lucky you didn't fry your eyebrows and lashes. A girl in class did that with a Bunsen burner. With the amount of hairspray she used, I'm amazed she didn't explode into a fireball."

I blushed. At least my eyebrows were intact, thanks to my martyred fringe. But I was guilty of using too much hairspray to keep my style. I changed the subject in case

Joe started speculating about that. "Oh – do you remember us talking about the lack of activities at the home? Did you manage to speak to Gloria?"

The barman interrupted us, putting my vodka and diet Coke and a bag of pork scratchings on the bar. He gave the pump handle a few pulls to top up Joe's lager. When Joe moved to fish in his pocket for his wallet, I spotted a familiar face through the archway between the bars. Great! That's all I needed. Had he seen Joe put his arm around me? More to the point, what was he doing here? Residents weren't supposed to be out at night. Even on days they spent with their families, they were under strict instructions to come back before seven pm, unless it was a special occasion.

I nudged Joe. "Isn't that Sir Bartholomew over there?"

He put his finger to his lips. "Keep it hush-hush. It's one of his few pleasures."

"What if he saw us together?"

Joe tapped his nose. "He won't say a word. Trust me."

I sighed. That didn't make me feel better. "But how did he get out?"

He mimed zipping his mouth but, when I wouldn't let up, he sighed. "Okay, you win. He uses the fire escape door. He puts a piece of cardboard on the inside so it can't click shut and a brick on the outside, so it looks closed but won't blow open."

"But what if there's a fire?"

"The brick wouldn't jam the door if someone pushed it open. Not the way he does it. When I caught him one evening, he showed me."

I pulled a face. While I admired Sir Bartholomew's ingenuity, I couldn't help worrying about the brick. Joe squeezed my hand. "Don't worry. It's fine. The brick would just slide across the concrete. There's nothing to stop it. Anyhow, going back to your earlier point, Gloria won't spend money on activities. The trustees have allocated all the unspent funds for a change in branding."

"Branding?"

Joe grimaced. "Welcome to Rockbeare Care Home. No longer will it be known as a residential home. That's too old-hat."

"They're changing everything for one word?"

"Signage, letter heading – you name it, they're doing it. It's all for show, just like the food. They don't see the value in other things, like keeping the residents stimulated. In fact…" He paused to chomp on a pork scratching, washing it down with a glug of his lager. "Gloria said the colour TV was more than most people had in their homes. Anyone would think a colour TV was something special."

I didn't tell him that we'd only got our colour TV a few years before. Mum had refused to pay the extra fee for a colour TV licence, saying our old black and white one was good enough. I'd been thrilled when it finally broke and she'd been forced to hire a new TV. I'd had to twist her arm for colour, though, moaning that we must be the only people in the world who had to view Bet Lynch – I couldn't think of her as Bet Gilroy – and her gaudy leopard-skin tops in shades of grey.

Someone slapped my shoulder. I swung around to find Tracey grinning.

"Blimey!" she said. "This looks cosy. What're you two doing here?"

Aiden hovered behind her, his bleached flat top almost touching the pub's low black beams. Had he emptied a bottle of Kouros aftershave over himself? It made my eyes water, especially when, not bothering to say hello, he pushed past us and waved a fiver at the barman.

Although he was hidden behind the pint of lager he sipped, Joe couldn't mask his raised eyebrows and bemused expression. How would I answer her question? I wouldn't tell all. Tracey might have been my best friend – she still was – but our friendship knot was loosening.

"Joe's meeting his friends."

She narrowed her eyes. "And you thought to join them."

I shrugged, uncomfortable under her scrutiny. "Why not?"

Tracey tugged at the sleeves of her off-the-shoulders top and arched her back, making her boobs stick out further. I chuckled. Was she doing this for Joe's benefit? I thought she'd got past that stage.

She turned her attention back to me, picking at the bow on my crimson headscarf. Mum had said it was the height of fashion, but I wasn't so sure. Fashion or not, I preferred the plain black one. I'd only worn it because Mum had bothered to stay up sewing it for another hour.

"You're looking very red," she said. "I would have gone for green with your hair."

"I like it." Joe held out his packet. "Pork scratching?"

"Don't mind if I do." She dipped her fingers in, pulling out a huge chunk, which she popped into her mouth.

Joe winked at me. He'd silenced her. He shook the packet, offering another one. This time she took two. When she'd finished munching, he said, "I thought you preferred the George and Dragon."

Aiden swung a half pint over my head, passing it to Tracey, not apologising when it dripped on my jeans. He didn't join us, but resumed his chat with the barman.

"Gary's meeting us." Tracey dropped her gaze, a flush rising to her cheeks. "He's bringing his new girlfriend. He wanted one drink here before we move over the road. You don't mind, d'you? I mean, about Gary."

I laughed. "No! He wasn't my type."

Her frown told me that wasn't the answer she'd expected. Did she think I was desperate enough to go for anyone? Little did she know I had the perfect man sitting inches from me: kind, funny and good-looking to boot.

"Here, Trace!" Aiden called her. "Dan was telling me about this new Indian place. Wanna have a mosey over there later?"

Joe jerked his head towards a table in the corner. "Let's get a seat." He slipped from where he'd perched on the bar stool, leaving his empty wrapper on the bar, its contents sacrificed in the pursuit of peace.

"I'll see you later," I said. Tracey nodded, then her face

fell. "You've taken that table. We were going to sit there."

Usually I'd apologise, perhaps offer to move. But her expectation annoyed me. Smiling, I pointed to another table beside the front window, well away from us. "That one's free, if you're quick."

I shot off to sit down beside Joe – not too close, in case it raised her suspicions. But it didn't stop him squeezing my thigh out of sight.

"You shouldn't let her get away with talking to you like that," he said.

"What? About the table?"

He frowned. "About your clothes. I don't know why she feels the need to put you down." His breath patted my ear as he whispered, "She's probably jealous of how gorgeous you are."

I blushed, wishing his words were true. No way could I ever match Tracey in style or looks. But I loved him for saying that.

Charlotte rushed in, drawing with her the chill of a damp evening. Wet tendrils clung to her forehead. She must have hurried here, as her cheeks were flushed and she panted as she brushed raindrops from her coat. She bent to kiss Joe's cheek, unaware that she was blocking Tracey's path. While Tracey waited patiently, clutching hers and Aiden's drinks, Charlotte draped her coat over the back of a chair.

"Just look at that sky! We're in for a belter of a storm. Dan needs to hurry up, or he'll get soaked."

I was just about to point out that Tracey needed to get

past when Charlotte turned to me. Her mouth dropped open.

"Wow! I love your look! Fabulous!"

I couldn't help glancing behind her to Tracey. It was a good thing she wasn't carrying milk. Her expression would have curdled it.

# Chapter 15

A new man sat at my table. I didn't know if he'd been given the chair of doom, or if a switch had been made, but no one at the table appeared fazed by his presence. Freda smiled and gave him her usual cheery welcome, Ernest and Wilf shook his hand, while Alice sat upright, a sparkle in her eye I hadn't seen in ages. Was she planning mischief?

"Peter Brenner." He touched his forehead to both women. "At your service."

Introductions made, the residents moved on to interrogate him about his past. He'd been in the RAF man during the war, followed by a career in publishing, and he'd been married until he lost his wife three years ago. She'd given him two boys, who'd given him four grandchildren. By the look of him, she'd also fed him well.

When Wilf and Ernest took their turn to tell their life stories, I felt for Alice. What would she say? Her story was about what other people had done to her. But when Ernest finished and Peter's gaze fell on Alice, she smiled.

"My life was one your publishing company would have paid large sums to offer to readers." Then she tapped her nose. "So, unless you're planning to do so, I'll keep it for someone who will."

Peter looked intrigued, but he didn't push further. After giving her a gracious smile, he moved on to Freda, whose tale seemed dull in comparison to the hidden excitement of Alice's. But I knew which I'd choose to have lived. While Freda's body might be gnarled and twisted, her gentle presence reminded me of a pebble rounded by the lapping sea, while Alice was like a craggy rock that had been beaten by angry waves. She might stand taut and proud, but the damage was visible to all.

Not that Freda had been awarded an easy time in the lottery of life. She was childless, now husbandless, with no family to visit her. When the others walked, she shuffled behind, her head bowed by that awful hunchback. Her arthritis caused her pain too. She never mentioned it, but I saw her rubbing her hands and wincing. She also brought what seemed like a Smartie tube's-worth of pills to the dining room; she had to take them with food.

I liked Freda's kind ways. She deserved to have friends who would wait with her – rather than stride ahead – as she would if the roles had been reversed. That gave me an idea. Would Gloria allow it? Probably not. But it was worth asking.

Joe got to me first, clutching my arm to stop me heading out to the kitchen with my laden tray. His expression was serious. "I need to speak to you."

I frowned. Gloria had seemed in a good mood at breakfast, so I'd planned on grabbing her before I moved on to the rooms. "Can it wait?"

"I want to tell you first, before Gloria."

Cryptic! Why hadn't he spoken to me last night when he'd driven me home after the evening shift? He'd been quiet, but I'd assumed he was tired. I placed the tray on the sideboard, ready to hear what he needed to say. "Okay."

Then Gloria swept into the dining room, glaring at us. Hastily, I picked up the tray and dashed to the kitchen. When I turned to back through the door, I found Joe behind me. He leaned across to push the door open, his expression serious. Thanking him, I swung into the bustling space, wondering if he'd followed me so he could tell me now. But he glanced at Tracey, who slotted plates into the dishwasher, then at the new worker, who loaded sparkling glasses onto trays.

"I'll speak to you later," he hissed. "We'll go to the café after lunch, if you're free."

Free? That was a laugh. Of course I would be. If Joe or Tracey weren't around, I searched for ways to waste the three hours between the first and second shifts. With Tracey spending rainy afternoons in her bedsit, Joe doing his articles, and the weather so miserable, I was often bored. The library closed three afternoons a week and there was only so much window shopping I could do. I'd come up with a solution, but Gloria had refused my request to sit in the residents' lounge, saying I would get in the way. I only wanted to sit in the corner to read a book – what was wrong with that? But I didn't argue.

Joe's vagueness left me unsettled. But I understood. With Gloria hanging around, anything longer than a brief chat was risky. The morning passed quickly. I didn't get to speak to Gloria, and neither did Joe.

As we headed out at the end of the first shift, Tracey hurried over. "Fancy going to the common?"

When I glanced across to Joe, who hovered by the doorway, she scowled. "I see how it is."

She went to push past me but I took her arm. "I'd already agreed to go for a coffee with Joe. How about tomorrow?"

"Maybe." She hitched her bag over her shoulder then marched past Joe.

He threw me an apologetic grimace, but it wasn't his fault. I could have been honest and told her we were an item, but I didn't trust her not to blab to someone at work. Being old-school, Gloria wouldn't be pleased about it. I couldn't risk my job – or Joe's. And I didn't want my fellow workers – or the residents – sticking their noses into our business. Their MI5 operation would go into overdrive.

Once away from the residential home, Joe took my hand. The rain had stopped, leaving an earthy smell in the air. Who would believe it was July? Roll on August and, hopefully, better weather. A gentleman as always, Joe walked beside the road, taking the brunt of the spray from passing cars.

We continued in silence until, impatient to learn more, I said, "Can we talk now?"

He shook his head. "I'd rather speak to you in the café. I hope you don't mind, but this will take a bit of time."

I shrugged away my irritation. I'd waited five hours, so what was another five minutes? My mind on Joe, I swerved to avoid an overhanging Leylandii branch, and didn't spot a puddle. It soaked my court shoes. Yuck! I grimaced as water bubbled between my toes, and my foot squelched with every step.

Lost in thought, Joe hadn't noticed. Now I looked more closely, he appeared strained. A knot bulged at the side of his jaw. Maybe he planned to end our relationship. But he held my hand – the only dry part of my body. Perhaps he was about to say he'd been two-timing me and ask for forgiveness, or even tell me that he had a child. I couldn't imagine any of those scenarios, though. Whatever secret he needed to share, I'd know about it soon.

The triangular common stretched from the residential home at the top of the hill down to town. An ornate clock tower stood at the bottom, by the junction to the high street.

Just fifty yards more and we stepped into the café, and were hit by smell of frying bacon. Workmen queued at the takeaway section, where delicious-smelling paper bags were swopped for cash. The café was busy, with suited office workers nibbling at sandwiches and baguettes, and older folk tucking into pies and pastries. At lunch we'd eaten shepherd's pie – or cottage pie, as Alice corrected me – so Joe and I plumped for coffee, although I didn't need the caffeine. My foot jittered in my soggy shoe and I worried at a loose thread to occupy myself. My nerves (Gran's favourite topic) were getting the better of me.

Joe sat opposite, steepling his fingers. After the waitress took our order, I gazed at him in expectation. I'd waited hours to hear whatever he had to say.

Finally, he broke the silence. "I couldn't tell you last night. I wanted to. But…" He let out a long sigh. "But when my boss told me it couldn't go on, I didn't know what to say."

Nothing he'd said made sense. Boss? Was Gloria sacking him? Why? Questions raced through my mind. Was she blaming him for the missing money? But he hadn't been in work that day.

He didn't look at me. Then he reached out for my hand. I let him, although I feared he was about to say something I wouldn't like.

"I've not been honest with you. But I couldn't. I'm sorry."

I swallowed, even though my mouth had gone dry. He'd stolen from the residents! But he had rich parents. The forty pounds taken from Arthur would be nothing to them. Maybe Joe had some sort of problem? Was he a magpie, like Alice, who didn't need what she took but wanted items for reasons only she understood? Shaking my head, I came to my senses. No way was Joe a thief.

He met my gaze and took a deep breath. "I don't work at the care home. Well, I do, but not like you think. I'm there for another reason."

# Chapter 16

The waitress placed our coffees in front of us, asked if we needed anything else, then hurried away after we shook our heads. Did she feel the vibes coming from our table? We'd moved our hands apart to make room for our drinks, but I didn't want to touch Joe now. Not until I knew what was going on. I tucked my hands into my lap.

"Does Gloria know this?"

Flushing, he shook his head. "As I said, I wanted you to know first. What I'm about to tell you … it's really important that you keep it confidential."

I frowned. What if he told me something terrible?

"I don't know. I mean, it depends."

He smiled. "That's why I like you so much. Why I trust you too." He leaned forward, gazing intently at me. "Please let me tell you the whole story. I hope you'll understand."

I sipped my coffee, surveying him through the steam. Inside I churned with anticipation and dread.

"I'm a journalist. I write exposés, as well as other stories. Well…" He bit his lip. "This is the part I need you to keep quiet. Someone came to my boss and raised concerns about the care home. My boss decided I should apply for a job there, try to see if anything underhand was going on. I shouldn't be telling you – or anyone – about this. But I can't not tell you. I… I…" His face reddened. "Love you."

Flipping heck! What a time to drop that four-letter word in! My face mirrored his – the heat in my cheeks told me that.

"You do pick your moments." I smiled, then unease settled over me. Had he told me he loved me to smooth his path? But I pushed the thought aside. Joe wasn't manipulative. Except – by omission – he'd twisted the truth. "You told me you were writing articles. Your friends must have known, so why hide it from me?"

"This is where it gets difficult. I'm sorry. It was important for us to find out the facts. I told Gloria I wanted to become a social worker – we had to find a reason for her to employ me. But I couldn't lie to you, which is why I said I wrote articles."

"So you're telling me now, because of what?" When my voice rose, I paused, fighting to keep calm.

He ran his finger around the rim of his cup in an incessant circle, going nowhere. A bit like our conversation, unless I let him talk.

"I wasn't allowed to."

"But you are now? Why?"

He grimaced. "I'll explain from the start. As I said, a man approached us – he knew my boss. His father, who had been a resident at the care home, had died. This man, Maurice Axe, was concerned – he thought his father's death hadn't been entirely natural."

"What? He thinks his father was murdered?" I gasped.

"Not quite. But he suspected abuse and neglect—"

I couldn't help myself. "But no one hurts them." I

couldn't imagine anyone being able to get away with abusing Wilf, Alice or even Freda. "And they all eat tonnes."

"The people you see do but, as you saw, there's a separate section of the care home for people with dementia and other illnesses. The cottage hospital won't take them, so the care home gets paid a pretty penny to look after them. At first they were kept with the other residents, but things kept happening, such as them going into other rooms and other incidents. But it was after a lady fell down the stairs during the middle of the night that it was decided to create a safe, enclosed wing, under the protection of nursing staff." He took a swig of his coffee. "The thing is, Maurice's father had unexplained bruising. And his ribs were showing. Rockbeare's solicitors state that the bruises were from a fall and that he often refused to eat. It sounds plausible, but Maurice told my boss that he didn't agree. There seemed no way for him to prove otherwise. He'd been working in Singapore for months, so he hadn't been able to see his father and he had to rely on updates from the care home. Then the care home rang to say that his father had been rushed to hospital. He came back then, but it was too late."

"I saw a solicitor's letter on Gloria's desk. I didn't read it, though."

"That was just a bit of argy-bargy over the amount the home charged for a past resident's care."

Startled, I gazed at him. So he'd been snooping in Gloria's office too. Of course he would, if he was a journalist. Maybe that explained why he knew so much about the residents too. After all, he'd been the one to tell me about Alice, when I hadn't heard a whisper about it elsewhere, no matter how much I tried to find out.

"The issue I'm talking about was well before you or I started. Maurice believed Rockbeare's explanation until he bumped into someone he'd met at the care home – another visitor. This person warned him that his father's death might have been more than it seemed. There's a particular nurse – a wife of one of the trustees – who this person named as being in charge. Julia. I looked into it. She's the one we saw with that lady. Do you remember?"

I nodded. How could I forget? The old lady had seemed so upset, even before the nurse had clamped her by her thighs to the bed.

Joe pulled a face. "My boss's friend asked him to investigate. My boss did say we had a newspaper to run – we weren't private investigators – but Maurice persuaded him by saying it could lead to a longer piece on abuse in care homes. So my boss agreed." He glanced down. "That's how I know about mental health institutions and how they treated people. The one thing we didn't realise until I started was that they have separate staff working in the nursing area of the care home. I tried to get moved there, but they only take staff who are trained – or, very occasionally, use chosen workers from the general area if they are really short-staffed. Gloria refused my transfer request. But, to be honest, I'm not convinced that anything major is going on."

"But that nurse … the way she held that woman?"

He nodded. "I know, but we don't know what was happening before we saw them. Or whether the constraint used was appropriate. It didn't look nice, but we only saw one small part of what took place. The rest of the care home does meet most of the residents' needs. Physical needs, anyway." He tapped his head. "It doesn't cater for what's up here, though. But we can't run an exposé on residents being bored to death. Even if they are. Literally."

I'd moved my hand to the table. He took it. "Look, I know this is hard on you. I've lied and I'm sorry. I should have known to trust you from the outset. I kept thinking that now was the day to tell you, but I couldn't see how without risking losing you. I really hope this won't change things between us. I've never met anyone who means so much to me."

What he'd said made sense. I was hurt by his deception, but I didn't want to have a row in the café. Or maybe at all. I'd mull it over in my own time and decide whether it was an argument to pursue.

I gave him a shrug and a flickered smile. "We'll work out a way."

His strained expression relaxed as he returned my smile.

Then I realised, I had another issue to deal with.

"Earlier, you said you were going to speak to Gloria?"

"I'm going to hand my notice in this afternoon. There's nothing suspicious going on as far as I can tell."

"Can you wait until after I talk to her? I have something

I want to ask her." I didn't know if Freda would agree, but I had to try.

♦

Gloria's expression moved through a range of emotions: surprise, disbelief and amusement. Joe had warned me what to expect. This time she wouldn't be able to make an excuse about funding. What I wanted would cost Rockdeane nothing. I'd be doing it in my own time too.

She tapped her biro on the table, gazing out through the rain-splattered window. I watched her. Her dark roots had lengthened. Her pixie style had grown too, curling at the nape of her neck and around her ears. Her earlobes hung low and flabby, her ear piercing no longer a hole but a deep line. Had she worn dangly earrings in her youth? I couldn't imagine it. She seemed older than the residents. Except she allowed us to call her Gloria, unlike my previous bosses who'd been sticklers for their titles being used.

She finally turned back to me, her face unreadable. "It's not a good idea. If something happens to her, we'd be held liable."

"I won't let anything happen. We'd just be across the road. The benches are no more than five minutes away." I couldn't believe I was arguing with my boss. Neither could Gloria. She blinked in shock.

"Pardon?"

"I'm sorry. But Freda's stuck inside with no family to

bother with her, and she struggles so much."

"Your last point is precisely mine. We've got a perfectly good garden."

"Can I try it once and see? I'll pick a nice day. If we have any problems, we'll come straight back. I know how sad she is about not getting out. It would be lovely for her to see the children playing and people walking dogs."

I didn't know if Freda liked children or dogs. Once I'd overhead her speaking to a visitor who arrived with a toddler. Wistfully, Freda had mentioned that she'd not been able to have a family. And animals? I'd never met anyone who didn't love a cute puppy.

Gloria scratched her head, then sighed. "No more than five minutes away?"

Those five minutes were my pace. Freda's shuffle would take double that or more.

"We won't go further than the play area."

She gave me a curt nod. "All right. Let me know when you're going."

I escaped before she could change her mind, pumping my fist in the air when I was safely out of sight. Joe was heading towards me, his expression tight.

"Good luck," I whispered.

Even if this had never been a proper job for him, if I were in his shoes, I'd hate to hand in my notice. Especially when Gloria was on the receiving end.

# Chapter 17

I would have liked to hang around to find out how Joe's chat with Gloria went, but I had to get on. The evening shift involved serving food to the residents and clearing up afterwards, which meant scrubbing the kitchen and dining room. Our final duty would be giving out cups of tea, but this took place in the lounge, where the residents sat in chairs lining the walls, squinting at the TV in the corner. Why we couldn't move the chairs closer to the TV, I didn't know. Once the night shift had arrived, we could leave.

As I handed Freda a cup of tea, I wondered if I should ask her about a trip to the common. But then I realised I didn't know her that well. I'd had the idea of taking her on an outing because I'd felt sorry for her. I'd have to ask her when we had a moment alone. Anyhow, her eyes were glued on *Wogan*, although she gave me a lovely smile and thanked me when the chink of crockery alerted her to my presence. On the dot of seven thirty, the TV would be switched over to *Coronation Street*, no matter what. I'd heard the old folk groan when the channel was changed and they'd been in the middle of watching something enjoyable. I knew the day and time by the programme that was on TV. When the credits rolled at eight o'clock, it would be time for me to go home.

I wheeled the tea trolley back to the kitchen. As usual, I backed through the kitchen door, so I didn't spot Gloria coming through.

"Mind!" she snapped. Then she pointed at my head. "Get that blasted bandana off. It must have healed by now."

I ripped the headscarf off and stuffed it into the pocket of my pinny.

Her eyes widened. "Put it back on! You can't be seen looking like that." Without another word, she stormed out of the kitchen.

I didn't look that horrific, did I? Frowning, I patted my hair and bent to assess myself in the oven's glass window. I pulled at the few remaining strands of fringe. My mum had hacked at it, insisting we needed to cut away the burned bits. She'd declared that I looked fine, but I cried when I saw her efforts. Not in front of her, though. I didn't want to hurt her feelings, especially when she'd cut up her shirt to make my headscarf. My tears hadn't flowed just because my hair looked dreadful, but also for the waste of money. For the first time in my life, I'd felt good about my hair. Gran, Mum and my auntie had all contributed by giving the little cash they had. And I'd wrecked it through sheer stupidity. In my bedroom, I'd tugged at my fringe, wishing I was like one of those dolls I'd had as a child, where I'd pulled its hair to make it grow longer.

My fringe was a semi-circle, making my forehead look like a reddened dome. Joe had been his usual wonderful self when I'd allowed him to peek beneath my headscarf, saying it would grow back and that I still looked lovely. No one mentioned about the money it had cost to have my hair styled a month before. Not even my gran.

But Gloria's spiteful comment had unravelled Mum and Joe's comforting words, revealing them for what they were. Lies. Of course, I looked a disaster. I *was* one. The dieting, the new clothes and hairstyle – I thought they'd given me Joe. But he had lied too. He wasn't working here to look after old people. He was working undercover to write an article about how people were treated in residential homes. But he *did* care for the people he looked after. I saw it in his actions, his kindness. He'd signed up to do this job because he wanted to help the residents by highlighting any abuse, although he hadn't found it.

I thought about the scene with the elderly woman. Her plaintive squeals were as vibrant in my mind today as they'd been then. I had no idea if the nurse had been unfair or not. Watching anyone being restrained was unpleasant. Joe had asked me to keep an eye out for anything suspicious now he wouldn't be here to do it himself. I would, although I didn't imagine that I'd find anything.

Joe swung through the kitchen door and put a tray down on the side. "That wasn't as bad as I expected."

"Really? Gloria was in a right huff when I saw her."

"She just said 'fine' and accepted a week's notice."

"She must like you. She told me to take my scarf off. When I did, she yelled at me to put it back on."

When Joe gave me a puzzled look, I added, "She must think I'll scare the residents."

He held my shoulders, gazing at me in sympathy. "I keep telling you. No one gives a fig about a few scorched hairs. Look, I'll drive you home in a bit. I won't stop, though. I have work to do." He gave me a wry smile. "*Work* work. How about we go out tomorrow afternoon instead?"

I sighed. "Sorry, no can do. I've promised to meet Tracey. I can't let her down."

"Okay. I can do my work then, and we can go out tomorrow evening if you're up for it." He began to stack the cups and saucers into the dishwasher. "When I said not to worry about your appearance, I meant it. You need to meet my mum. You're similar in so many ways." He turned, grinning. "That sounds a bit Oedipus complex, but it's nothing like that, honest!"

I chuckled, until he added, "Let me know what day you're off next week. I'll arrange time off work. You could have dinner at mine. Mum's been asking when she'll get to meet you."

# Chapter 18

Freda's eyes had sparkled when I asked her about a trip to the common. She'd laid her gnarled hand on my arm and twisted her head to look at me. I felt bad then. I should have waited until she was seated in the lounge, rather than following her when she shuffled behind the others. She'd left the dining room before the rest, but now she'd be the last to find a chair. It meant she would view the TV – and the garden – from the other side of the room.

"That would be lovely, duck." She'd chuckled. "Simply wonderful. Ooh, I'll have to get out my glad rags."

I hoped I hadn't over-sold my invite. "It's only a cream tea on a bench."

"It's a day out. A special occasion." She patted my arm. "And I don't get many of those."

Thanks to Gloria insisting that Freda used her Zimmer frame – rather than my arm – it took us five minutes to get out of the door, never mind across the potholed, mossy driveway. After spending an anxious morning watching rain pelt the windows, I gazed up at the clumps of slate clouds. I wished they would scud off and leave us with the promised 'overcast with sunny spells'. I knew better than to trust weathermen. I'd been at poly last October when Michael Fish assured viewers that we wouldn't be in for a hurricane, just a bit of wind and rain. He'd been right about the rain. I'd got drenched that night coming back from the SU bar, but I'd woken to felled trees and a power cut. Back home, Mum hadn't fared any better: a row of her fence panels had landed on next door's prized rose bushes (which, thankfully, survived the encounter). In turn, Gran moaned about the loss of her umbrella, which flapped inside out and couldn't be mended. When Mum pointed out it was hardly the same, Gran wouldn't have it, saying it was her favourite brolly.

Through a break in the trees, I spotted a strip of blue. A rainbow began to shimmer, touching the roofs on the other side of the valley. I tapped Freda's shoulder and pointed to it.

"Lovely, duck." She resumed her painful walk, lugging the frame forward, then slowly catching up. When she began to wheeze, I wondered if Gloria had been right to cast doubt on our expedition.

I'd never spent much time looking around at the driveway before. It was something to be hurried over – either in my haste to get into work on time or the rush to get away. Beneath the tall trees was a bed where wildflowers fought with weeds. Gran would tut. She loved her little garden. Beside the entrance nestled a straggly lavender bush, wafting a gorgeous scent in the air. It had been planted too close to its hydrangea neighbour, so silvery stems with delicate petals pierced the gaps in the lush foliage and abundant pink blooms.

We finally made it to the pavement, where we had to wait a while until the road was clear. Even so, we were still crossing when a white van roared towards us. I wanted to pick Freda up and dash across the road, but I daren't. Instead, my hand hovered behind her as if I could somehow propel her forward. Rolling my eyes, I sent her a silent plea. *Please get a move on!* But neither she or the van changed their speed. Couldn't the driver see us?

I shouted, "Slow down, idiot!" but the van swerved around us, blasting its horn.

"Dickhead!" I screeched, anger making me forget myself. I clamped my hand to my mouth. "I'm so sorry, Freda."

"I couldn't agree more, duck." She hefted the heavy metal frame onto the kerb then paused to take a breath, panting as she spoke. "That reminds me. I once knew a Dick Stain." She chuckled. "Can you believe he answered the phone by saying 'Dick Stain speaking'? His name was Richard."

I laughed. "Really? If I was called Richard Stain, I'd never call myself Dick."

"His parents should've known better. Poor man. For the life of me I can't understand why he shortened it to Dick. But, even worse, letters would be addressed to Mr R. Stain."

I had to think for a moment, repeating the name, Mr R. Stain. Then it clicked. "Poor man! I'd have wanted to murder my parents if they did that to me."

We giggled all the way to the bench. If I'd been worried about finding things to talk about, I couldn't have been more wrong. Freda was hilarious. What a shame she was overshadowed by her more confident companions at the dining table. She'd have them in fits of laughter.

Although there were picnic tables, we chose a bench, as it didn't sit in a muddy puddle. Once I'd wiped the seat dry, I unwrapped the scones, jam and clotted cream I'd packed. Freda smacked her lips, her grey eyes sparkling. I noticed that she'd styled her hair into soft waves. How had she managed that with her arthritic hands? When I complimented her on it, she waved me away, smiling as she scooped a spoonful of jam onto her scone.

"The last time I had a cream tea, I was in Cornwall with my Jim."

I balanced my paper plate on my lap and scraped a smidgen of cream onto each half of the scone. This picnic would do my diet no good, so I was determined to lessen the damage.

Freda pointed her spoon at my scone. "Going for the Devon way?"

"Eh?"

"In Devon they put the cream on first, then add the jam. In Cornwall, it's the jam first then the cream."

I shrugged. "It all tastes the same."

She chuckled. "Don't tell them that. They get quite het up about the right way to do it." She took a bite of her scone and settled down to munch in peace. Nearby us, parents stood in groups while children raced around the park, queued for their turn on the slide, or stood at the top of the climbing frame, shouting to each other.

An elderly man with a small black and tan dog sauntered past, whistling. He lifted his cap and gave us a cheery, "Good afternoon. I'll have some of that if there's any going spare."

Freda held up the second half of her scone, not yet coated in cream and jam. "You're very welcome, duck."

"Oh, I wouldn't deprive you." He chuckled. "Rover here would make fast work of it, though. He's a food fiend."

The dog didn't seem that bothered by our cream-tea picnic, choosing to sniff around the neighbouring picnic table instead. When the man walked on, his dog wagging its stubby tail beside him, Freda watched them. "I used to have dogs. Bertie and Basset were my first ones. Then my husband chose the names for our others. It went downhill from there. Pirate – he thought Patch was boring. Piglet – that one looked all pink like a pig when we chose him as a puppy. Last of all we had Poppy."

"Poppy's sweet," I said.

"She started out as Petra – my choice – but she suffered with wind, so Jim renamed her Pop-off. I told him he couldn't go around town calling her that, so we settled on Poppy."

While I opened the flask and poured our tea into two plastic cups, Freda took another bite of her scone. Then she swiped a dollop of cream from the corner of her mouth and chuckled.

"Did you spot Alice's sour face when I said I'd see you at two o'clock?"

"Should I have asked her too? "

"Not this time, duck. It's lovely to have someone to

walk alongside me. It gets a bit tiresome looking at the back of people's legs all the time." She lifted her feet a few inches, then dropped them back to the ground. "This hump means I get to see a lot more than people realise. You can tell a lot about a person by the way they keep their shoes."

That was one of Gran's favourite expressions. A few years earlier, I'd gone round her house wearing a pair of winklepickers whose tips had bent upwards. She'd told me that in her day she'd not let a man near Mum if he arrived on her doorstep with curled winkle-whatsits. And woe betide them if their shoes weren't polished and buffed to perfection.

"I told your mum and I'll tell you the same," she'd said. "It's no good him spending time curling his hair into a daft quiff, spraying Old Spice or whatnot, putting on his best shirt and shiny trousers if his shoes don't match." She'd pointed at me. "Hark at my words – that's a lesson for the whole of your life."

One that I'd forgotten until now. When I passed Freda a cup of tea, I made sure I tucked my shoes beneath the bench, out of sight. Although Mum had a box full of polish, I preferred to use the black dabber to cover the scuffs. It didn't make them shine, but it was quick.

Thinking about Gran made me wonder why I'd never thought to ask her if she'd like to go for a walk to the park. Perhaps I'd invite her on my day off next week. It couldn't be before then. Today was Joe's last day at the residential home and he'd taken tomorrow off his usual job so we could have the same day off. I grimaced. I'd never had to face dinner with a boyfriend's parents before. Just the thought made me tingle with nerves. One thing was certain – I'd get the polish out later and buff my shoes.

# Chapter 19

The *Our Tune* theme blared on the radio. Mum and I loved Simon Bates, especially the stories on *Our Tune*. She switched off the kettle – my tea could wait – and sat down beside me at the small kitchen table, where we listened to a sad tale about a parent losing their only child. When the Elton John song 'Daniel' played at the end, we were both in tears.

Sniffing, she pulled a tissue from the box. "That poor family."

A lump filled my throat. "I wouldn't wish that on anyone."

At least our wallowing had taken my mind off the coming afternoon, but now it came back to me. I glanced at the clock and frowned. Mum got to her feet and squeezed my shoulder. "You'll be fine, love. I can't imagine anyone wouldn't want you as a daughter-in-law."

"Hold your horses, Mum! We've not been dating that long."

She chuckled. "Well, I've been keeping my fingers crossed. He's perfect son-in-law material. Especially being a journalist too."

I tapped my nose. "That's hush-hush."

As she pulled on her supermarket overcoat, she shrugged. "A woman can't help but hope." She bent to kiss my forehead. "Good luck, love. Just be you and you'll be perfect." She paused by the back door. "Sorry, I didn't get around to making you that cuppa."

"I think I can manage." I smiled.

Determined not to let my nerves overcome me, I headed off to the bathroom, Jif in hand, to scrub the bath and sink. A busman's holiday of sorts. And, just like we did at work, within minutes of cleaning I had dirtied the bathroom – by washing my hair and having a quick bath. Joe had proper shower fittings in the en-suite I'd stayed in, but Mum improvised with a rubber fitting that slotted onto each tap to mix the hot and cold water. That was fine until, like today, one end came loose, so you risked being scalded or frozen. In my case, the latter.

At least the bath was hot. While I lazed in the bubbly water, my clean hair tucked into Mum's frilly shower cap, I kept an eye on the time. Another bonus was that, since it was summer, I didn't have to race to my bedroom to get warm when I got out of the bath. For some reason, we had no radiator in the bathroom, so it got chilly in winter.

To the sound of bath water gurgling down the plug hole, I wiped the steam from the mirror and inspected my fringe. Gloria was right. It looked awful. Would it ever grow back? Mum had made me another two headscarves – one flowery, the other a gorgeous emerald, which would coordinate with the green top I'd chosen for today. I wanted to impress Joe's mum. Hopefully, she wouldn't notice that my top came from C&A rather than one of the posh shops she must frequent.

Punctual as always, Joe arrived on the dot of one. He grinned when I told him for the third time how nervous I felt, and patted my hand.

"Don't worry. Mum won't eat you. Dad might," he joked. "But he'll be at work until goodness knows what time."

We pulled up in front of Joe's parents' house, which was as large and impressive as I recalled. Joe led me into the hallway with the chandelier hanging above. The kitchen door stood ajar and I could smell baking. After toeing off my shoes, I followed Joe, feeling more bashful with each step. Princess Diana's shyness looked charming, whereas I… let's just say, I went every shade of red imaginable.

Spotting us, Joe's mum put her baking tin on the side and hurried over. She rubbed her hands down her apron then held out a hand to me. Hers was surprisingly cold. Perfect for pastry making, my gran would say.

"Hello, Mrs Good," I said.

"You must be Belinda. Call me Harriet. I'm so pleased to meet you."

I gazed at her in surprise. If she'd been twenty years younger, we could have passed for siblings. Her hair was more ginger than mine. The hairdresser had told me I was lucky to have chestnut auburn hair, which was a lovely way of putting it. Harriet was a little chubbier than me – she looked like I had before starting my diet – and we were the same height. There the likeness ended; her eyes were startling blue, while her foundation masked her freckles, the giveaway being her chest and hands. Even though Joe had said we were alike, I hadn't expected such a similarity. I found it disconcerting, yet comforting. After all, Gran had said my dad and Mum's father were the spit of each other. Mum never got to meet hers, though. He was a GI stationed at a small base in the village neighbouring the farm where Gran had worked during World War II. Gran fell for his strange accent and easy manner.

"Stuff the nylons," she'd once said. "I was more interested in being taken to the pictures."

Sadly, Gran's GI didn't make it back from the war, so he never knew that Gran was pregnant. She had to face the shame of returning home to become a single mother. That's why she just got on with it when Mum got pregnant and the feckless jack-the-lad wouldn't do the right thing. Or that was Gran's version of events. Mum told me she screeched and hollered so loud at her, calling her a silly cow, that half the street must have heard.

Harriet blinked, bringing me back to the present.

"Me too," I said. "I've been looking forward to it."

Joe grinned, but he didn't contradict me. Although if his mum saw his expression, she'd know the truth.

"I was going to make an apple pie, but I've searched high and low in the chest freezer and the apples aren't there. They couldn't have vanished." She frowned. "You haven't used them, have you?"

Joe chuckled. "Do you think I'd need stewed apples for a wild party or something?"

"Well, we all know you wouldn't need them for cooking," she said. "I never have to worry about coming back to a messy kitchen." She spoke conspiratorially. "He can cook if he tries. He made a wonderful beef bourguignon for our anniversary meal. Ask him to make it for you."

I turned to find Joe shaking his head. But when his mum looked at him, he stopped and gave her a pleasant smile.

She wagged her finger. "It's no good pretending you can't. You let the cat out of the bag with that dish. Now, why don't you take Belinda off into the garden while I get this lot finished." She looked at me. "You have eaten lunch?"

When I nodded, she smiled. "That's good. I've told Ron he's to be back for five thirty or he's in trouble."

Joe's dad would be coming for tea? I'd got over the ordeal of meeting his mum, only to face a worse one later. Joe looked surprised too, but he didn't say anything. He led me through to the plush lounge and slumped onto the settee, patting the seat beside him.

"Are you okay if we stay inside for a bit? I thought you might like to watch a video. I've rented *Dirty Dancing* but it has to go back later."

Would I mind? I'd love to! My expression told him as much.

"Before we watch it, I've a confession to make. That beef bourguignon? I got it from the posh nosh shop in Bilton where they make home-cooked food that you reheat. Mum was so thrilled that I'd bothered, I didn't have the heart to tell her I cheated."

I chuckled. "Maybe it's time to find out how to make it."

"Maybe." He slid off the settee and headed over to a cupboard, which he opened to reveal a TV and video unit. Kneeling, he pulled a video from its case and pushed it into the slot before plumping back onto the settee, where he took my hand.

After the film ended, we sat for a few minutes, enjoying the afterglow of the romantic film. Joe kissed my cheek. "Fancy seeing if I can lift you in the pool?"

"No way! Anyhow, I haven't brought my costume."

"My mum used to be your size. She's probably got one stuffed away in the back of a drawer somewhere."

"I couldn't."

It would be too embarrassing to ask to borrow his mum's costume, let alone for Joe to see my body, warts and all. And no, we hadn't got that far yet. Close, but not the full hog. While I wasn't into the whole 'no sex before marriage' thing, I was old-fashioned in the sense I wanted it to be right. And a quick fumble in Joe's car didn't match my expectations. I chuckled to myself. Going by my family history, I was even more behind the times than my mum and gran – even though women now were lucky enough to have the pill. Some of my innocence had been by mum's design – determined that I wouldn't follow in their footsteps. But she needn't have worried. The bullying and fat shaming at school had made me keep males at arms' length more than her constant warnings ever could.

"I'll deal with it. Give me a minute."

Joe must have mistaken my expression for shyness – after all, it was my default mode. Ignoring my plea not to worry, he rushed off to persuade his mum to rifle through her drawers. And, yes, I did mean to phrase it that way: my swimming costume was stuffed in my knicker drawer along with the suspender belts Tracey had persuaded me to buy, after telling me that men loved them (even though they'd have to look at me first to know I wore one).

Soon his mum's voice echoed from the hallway. "But you'll freeze! I told your tight git of a dad we needed pool heating, but he wouldn't have it."

I glanced outside. During *Dirty Dancing*, the sunlight had streamed through the huge patio windows, dazzling the screen, forcing Joe to draw the curtains to shade the TV. Puffs of clouds now littered the sky, dappling the lawn in a mixture of sun and shade.

When Joe reappeared, he took me to the room I'd stayed in after his party. A black and white swimsuit lay on the bed beside a folded white towel. Once changed, I twisted around in front of the full-length mirror. I was thankful to see that it covered my bum, although it made my middle look like a zebra. All the physical work I'd been doing at the residential home had made my legs thinner, and my arms. Only my stomach needed work. I wrapped myself in the huge bath sheet he'd given me, determined it would stay in place until the last possible moment. When we stepped outside, through a side door rather than via the lounge, I waited until he'd folded his towel over a patio chair and turned to lower himself down the steps before I removed my towel – and headscarf – and jumped straight into the water.

He gazed at me in admiration. "You're brave!"

I struggled to smile while gasping with shock at the cold. Flaming heck! My body burned with cold, while mountain ranges of goosebumps fired across my skin. "It's not so bad." But my chattering teeth gave me away.

"Start swimming and you'll get warm."

How? My legs had seized up, thanks to the Arctic temperature. But I did as he said, while he clung to the rail, most of his body out of the water. Until I splashed him. Then we started to duck each other. Before long, I had forgotten the chill, although I didn't enjoy our attempts at the lift from *Dirty Dancing*, which resulted in repeated icy duckings. When we changed places, it was even more of a disaster, so we played other daft games instead. He chased me around the patio, where I divebombed into the pool to escape him. It was only when we stopped for breath that I realised I'd been having too much fun to worry about my stomach.

Joe's mum came outside carrying a tray of drinks and biscuits, which she laid on the patio table. "You are honoured," she told me. "Ron's come back extra early. He's gone for a shower."

In all the fun, I'd forgotten about him. My knowledge of fathers had been gleaned from the stern figures in childhood books. My friends' dads ranged from those who sat in 'their' chair in the corner, eyes glued to the TV, to the ones who said hello and smiled. Except for Caroline's dad, who'd been the chief cook in their household. A big man, whose booming welcome scared me, so I scuttled behind her out to the safety of the garden. I think he found me hilarious, as he took great delight in searching me out, so he could bellow, "Can I get you a bacon butty or sommat?" He came from Lancashire and once, when he spotted me sniffing the air, told me he was cooking lambs' bollocks for tea. I still have no idea if he was kidding.

But no one had ever made a point of returning from work to meet me. The thought unsettled me more than I could believe.

# Chapter 20

Joe hadn't shown me the dining room when I went to his party. Again, the contrast between his house and mine was stark. The room didn't seem to suit his down-to-earth mum either. It was all burnished mahogany, like a stately home. A velvet easy chair sat in the corner, tucked behind the polished oval table which was surrounded by eight chairs. While the lounge had been the height of modernity, this room felt cosy, the furnishings dated, but in a nice way. A dado rail ran the length of the room, separating the burgundy and cream wallpaper at the top – which featured a floral pattern between the thick stripes – from the block burgundy below.

"Dad hates this décor. He says it makes the room too dark and the stripes should be at the bottom. But Mum reckons it's the new fashion." He shrugged. "Just a warning in case you mention it. That, along with the lack of pool heating, tends to start World War III."

Beside him stood a large bookcase packed with paperbacks that, on closer inspection, got my seal of approval. I'd enjoyed James Herbert, Stephen King, Danielle Steele and Jackie Collins books in the library while waiting for my second shift to start.

Joe crossed over to a sideboard and took a handful of cutlery from one of the drawers, which he held up. "Only for special occasions: Christmas, birthdays, dinner parties and the introduction to my lovely girlfriend."

I wilted. All this for me? Instead of making me feel special, it heightened my anxiety. What if I did something stupid, like spilling my drink? Or worse. I took the place mats from Joe and set them around the four seats in the middle of the table, then helped to put out wine glasses and flutes beside the knives. I laid them down as if they were precious newborns. Joe had positioned all the cutlery on either side of the placemat, whereas at the residential home we put the pudding spoon and fork facing in opposite directions at the top. When he showed me to a chair, I sat bolt upright, keeping my hands in my lap in case my fingerprints marked the wood. My stomach churned, and not with hunger. If only I could fast-forward an hour, maybe two, and get this over and done with.

Joe returned carrying a tray of short-stemmed dessert dishes, heaped with green and topped with pink stuff. On closer inspection, it was prawn cocktail served on a bed of lettuce. I wasn't a fan of prawns, but when Joe had asked if there was any food I didn't like, I'd shrugged and told him any food was good. Now I wished I'd been more specific. Any meat and veg was good.

His mum bustled in with a bottle of bubbly in a silver bucket. His dad would follow soon. Why on earth had I agreed to this? Stupid. To think I could be sitting at home, feet up, watching TV, snaffling chips out of newspaper. Okay, that wouldn't help my diet, but I couldn't imagine that this dinner would do much good either.

A door creaked, like something from a horror movie. A man's voiced echoed in the hallway. Joe gave my hand a squeeze, only releasing it when his dad appeared holding a bottle of red wine and a corkscrew. He was taller than Joe, a thick-set man with salt and pepper hair. Like me, he had wide brown eyes, but his skin was tanned – perhaps from their recent holiday, where they had been when Joe had his party. Joe had said he spent every possible minute working.

"Dad, this is Belinda," Joe said.

Smiling, his dad held out a large hand and enclosed mine, introducing himself as Ron. His skin felt coarser than I'd expected. He must have started at the bottom and grafted his way up before his pools win meant he could buy out the company. I hadn't asked Joe what his dad's work involved. Maybe he still did his fair share of manual work.

Once he'd poured the drinks – a flute of bubbly for me, with a glass of water – we tucked into our prawn cocktail starter. Thankfully, the sauce obliterated the taste of the prawns, which were small enough to be cut in half, swallowed without chewing and washed down with a liberal glug of water. I finished before everyone else.

Joe looked at me in surprise. "You must have liked that."

"I loved it." Well, I liked the lettuce.

Across the table, his mum beamed at me. "I hope you like duck. Joe said you're not a fussy eater, which is lovely."

"I love duck." This time I spoke the truth. Pre-diet, my mum and I often had duck with pancakes from the local

Chinese. But the duck Joe's mum brought out didn't look much like the crispy shredded duck we took home in foil trays. Perhaps it would taste the same. It didn't. It had a strange bloody taste, too strong for my liking. But, following my childhood mantra of saving the best for last, I sawed my way through it, keeping the broccoli, carrots and the creamy potato slices – which tasted lovely, even though I had no idea what they were called – to savour at leisure.

Until now, the conversation had centred around Ron's day, but now he eyed me. "What do you think about the rumours about the old folks' home?"

Of all the things I'd expected him to ask me, it hadn't been that. I glanced at Joe, uncertain what I should say.

"Dad thinks I might have missed something," he said. "I didn't realise at the time, but Dad knows my boss's friend, Maurice. You know, the one who asked my boss to look into it—"

"Sensible bloke. He wouldn't make a mountain out of a molehill for no good reason." His point made, Joe's dad forked a mound of duck, potato and veg into his mouth, his gaze trained on me. Joe's mum – I must get used to calling her Harriet and his dad, Ron – surveyed me from above the rim of her wine glass, which she held to her lips.

I flushed. "I've not seen much go on." Talk properly, I reprimanded myself. They might not speak posh like Charlotte or Dan, but they moved in wealthy circles. "I mean, I haven't seen anything really suspicious. There was the time we saw the nurse holding down a lady who had dementia. And money and a watch have gone missing." I frowned, trying to think if I'd seen anything else. Nothing came to mind.

"They're more likely to die of boredom in the home, not neglect." Was that an inappropriate joke? I amended it. "I mean, they don't get to do much other than eat and watch TV. There are no activities for them to do. I took one of the ladies, Freda, over to the common the other day for a cream tea and she loved it. She didn't mention anything terrible happening at the residential home, though. Not that I asked her."

"Perhaps you should," Harriet suggested. "It's amazing what you can learn from an off-hand remark or by planting a seed of a question that might lead to something."

As Ron scraped the last of his potato onto his fork, she turned to me. "Finished? I hope you've got room for dessert."

I hadn't eaten this much in ages. The cream in the potatoes and in the prawn cocktail sauce must have contained a zillion calories. But it wasn't just that. My stomach felt like a lead weight at the thought of the prawns congealing beneath the bloody duck. Yuck! I swallowed back a fish-and-duck-tasting burp and smiled. "I'd love pudding."

She beamed at me. "Pineapple upside-down cake with custard."

Until now, I could have sworn that I wasn't – as she put it – a fussy eater. But why oh why had she picked pineapple? It was the only fruit I detested. At least when

I'd had gammon at a restaurant, I could slide the pineapple to the edge of my plate, but here it would be embedded in the blooming thing.

"Delicious," I said.

Ron looked at me. "Nice to see a girl with a healthy appetite. None of this dieting business. Harry's always on some diet or other."

Harriet rolled her eyes. "He likes me to look nice, but he doesn't want to pay for it. Same as the pool. What's the point of having one if you can't use it without freezing to death? Poor Belinda went blue out there today."

Joe gave my thigh a warning squeeze. Don't say a word. I didn't. Instead, I gave Harriet a bland smile, even though it felt rude not to respond.

Joe saved me by standing up. "Belinda and I will clear the plates."

I followed him out to the kitchen, where I was surprised to find there was a dishwasher hidden behind a cupboard door. No one I knew had one in their kitchen, while the one at work was huge. At Rockbeare, the inside of the cups sparkled white, unlike ours at home which were tea-stained, no matter how hard we scrubbed them.

Harriet put a Pyrex jug of custard in the microwave, which was fitted into the units, just like the oven. Mum had been talking about getting a microwave, but she was worried about it exploding or setting on fire. She said she'd read an article in her paper that had mentioned dangerous rays. With a small kitchen like ours, she didn't want to risk it. But in reality, it came down to the price.

We couldn't afford one.

Leaving his mum beside the whirring microwave, Joe carried the pungent pineapple upside-down cake through to the dining room, while I followed with the dishes. Minutes later, Harriet placed a steaming china jug on the table.

"Just a small slice," I pleaded as his dad went to dish up.

He and I had different ideas about what constituted 'small'. And Harriet didn't help by telling him to, "Give Belinda that bit. She'll want pineapple."

I gave her a gracious smile. "Please, don't worry about me."

"Nonsense!" She flapped me away. "You're our guest. The first girlfriend Joe's brought around too."

That stunned me. And Joe too, by the look of his cheeks. Wow! Me? Special? No one had ever treated me that way before. But they didn't massage my ego by saying more. Instead, Harriet changed the subject.

"I hear that you used to work in an office and you went to poly for a while. What made you decide not to continue with your course?"

Her words smashed into me like a tidal wave. Flipping heck! Could this evening get any worse? Prawns, duck, pineapple and now this. No way could I tell them the truth. They'd never have me over to dinner again. And what would Joe think? He'd asked me once what had happened, but I'd changed the subject and he hadn't pressed the point.

"I … er…" I couldn't think of a plausible explanation, even a lie. Unable to come up with anything, I shrugged. Across the table Ron gazed at me with interest, his eyebrows lifting as I stuttered into silence.

"It wasn't for you?" Harriet offered me a spade to dig myself out of the hole she'd created.

"It wasn't what I expected."

Looking curious, Harriet leaned closer. I winced. Great! I'd only gone and opened up another line of enquiry. This time Ron took up the challenge. His laden spoon hovered in mid-air. "What did—"

"Where did you get this custard?" Joe said. "Is it that Ambrosia tinned stuff again? It's delicious."

"Yes." Harriet turned back to me, her eyes alert with interest. "So—"

Joe jabbed his fork into his sponge. "This pineapple's lovely too. I was thinking of baking something for Belinda when she takes Freda out again. Will you show me how?"

For a man who didn't cook, maybe he realised what an odd remark this was, as he went on to say, "That reminds me. I've got an interview on Monday with a chef who's been having an affair with a married MP."

His dad's lips thinned. "I didn't know you were into that sort of tattle."

"Usually not, but this MP voted for Section 28 – a bit hypocritical if he's homosexual. But we won't run the piece if there's no evidence."

His dad pulled an unimpressed face. I cringed. By deflecting the conversation, Joe had brought grief on himself. I'd thank him later but, for now, I had to eat a whole ring of disgusting pineapple. At least, if my mouth was full, Harriet couldn't interrogate me further. Because I really didn't want to explain what had led to me leaving poly.

# Chapter 21

On the way home, Joe asked me the question I dreaded. He guessed he'd hit a nerve, as he told me it could wait if I wished. While I didn't want to tell him, neither did I need it looming over every future date. I'd always be on tenterhooks worrying about when the question might spring up. Should I get it over and done with? Would he want to be with me if he knew what I'd done?

"I don't know." I squirmed in my seat. "I did something out of character."

He didn't take his eyes from the road as he said, "You got kicked out?"

"Flipping heck! You guessed!" He'd hit the nail, but I'd responded in a jokey way, hoping it might deflect him. In truth, I felt close to tears.

He squeezed my thigh. "Do you want to go for a drink before you go home?"

It was the last thing I wanted. But I couldn't prolong this agony.

I nodded. "Not the Nag's Head, though. It's my gran's friends' local."

He chuckled. "What about the Ivy Tree? I can't imagine them there."

"At those prices, I can't believe anyone can afford to drink there. It'd have to be your shout. Or how about the Rose and Crown? I could stretch to that."

"Do you go there often?" His eyebrows raised, but a

smile played at the corner of his mouth. "My mum says it's the type of place where you wipe your feet before you leave."

I shrugged. "I've been there once or twice. The carpet is used as an ashtray and the glasses have more lipstick than a cosmetics counter. But it's handy for building the immune system."

He indicated to turn down Ivy Lane. "I think I'll make it my shout."

Many a time I'd been driven past the Ivy Tree and admired the beautiful brick and flint building with its leaded, arched windows and ivy climbing around the entrance door. I'd never been able to afford to go there.

After his small glass of wine during dinner, Joe opted for an orange juice, while I stuck to a half of lager. When Joe received a few pound coins and coppers as change from a fiver, I wished I'd gone for tap water. The cost was worse than the fabled London prices. We chose a small table in the corner, where I nursed my amber nectar as if it were gold dust. Outside an apricot sunset glowed across the valley, the nearby moon waiting to beam upon the patchwork fields and clumps of trees.

"You don't need to tell me if you want," Joe said.

But I knew I had to. I cleared my throat then shrugged. "It's nothing, really."

Condensation soaked my glass. I wiped my hand on my trousers, leaving a smear. This was hard. Even though I'd confided in two people, I'd never told them the whole story in one go. Tracey knew most of the sorry tale, while

Mum had fitted together the pieces of the jigsaw. I took a deep breath.

"I was bullied at school – I was called 'chubby', 'ginger', 'goofy' and 'metal mouth' when I got braces. It was horrific. Boys were the worst. I had a few friends who told me to ignore them, but at seven it's quite hard to do."

"Seven?" Joe sounded astonished.

"It started at infants and never stopped. In the end I dressed to disappear. If you see photos of me from back then, I'm always in black."

He smiled, gazing at my emerald top. "But not now."

"That's another story. I have the lady at the charity shop to thank for the idea behind the brighter colours and my new wardrobe. And changing my hairstyle." I patted my headscarf. "I had me to thank for wrecking it, though."

Bits of the paper coaster were scattered around the table. I hadn't realised I'd been tearing it. I put the remaining bit down and scooped the fragments into a tidy pile. We'd moved off topic. It would be so easy to laugh, let our chatter turn to hair and fashion, but Joe wanted to know the truth. I found it hard to accept what I'd done. Tracey had roared with laughter when I'd told her, slapped me on the back and congratulated me. But she was wrong. I'd lost my temper and had released years of anger on that man.

"Anyhow..." I knew it would be difficult, but I hadn't expected to feel so much emotion: anger, fury, shame. I took another deep breath. "I went through school being the class fatso, carrot head … freak."

Just admitting that last one made me cringe with embarrassment. I mean, I was a child. How many stupid adults told me, 'Sticks and stones will break your bones, but words can never hurt you'? What rubbish! They branded you for life. I could feel my cheeks burning. They'd be the colour of Ribena bubbles – the awful nickname that my lecturer had given me, which had stuck. It might be a tasty drink, but the adverts had done me no favours.

I ached to press the chilled glass to my hot cheeks, but thought it might draw more attention to them. Instead, I took a sip of lager. "Anyhow, when I went to work in the office, all that ended. I could forget my past and be me." I allowed myself a chuckle. "Although I still dressed in black." Now to the hard part. "Then my boss persuaded me to go to poly. He said it would be good for me and my prospects. There was this lecturer there. Thought he was God's gift – flirted with all the girls, acted like he was the boys' best mate." I paused to stop myself from gabbling. "But, for some reason, he decided to use me as a prop for his jokes."

Joe's face swam before me. Stupid, stupid! Why on earth was I crying about this? A tear trickled down my cheek. I dabbed at it.

Joe reached for my hand. "I'm sorry for making you drag all this up. If you don't want to go on, I'll understand."

I shook my head, sniffed, and forced a smile. "No. I have to deal with this one day. It might as well be now."

My lips trembled, but my voice rang clear. "After spending lecture after lecture being the butt of his humour, I'd had enough. He was vile – worse than the kids at school. He should have known better, for a start. But he was clever. He picked on every single thing I hated about myself."

The memory of the first incident came to me. I'd been late for class that day, rushing in all apologetic, my bag sliding down my arm. My bag had bashed against the door frame and a book had fallen to the floor. I'd stooped to pick it up.

"It must be some door to withstand that," the lecturer had joked to the class, who'd sniggered with him.

Then when I'd dropped into my seat, he'd added, "The chair too. It must be made of reinforced steel."

Of course I'd blushed, giving him more ammunition.

"The heat! The heat!" He'd held out his hands, as if to ward it off. "It's burning me."

To the sound of roaring laughter, I'd fired barbs of hatred at him. He'd chuckled. "Watch out you don't kill me with that stare. Has anyone told you that you look like an orange version of Medusa with that hair?"

Each incident wasn't terrible, in itself. But it got tiresome. More than that. It was humiliating. And it got worse when a few lads decided to carry it on when he wasn't around. I couldn't believe the lecturer could get away with it, but my friends told me not to worry. He was just joking.

I sighed and turned back to Joe. "He started by

mocking me in front of the class on the odd occasion, but it soon became a daily thing. At the Hallowe'en ball, he asked me which one of the Addams family I'd come dressed as. I was in my usual clothes. But I had no idea what he was on about; I hadn't seen the programme, so I told him so. He used that to taunt me in the next class, even though most of my friends had never seen it either."

I took another glug of lager. I needed to get this over and done with. "Anyhow, this went on for ages. One evening a hypnotist was at the SU bar, and my friends forced me onto the stage with them. But I couldn't be hypnotised as I'd been drinking, so I got sent back to the audience. My friends were still on stage, which meant I was alone – until the lecturer came over."

Flipping hell, this was hard. I forced myself to carry on. But I couldn't meet Joe's eyes. "He stood for a moment, smiled at me, then breathed in my ear. 'Fancy a shag?' I was so shocked, I said, 'No, why on earth would I?' And you know what he said? 'Believe me, I'd be the one doing you a favour'."

"Did you punch him?" Joe's eyes were bright with fury.

I gasped. "How do you know?"

"I don't. But if he did any of those things to one of my friends, I'd want to do that."

I'd thought Joe would hate me after he heard my story. What sort of person resorts to violence? The head of department said I was fortunate that the lecturer decided not to press charges against me, as this would harm my chances of getting work in the future. But I didn't feel lucky. I'd never touched anyone in anger before, but all my pent-up fury had spewed out and I'd given him a black eye. I ended up with bruised knuckles. If I'd slapped him across the cheek, it might have been better. That's the sort of girly thing women are supposed to do. Not a full-blown, pull-your-arm back, fist in the face. I'd been shocked at the level of rage I'd felt. The lack of control. The look on everyone's face.

My gran's surprised face appeared in my mind. I'd returned home to find her sitting in our lounge having a cuppa. I'd got the train home. Of course, I hadn't told her or Mum the real reason I'd come back. They'd have gone mad, phoning the poly, causing a scene. Instead, they'd gazed at me in shame. I'd given up on yet another thing. Would I ever grow up? Do something to make them proud?

I stared at the table, my voice low. "No one believed me when I told them what he'd said. Not even my friends. Nobody. Why would they? I mean, why would he want to be with anyone as disgusting as me?"

"You're not disgusting. You're beautiful."

"Thank you. But we both know that's not true."

He grasped my hand more tightly. "Don't you ever, *ever* think like that. You are gorgeous, inside and out."

He was lying, of course. But it made me feel a little better. I gave him a wan smile. Now I needed to finish my story. To explain why I'd left my course at poly. "The lecturer lied. He said he'd simply asked why I'd left the stage. Said I must have misheard him. It was loud in there, after all. Apparently…" I puffed out a breath. "He wouldn't press charges on the proviso I didn't re-join his class, but he had no worries on that score. It was made very clear that I should leave. So I did. I couldn't stay, anyhow. Not a single person believed me."

"I believe you."

I shook my head. "That's easy for you to say."

He frowned. "You're not lying, though."

"No, but even my so-called friends thought I must have misheard because I was drunk. I was, but his words were as clear as day. The thing is, he was so mean to me all the time that no one believed he, of all people, would say that to me."

I rubbed my fist, remembering the pain I'd felt after I hit him. He'd staggered backwards and clasped his face. Then the uproar started.

Joe reached for my hand. As I took it, I realised something I'd never thought about before: the worst night of my life had led me here. If the lecturer hadn't been so awful, I wouldn't have met Joe. Although there were better ways of meeting people than being kicked out of poly and ending up cleaning toilets.

"Didn't the poly reprimand him for bullying you? No, don't answer that. You wouldn't be sitting here if they had. What's his name?"

Surprised, I gazed at Joe. "Why do you need to know? You're not going to do anything, are you? I don't want all that dragged up again. I'm so ashamed of what I did. I can hardly talk about it." I took my hand from his, rested my elbows on the table and covered my face. "I just want to forget it."

He gave me a moment before he drew my hands away. His fingers entwined with mine, his eyes searching my face. "I've been wondering what you did that could have been so terrible. But it's not your fault. What I *can* tell you is that it's not worth wasting any more time worrying about it. Ever. Your lecturer, on the other hand – his actions were appalling." He released my hand to make a cross on his chest. "I promise that I won't do anything that causes you any trouble. Please tell me his name."

# Chapter 22

Peter, the new resident, liked to hold court at the dining table. The others didn't seem to mind, especially as he told such interesting tales about his life in the RAF and in publishing. Even Alice hung on to each word. Today, he was telling a story about his mother, who had moved from the Netherlands to London in 1910 after his father died, while pregnant with Peter. She had left behind Peter's grandparents, aunt and cousins. His mother was English and, although his family wanted her to stay in the Netherlands, she'd been terribly homesick. She remarried a wealthy man when Peter was a toddler, who'd adopted him. Peter said that, his British passport and his public school upbringing had opened paths to him that might have been closed by his heritage. I didn't ask what he meant, but it became clear as his story moved along.

Peter's brow furrowed and his face darkened as his story moved into the 1930s and he told us what had happened to the rest of his family. His grandparents weren't Dutch; they'd moved from Berlin to Rotterdam years before. When their son reached his late teens, he returned to Germany. Peter looked close to tears as he told us how life had become ever more difficult: his uncle had been beaten on the streets, then his business had been forced to close after what Peter called Kristallnacht (I'd never heard of it, so decided to look it up in the library. The others seemed to know). His uncle had been taken away to what they now knew had been a concentration camp. From the seeming refuge of the Netherlands, his grandparents could only look on in horror. But none were safe, even in Amsterdam, as they were about to find out. His trembling hands rested on the table.

"Some were taken to Theresienstadt – where my grandmother died. From there they were transported to Auschwitz. The others went straight to Treblinka. Later we discovered that my uncle had been selected to work, but he didn't survive; my grandmother, aunt, cousins – even the little one at just two – were sent to be gassed." He thumped the table, making me jump, Freda gasp and people on nearby tables turn around in surprise.

"Two years old! What sort of person murders an infant?" He shook his head, his eyes glistening. "But time moves on. My daughter is married to a lovely German who is just as horrified by what happened then as I am."

Alice reached out and clutched his sleeve. "Terrible times."

Peter gave her a thin-lipped smile. "They were."

I sat stunned. All the people in the dining room had gone through so much, most living through both wars. Their stories put my issue with my poly lecturer in perspective. It might have been a horrible period in my life but, as Joe said a few evenings ago, it was in the past. I didn't have to make it my future too.

The conversation moved on to Wilf's outing with his daughter. For once, she'd turned up as promised and they'd gone to a local pub for Sunday lunch. Beaming, he told us it had been delicious. The best meal he'd had in ages.

Alice's expression soured. "You're lucky. No one ever takes me out."

Freda stilled, her fork hovering in mid-air. As her lips parted, a shudder ran through me and I sent out a silent plea. Please don't ask Alice! It had been hard enough getting Gloria to agree to one person, let alone two. And Alice of all people. If Gloria didn't trust Alice with a butter knife – I still didn't understand why – no way would she want her going on an outing.

"Why don't you come with us? We're going to the common on Saturday."

Alice sneered. "Across the road? That would be exciting."

I breathed a sigh of relief. Problem solved.

Alice sank back into her chair. "Even so, it would be better than doing nothing. What does this trip involve?"

I left Freda to tell her about our afternoon at the common. She spoke of clotted cream (an expense I could barely afford from the posh deli in town), the softest of scones – which I'd got from the supermarket – and delicious jam. Her tale could have come from the pages of a Mallory Towers midnight feast, although we'd had a flask of tea rather than lashings of ginger beer, and thankfully no anchovies.

Alice's eyes gleamed. Freda must have known that mentioning food would sell it to her. But why would she want Alice to come? Surely she must realise that Alice would want to take charge, telling her to get a move on, swiping most of the food, talking over her like she often did.

I butted in. "I'll need to check with Gloria."

Thankfully, she wasn't nearby to overhear us. A new worker sat on Joe's old table, which meant I'd been promoted to tea duty and room cleaning while she was tested with the toilets and commodes. How long would she last? She seemed too timid to deal with the more bolshy residents. Then I thought again. Hadn't I'd been the same? I should do what I could to help her, starting with warning her to hide her hoover from Alice.

Wilf cleared his throat. "If that woman had her way, we'd all be locked in our rooms."

"Glo's waiting room, I call it," Ernest said. Then, in case none of us understood, he added, "Because she acts like God at times."

They became background noise to Alice whose morose silence leeched the air. I wished I hadn't mentioned the need to get permission – although it was true.

Before I could think about the implications of my words, they spilled from my lips. "It's not that bad. She was fine about Freda coming. I can't see why there would be an issue with one more."

Wilf raised his eyebrows, but Alice didn't notice. I'd told a lie, but it did the trick. Perking up, she awarded me a rarely seen, generous smile. Then she reached out to snaffle the solitary jam tart left on the plate. "Waste not, want not."

I'd need to buy extra food for our next outing. Maybe I could find a bigger tub of cheaper cream somewhere. Although I couldn't imagine I'd need it. After I'd spoken to Gloria, I'd be returning with her sharp refusal to prick Alice's bubble of hope.

♦

If there was ever a good time to ask Gloria, this wasn't it. As Sally stormed from her office, throwing me a strange smile as we passed in the corridor, I wondered whether I should come back later. Perhaps I'd missed an item of cutlery when counting the pieces after breakfast. I hesitated, then carried on. After all, if Alice had pilfered another knife, she only had herself to blame if Gloria vetoed her picnic trip.

Through the open office door, I found Gloria gazing out of the window. The sun dazzled through her blonde hair, giving a halo-like effect. I chuckled, remembering the previous evening's comments about her being godlike. She turned, pursing her lips when she saw it was me. I *had* done something. But what?

"Yes?"

"I can come back later if you've got other things on."

I hoped she'd send me away. Instead, she swept her hand through her hair and sighed. "When haven't I? Is this about a resident?"

I grimaced. "Sort of."

That gained me a raised eyebrow.

"It's about Alice."

She groaned and slumped into her chair. "What has she done now?"

"She wants to come to the next picnic with Freda."

"*No!* It's out of the question." She planted her hands on the desk. "No. *No!*" Then she seemed to deflate. "We simply can't risk it."

Between us, dust motes danced in the air. Perhaps I should just leave and get on with cleaning the bedrooms. Then I felt bad. I should try a bit harder for Alice, even if I didn't feel inclined to do so. It would be like taking a porcupine on a date and hoping you didn't upset it. Except, unlike Alice, they looked cute.

"What if I brought Joe along? Or Tracey?" No way would Tracey want to join us, and the mention of Joe might raise her hackles, but what choice did I have? "If there's two of us, we should be fine. Freda loved it last time and I think Alice needs to get out. She hasn't got anyone."

Gloria's face clouded and she shook her head, slowly this time, as if she was less certain. "You must think me an ogre. But I'm looking after their best interests." She swung around in her chair to face the window. From her seat she could see the common through the trees, maybe even the bench where Freda and I ate our cream teas. After a moment, she steepled her hands and shook her head. "I can't believe I'm saying this, but…" She pointed her finger at me. "I'm agreeing on the proviso that there are two of you with her and Freda. Just make sure nothing happens. And don't leave Alice alone for one minute, no matter what the pretext."

I fought to hide my alarm. "You'd don't think she'll run off, do you?"

Gloria scowled. "I wouldn't put anything past that woman. On your head be it if anything goes wrong."

After thanking her, I scarpered from her office. On the way out, I heard her mutter, "And mine."

# Chapter 23

I bumped into Tracey in the cupboard, where she fished out my cleaning bucket and handed it to me, saving me from squeezing into the small space with her.

"Are you still on for this afternoon?" I asked.

Her eyes narrowed. "Now Joe's gone, I'm back on the scene, am I?"

"You know it's not like that. You can't go out with me all the time. Do you expect me to sit on my own on the common every afternoon?"

She shrugged. "Fair point. It's just that you seem more fussed about him than me."

"You've got Aiden now."

She reached to the back of the shelf to pull out a bottle of bleach, pulling a face. Were they having problems? I didn't have time to pursue it, but I'd ask later. I picked up my cleaning bucket and the hoover and staggered off in the direction of Mr Pengelly's room. The first on a long list. With our staff numbers down, I'd be working alone. So would Tracey, while Sally 'supervised' the new woman on commode-emptying duties.

Later, Tracey and I met in our usual spot in the park. The drone of the council's mower quietened as it moved away, leaving us with the fresh scent of cut grass. Tracey rolled her cardigan up to act as a pillow and lay down on her back, hitching up her top to tan her stomach. I sat on a carrier bag, gazing at her in envy. No matter what I did, that final half a stone was refusing to budge.

"Did you hear what Sally did to me?" She kept her eyes shut as she spoke, the sun making her face gleam. "Flaming cow! Up to her old tricks again."

I used my hand to shield my eyes, then decided it was easier to lie down too so we could chat. "No. What?"

"She only went and grassed me up for forgetting to give Mrs Morris a cup of tea this morning. Why didn't she just tell me?"

"Oh, so that's why she looked so happy when she came out of Gloria's office."

"Nah, she snitched on me upstairs, when Gloria walked past. Her being in the office was probably to do with getting the deputy warden job. She's been on Gloria's case for ages about it. It's been her game plan all along, ever since she moved from Julia's section cos there was no chance of promotion there."

My ears pricked up at that. Sally had worked with the dementia patients and those who needed extra care? They must have had a party when she left. Tracey's arm covered her eyes, so she didn't spot my surprise.

"Apparently…" Her voice was thick with sarcasm. "The care home has spent all its money on rebranding so we can't have a pay rise. But somehow, Sally's convinced Gloria she needs a deputy, rather than just a senior residential worker."

"Flipping heck! Can you imagine her with more power? She'll be a nightmare."

"Tell me about it." Tracey sighed. "So what were you

doing hanging around Gloria's office?"

There were no flies on her! At least it gave me the opportunity to see if she would help.

"Alice is coming along to the next picnic. It'll probably be Saturday afternoon, if it's dry. Do you fancy joining us?"

"You're having a laugh, right?" She squinted at me. "Blimey, you're being serious. Don't drag me into your nutty scheme. I mean, who in their right mind wants to spend their few hours off playing nursemaid to a bunch of old fogeys?"

I felt strangely defensive of the quick-witted Freda – once freed from the confines of the home, she'd been an interesting companion – but less so about the sharp-tongued Alice. But still. One day I might be in a residential home and I'd want people to bother about me: to remember that I hadn't always been old, that I was still important.

"They're not fogeys."

She chuckled. "Old farts then. Is that better?"

There was no talking to her when she was in this mood. Grass embedded my calves, leaving a criss-cross pattern. I brushed myself down and sat up, holding my knees close to my chest. Still feeling needled by her remarks, I sat in silence, wondering what to say until inspiration came. "How's it going with Aiden?" I knew the answer. It had shown clear as day in her face earlier.

"Flaming 'eck, Bee! Are you trying to wreck my afternoon?" She shifted around to pull her fake Ray-Bans from her handbag and put them on. Now her eyes were hidden from view, she faced me. "If you must know, we're going through a bad patch. Not helped by Luscious Lucy."

I hadn't heard of her. But then I hadn't been out with Tracey since the night she'd tried to pair me off with Gary. "Who's she?"

She grimaced. "Some tart friend of Gary's new bird."

I winced. I hated that term. Freda could call me 'duck' all she liked. It was a lovely expression, but 'bird' was horrible.

"Does Aiden like her?"

"Who knows?" She shrugged. "I told him to take his eyes off her cleavage." She cupped her hands over her own boobs. "They're, like, out here. She might as well be wearing bits of string to cover them for all the good it does. It does my head in the way he looks at her."

I chuckled to myself. While I felt for Tracey, she'd spent her life outdoing other women and now, it seemed, she'd met her match. Now wasn't the right time to tell her my news about Joe – old to me, but new to her. Since he was no longer working at the residential home – I couldn't get used to it being called a care home – we didn't need to hide our relationship. But if I told her now, I'd be putting the knife in. I had a lovely boyfriend, while she was stuck with a lad who was more interested in other women's boobs than he was in her.

Her next comment surprised me. "Are you still seeing Joe and his posh-knob mates?"

"Yes."

Her eyebrows raised above the rim of her glasses. "Still just good friends?"

I'd made my mind up not to tell her, but her question had blown that decision out of the water. What should I do? Go the whole hog and admit everything, or play it cool? I decided on the latter, smiling coyly. "I'm hoping for more."

It wasn't a lie. The other night, after we'd left the Ivy Tree, we'd snogged for ages in his car. I'd wanted him so badly. By the feel of him, he felt the same way. We'd gone further that night. Not the whole way. That wouldn't be right. For a start, I hadn't seen the doctor yet to get the pill. I'd read that I could go to the family planning clinic, which might be better than seeing my ancient doctor.

Joe had pulled a condom from his glove box, but I'd shaken my head. Not here – in a car, of all places. What if we were seen? Luckily, we'd steamed the windows up… At one point, I'd almost begged him to unwrap his condom, but I'd held off. Everyone made such a big deal about the first time, I wanted it to be special.

Tracey frowned. She didn't seem pleased by the idea of my developing relationship. "Have you kissed?"

Her downbeat expression made me decide not to tell her the whole story. "The other night. But I don't know if we'll take it further."

I was getting good at playing with words. But it made me uncomfortable. A change of subject was in order. "You sure you don't want to help on Saturday?"

"Give over, Bee." She sighed. "Ask Joe. He seems to like old people. It'll be a good excuse for you to see him again."

She didn't mind, after all. I was about to spill the truth when she ruined it by lowering her sunglasses to gaze at me. "Just don't get your hopes up, Bee. Speaking as a mate, you'll end up his bit on the side while he hunts for a Miss Fancy Pants like that Charlotte."

♦

Of course Joe said yes. During our conversation, I'd mentioned that Sir Bartholomew was laid up after a fall, so Joe wanted to pop by to check on him first. When I saw Joe chatting to one of the residents in the lounge after lunch, I gave him a wave and got on with my work. Once he'd seen Sir Bartholomew, he met us by the front door. He clutched a piece of paper and a five-pound note.

"I've promised to put his bets on."

"What? This minute?"

"They're for next week's races, so it's not urgent." He turned to Freda and Alice and gave them warm smiles. "Ready?"

Alice didn't need asking. She hopped on the spot, buzzing with excitement. I'd never seen her so happy. Maybe it was the sugar hit. When Freda and I had turned down the spotted dick pudding, she'd snaffled both of our helpings before anyone else got the chance. Wilf moaned at her, saying it was his favourite and, besides, she was going out. He'd got his own back by pouring the last of the custard into his bowl, filling it to the brim, then chuckling when she pointed out that he'd left her with a few drips. When she scraped the dregs from the jug, I wondered if she'd be able to fit in the cream tea too. I hoped so. I didn't want to be left with wasted food.

We set off at Freda's slow pace. Alice bounced three steps to each of ours. When she put her foot on the pavement, she squealed in glee.

"I'm free!"

"You sound like John Inman," Freda said.

It took me a while before it came to me. It was a character's catchphrase in the old show *Are You Being Served?* Mum and Gran had adored it. It wasn't to my taste, but I'd watched it. In return, Mum sat stony-faced through *The Young Ones* and, more recently, *Spitting Image* – although she loved the caricatures of Maggie Thatcher and other politicians.

When Alice started huffing about our speed, Joe distracted her by asking about her day. But she didn't have much to say, other than the food had been better than usual, if only Wilf hadn't been such a glutton. When we finally crossed the road to the common, we agreed that Joe and Alice would grab the last unused picnic bench beside the play area. Alice darted worried looks at the children, but Freda assured her it would be fine. At least it would mean we could talk and put our food on the table – much easier than eating off paper plates on our laps.

By the time we caught up, with Freda wheezing but

chirpy, Joe had set out the picnic. Laughing, he stretched out his arms, pretending to block Alice from the food. She slapped him away with a "Cheeky rascal!" and beamed. Not her usual sarcastic or tight-lipped smile either, but a real one, with teeth and gums. She waited until we had each taken a scone and didn't overdo the cream and jam, although I'd pre-empted her by portioning them out into ramekins borrowed from the kitchen at work. At first each question Joe asked her was met with a yes or no, but then Freda spotted a nearby plaque in front of a spindly tree, commemorating the Chairman of the Parish Council, who'd died the previous year.

"I knew him! He used to be a Wellington bomber pilot. A member of the gardening club too. That's how he knew my Jim." She turned to Alice. "Were you here when the Germans released their unused bombs after attacking London?"

She flushed. Of course Alice wouldn't have been here. She'd have been tucked away in the mental hospital in the back of beyond. Kept away from friends and family.

I waited for a snarky retort, but she surprised me with her tone. "Unfortunately not. But do tell me about it."

With a flicker of surprise, Freda did so. "We had three hits in this area. One in the fields by what is now Marsham Rise, one that killed a gardener at Perry Manor – in the days when it was one house – and the other was where you live, Belinda." She nodded at me. "You must have heard about that."

I had. Until now, I'd forgotten about it. "Yes! Gran told

me it hit the village pond and killed the ducks and a few sheep in the next field too."

Our chatter strayed from talk about the war to politics. Freda and Alice had different opinions, but they put them across without raising their voices.

"Well, I admire Margaret Thatcher," Alice declared. "She's given people a chance to buy their council homes. That's a good thing."

"But what about the next generation?" Freda said. "Where will they live? It's all about now. Like the utilities. They're making a fortune selling them, but there'll be nothing left in the future."

"I don't know why you're worried. It's not as if you or I have progeny to be concerned about. However, I'll grant you those points, although she's done many good things too." Alice pushed away her plate and rested her elbows on the table. "What do you think of Tony Benn's challenge for leadership of the Labour Party? Do you think it will fail like last time?"

The conversation sallied back and forth. Joe grinned at me. We weren't needed, but we couldn't leave them and go for a wander. Gloria would kill me.

An hour later, Joe pointed at his watch. "We'd better head back. I need to get to the betting shop before it closes."

"For your Sir Bart," Alice said. "What will he do without you to keep his fire escape shenanigans secret?"

Joe's eyebrows shot up. "You know about that?"

She tapped her nose. "There isn't much I don't know."

He glanced at me and cleared his throat. I guessed what he was about to ask.

"What about the patients in the other area? Do you know about them? The ones with dementia and suchlike."

Alice scrutinised him. "Why do you ask?"

He kept his demeanour relaxed, but his eyes were watchful. She knew something, he was sure of it.

"How about we swap confidences?"

She gave him a slight nod.

"I once saw something that made me uncomfortable. I didn't like the way a resident was being treated," he said.

She didn't answer but swept some crumbs onto the ground. Freda frowned. No doubt she was thinking the same as us. What did Alice know?

"I wasn't meant to be there," she said. "I don't want to get into trouble."

The usual Alice was back. Thin-lipped, her beady eyes assessing us.

"Tell him, duck," Freda said. "They won't say a word. Nor will I."

Alice sighed. "I saw one of the staff slap Cyril Axe." She turned to Freda. "Do you remember him?"

Freda frowned. "I don't think so."

Freda might not have known him, but Joe leaned forward, alert.

"He must have been moved before your time," Alice told Freda. "He deteriorated quickly. One minute he was fine up here." She tapped the side of her head. "And the next they carted him off to the dark side. I'm telling you now, I do not want to go there. It's run like a separate business. Gloria might be in charge, but she's kept at arm's length from it."

Joe's face remained expressionless, but watchful. "The worker who slapped Cyril – is she still working at Rockbeare?"

"Yes!" Alice's voice quivered. "But I'm not saying anything more. She's a nasty piece of work."

"Julia!" Joe hissed. "It must be her."

Alice mimed zipping her mouth and folded her arms. "That's all you'll get out of me. I don't want to spend my last years like so many others."

# Chapter 24

I had an hour until my next shift started so, after Alice and Freda were safely back at the residential home, I offered to go to the betting shop with Joe. Having never been in one before, I was intrigued. Mum and Gran refused to go inside betting shops, but they'd never explained why. Gran did the pools – a man came around once a week to collect her stake. Mum bet on the Grand National – although she went around to see Gran's next-door neighbour, who laid off bets with a local bookmaker. So it couldn't be an issue with gambling.

I went to ask Joe what to expect, but he cut in. "Did I tell you that my boss's friend was Maurice Axe? His dad was Cyril Axe."

I vaguely recalled the name, but I couldn't say for sure.

Joe's grip tightened on the steering wheel. "It looks like Maurice might have been right. It's a pain that Alice has clammed up. We need a name at the least before we can investigate further."

"Maybe Alice will change her mind? If we get her to tell Gloria, she'd have to listen."

He grimaced. "Alice's word is worthless. We need evidence."

"Why? Alice actually saw a nurse slap him."

"Alice was a patient in a mental hospital." Joe flushed. "There was a letter in the file in Gloria's office from her GP. To summarise it bluntly, it said that she was unstable

– I can't remember the exact wording – and should be watched at all times."

"Unstable? That must be why Gloria was so worried about me taking her out, and her having the knife in her room."

He shrugged. "I didn't read any more. I didn't go in there to snoop on everyone. But we'd just had a conversation about her. It sparked my curiosity when I came across her file. Then I felt bad. I mean, it wasn't any of my business. Anyhow, I was supposed to be looking for information on Cyril. That was my priority."

"Did you find what you needed?"

He shook his head, but then it occurred to me that he might have gone through the staff files too. Had he come across mine? While I couldn't imagine there would be much in there for him to see, I didn't like the idea of him prying.

"Did you read any others? Such as my one?"

We'd reached the car park behind the supermarket. Joe pulled into an empty space across the road from the betting shop. When he turned off the ignition, the engine noise died, leaving us in silence.

"Well?" I gazed at him.

He put his hand to his chest. "I swear, I did not touch your file."

"But you looked at other people's?"

"Julia Bovingdon's – but only after we saw her holding down that woman. It showed exemplary service, apart from one unfounded complaint in the past." He sighed.

"Let's go and place these bets."

I'd passed the betting shop before. Not often, though. It lay off the high street, next to a solicitor's and a funeral parlour. Beyond them sat a small car showroom, set back from the road, then a row of cottages. As you moved down the road, the houses got bigger, becoming a typical suburban sprawl.

We crossed over to the betting shop. In winter the doors stayed closed, while in summer chains – metal versions of the red and yellow plastic strips Gran had to stop flies coming through the open back door – hung across the entrance, concealing what lay behind. The law, apparently. No one under eighteen could see inside. But the betting shop had tried to make their entrance more enticing – the chain curtain showed an image of a horse racing towards the finish line. Since it was summer, the door had been jammed open and the excited pitch of a commentator cut through the air. As we stepped inside, the fug of cigarette smoke made my eyes smart.

Joe ripped a betting slip from a dispenser and picked up a pencil. While he transcribed Sir Bartholomew's bets onto the sheet, I gazed around in fascination. The floor was littered with crumpled betting slips, although a bin sat nearby. The walls were lined with pages from the *Racing Post*. Behind the glass-screened counter stood two people, above them a woman on a raised platform. As the commentator on the radio called out the odds, she scribbled them onto a huge whiteboard, for some reason using two colours. It took me a while before I realised she was marking the favourite in red, the rest in blue. Her knowledge of fractions was impressive. It would have taken me ages to work out the difference between 7/4 and 13/8.

Transfixed by her, I hadn't seen the huddle in front of a TV screen in the corner until I heard urgent cries of "Come on my son!", as if they were the jockeys geeing on the horses. They weren't all men. An older woman in a flowery dress had her back to me. When a man shifted to toss his slip into the bin, he revealed another woman, this one in a black skirt, her dark bob curling over the collar of her blouse as she watched the screen. I frowned. Surely it wasn't… On the screen, a horse galloped past the winning post to groans and roars of "Yes!" She shook her head, crumpled the betting slip in her hand and let it drop to the floor. As she turned, she met my eyes, and her lips formed an 'o' of shock.

Sally! Of all the places to bump into her. I headed over to offer her a lift back to work, but she ducked past a man and shot through the chain curtain, which rattled in her wake. What on earth?

Joe placed his hand on my shoulder. "All done."

I pointed towards the door. "That was Sally."

He shrugged. "I didn't see her."

Blinking, we stepped out into the bright afternoon. Sally was nowhere to be seen. Either she was a fast walker or she'd brought a car, although I'd never seen her with one. She lived nearby and walked to work. Still, I kept an eye out for her as we crossed over to the car park. A gentle breeze wafted over us, but I could still smell cigarette smoke.

When we got into Joe's car, I wound down the window and flapped my hand. "I stink. What will Gloria say?"

"Stand next to Sally. She'll smell the same."

I chuckled. "I wonder why she rushed off."

We'd turned down the radio to talk as we drove here, but I could just make out the tinny sound of Patrick Swayze crooning 'She's Like The Wind'. A favourite since we'd watched *Dirty Dancing*! I longed to turn up the sound, but I was too puzzled by Sally's actions to pause the conversation, even for this song.

"Has Sir Bartholomew mentioned seeing her in the betting shop before?"

Joe grinned. "Why the big fuss? It's not a crime to place a bet. Anyhow, Sir Bart wouldn't tell. He believes that discretion is a matter of honour. One tap of his nose and it'll never be spoken about again."

♦

Freda's bottom lip quivered. Gone was the smiling woman I'd left on the doorstep of the residential home just a few hours before. She sat at the dining table, her eyes welling as she pushed her food around her plate. I didn't want to bring attention to her, so I said nothing. But, while the men gazed at each other and shrugged, Alice lifted a tentative hand to touch Freda's sleeve. "Are you feeling unwell?"

Freda shook her head and gave her a watery smile. "No, duck. Thanks for asking."

"The picnic not too much for you?"

"No, no. It was a wonderful afternoon."

"Then what?" Her tone was sharp, but she softened it. "There must be something. It isn't like you to be upset."

With a trembling hand, Freda pulled a hanky from her sleeve and dabbed her eyes. "I'm being silly. I'm sure I'll find it somewhere."

Before Alice could ask, I said, "Have you lost something?"

"My engagement ring. It no longer fits, but I like to get it out to remember my Jim." Her gnarled fingers caressed her wedding ring. "I had to have this one resized."

Freda was the only person on the table wearing a wedding band. All the men had been married, but none wore rings. They gazed sympathetically at her.

I tried to be helpful. "When did you last see it?"

Alice huffed. "If she knew that, she wouldn't be looking for it, would she?"

I rolled my eyes. While Rockbeare was a huge building, there were a limited number of places Freda could go. But it would be useful to have a starting point. "Sorry, Freda. When do you *remember* last seeing it?"

"In my bedroom, duck." She sighed. "I keep it safe in my drawer. I don't get it out every day, as I have a photograph of Jim on my bedside table to remember him."

I'd seen the photograph of her Jim, a smiling man with twinkling eyes. From what she'd told me, they'd had a loving marriage. She said she couldn't have been given a more wonderful husband. Tears spilled from her eyes, and she brushed them away with her damp hanky. "I can't think why I would, but what if I left it on my bed and it was taken away with the laundry? It's been three days since I saw it. You've changed my linen since then."

By 'you' she meant the wider team. She wouldn't know which of us cleaned her room. With the new worker on commode training with Sally – I'd return to that duty tomorrow – I'd been assigned the rooms on the other wing and Tracey had been left to do the rest. We worked without interruption from the residents. They stayed downstairs between breakfast and lunch to enable the staff to get on. Some sat by the entrance, watching people coming and going, others in the huge lounge, and a few went into the garden. Although the rooms were left unlocked, it was unlikely that anyone other than staff would have entered her room.

"I'll speak to Gloria," I said. "Tomorrow we'll give your room a thorough going over to find it."

# Chapter 25

An intensive search didn't find Freda's ring. The laundry company said they hadn't come across it, but promised to call if it turned up. Although she tried to put a brave face on her loss, it took Freda a few days to perk up.

"Perhaps someone stole it," Alice said.

Freda flapped her away. "Don't be silly. No one would do such a thing. It must have been me having a daft moment and leaving it on the bed."

"What about Edith Irving's watch? And Arthur's pension money? That went missing after he died."

But Freda wouldn't have it. In her view, it wasn't fair to blame others. She blamed herself. "Next time I'll be more careful. Except…" She twisted her wedding band. "This is the only item of value I have left. At least it's impossible to lose. I'd have to chop my finger to get it off."

Later, when on commode duty, I bumped into Sally coming out of Freda's room with the new woman, Elspeth, in tow. Thankfully, I was empty-handed.

"Watch it!" she hissed. Then she turned to Elspeth, who was laden with the cleaning bucket and hoover. "Get a move on. We haven't got all day."

Other than to tell me what to do, Sally hadn't spoken to me since I'd spotted her at the betting shop. When I moved on to cleaning the reception area, Sally stomped past, minus Elspeth. Without knocking, she disappeared into Gloria's office and shut the door. Snippets of angry conversation filtered through the wall. Her voice, not Gloria's. Behind me a trio of residents speculated on what might be afoot, but I kept my head low, concentrating on polishing the table on which the visitors' diary sat, before moving on to the squat bookcase, full of faded tomes that were there for decoration rather than pleasure. The pile of dog-eared *Reader's Digests*, other magazines and paperbacks in the lounge better served the residents. When I started to vacuum the carpet, one of the ladies waved at me. I switched off the hoover.

In a petulant voice, she said, "Can't you do that elsewhere?"

I pointed to the clock. "I have to get finished or else you won't get your lunch on time."

"We're trying to listen," her companion said.

At that moment, Sally appeared, her cheeks flushed. Spotting us all staring, she snapped, "What?" Then she strode away, fists clenched.

One lady gasped. "Well, I never!"

The other agreed. "How rude!"

I just shrugged and turned the hoover back on. If it had been anyone but Sally, I might have been offended.

♦

At two o'clock, I left with Tracey. She was heading home for a wash and change, while I would spend the next three hours in the library or wandering around the shops. I asked what her plans were for later. Not bothering to answer, she checked behind us and cupped her hand to her mouth. "Did you hear about the row between Gloria and Sally?"

I nodded. "I don't know what it was about, though."

"I do." Again, she glanced around. "You know I thought Sally was being given the deputy warden job? Well, I got it wrong. Apparently, it was up for discussion at the trustees' meeting, but they reckon there's no money in the pot for a wage rise."

"Is the residential home in trouble? Financially, I mean."

"Doubt it. The residents pay a fortune to stay here. Not as much as some places, but enough."

She pointed to the smart new sign. It said 'Rockbeare Care Home' with a stencilled image of the frontage and the words 'Excellence in care' below.

"They've spent it all on the rebranding. Blimming waste of money, if you ask me."

"No wonder Sally's not happy."

"From what I heard, she needed that pay rise. Don't tell anyone, but I saw her coming out of a pawn shop in Bilton. She didn't see me."

A pawn shop? Why would Sally need to pawn possessions if she had enough money to bet?

"When was this?"

Tracey shrugged. "Last month sometime."

We'd reached the road that I crossed to go to the town centre. A van zoomed past tooting its horn. Tracey waved.

"Do you know them?" I asked.

"It's one of Aiden's mates. I'm seeing him later."

"You've made up?"

She pulled a face. "Let's just say we've come to an arrangement. He won't stick his nose in that bird's cleavage, and I won't punch him. A win-win all round."

"Tracey!" We turned to see Gloria standing by the driveway, waving her hands. She hurried over. "I don't suppose you could come back earlier to give me a hand? It'll mean leaving an hour later too. Sally's had to go home with a headache."

Tracey winced. "Sorry. I'm on a half day." She checked her watch. "I'm going to be late as it is. I've got plans I can't change."

"Damn!" Gloria hissed. She rubbed the side of her face, thinking. Then her gaze fell on me. "What about you? Can you get back here for three? And work until nine?"

She knew I'd have little on. With Joe at his new nine-to-five job (or so she thought) and Tracey out for the afternoon, I wouldn't be able to find an excuse. I wasn't too bothered. While I didn't mind spending a few hours in the library, it was boring doing the same thing each afternoon. The only issue was the bus home. It left at nine.

"I can work until eight fifty. I'll need to leave then to get the bus."

She heaved a sigh of relief. "We're one nurse down too, so we need to get ahead of ourselves. You'll need to assist Julia later."

That meant working in the other area for the first time. Part of me wanted to leap at the chance, while my more sensible side wilted at the thought of working with Julia. Would she remember the time Joe and I had seen her dealing with the resident? I couldn't imagine she would have forgotten, especially as she'd complained about us to Gloria afterwards. After instructing me to be back by three on the dot, Gloria walked away.

"Sorry for dropping you in it there. To be honest, I'm glad I dodged that one. I've worked with Julia once, and that was more than enough for me." Tracey gave my arm a squeeze. "You'll be fine, though. I'm sure of it." Then she tapped her watch. "I wasn't joking about being in a rush. Aiden's picking me up at six and I need time to make myself look good."

# Chapter 26

Gloria pared down that evening's work and called Polly in from her day off, so it was manageable between the four of us. After we finished serving tea, I was sent off to Julia without having to worry about clearing up. Joe's earlier excitement when I'd phoned him had made me feel less apprehensive, but Alice brought me back down to earth by wishing me luck.

Gloria had told me to go through the double doors by the independent living area. I'd never been in this section before, so I was surprised to find a small staff room with TV and kitchenette just beyond the doors. I found Julia washing up a mug, which she dried before turning to me with a frown. "Gloria promised me Tracey. I don't have time to train you." Without another word, she unhooked a sky-blue uniform from the coat rack and passed it to me. I removed my pinny and slipped my arms through the sleeves, buttoning up the front. Unlike the sleek nurse's uniform she wore, buckled with an elastic belt, my outfit hung off me like a sack.

Julia glared at me. Was I being too slow? I tried to speed up.

"We've got five residents to wash and put to bed. Jackie's dealing with two others. It sounds easy but it's anything but, so you need to do exactly as you're told."

Jackie? I'd never met her. Did she come in and out through a separate entrance? It was strange that I'd been here for months yet I knew so little about the wider business. Joe had asked me to keep my ears and eyes open to anything unusual, but this was a whole new world. Everything seemed different. We didn't have to do personal care in the main section. Most of the residents were able to do this themselves, although we helped a few residents, including Freda in and out of the bath. Not that they seemed to bathe often. I usually found the baths as pristine as I'd left them the day before, a heap of flannels in the basket. Most preferred to strip-wash. The bathroom Julia showed me had hoists and other equipment I hadn't a clue how to operate.

"Right, we're going to get Mrs Kehoe. We do the residents on this floor first, then we'll go upstairs."

Mrs Kehoe sat beside her bed in an armchair that faced the room, rather than the large window, through which she could watch people passing and the birds flitting through the trees. Instead her view was of magnolia walls on which two pastel prints hung, a wardrobe, a commode, a sink and a bedside table. I longed to ask why she couldn't be turned around, but dared not. Julia wasn't one to be questioned.

When we knocked on residents' doors to give them their morning tea, we always greeted them with a smile and a 'good morning' but Julia didn't bother with pleasantries. Mrs Kehoe raised milky eyes to mine, but didn't return my smile. Without ceremony, Julia placed her arm beneath the woman's armpit and instructed me to do the same. Her frail body was much lighter than I'd anticipated.

Julia spoke over Mrs Kehoe's head, as if she wasn't there. "Right. Now we move her to the bathroom. Keep a tight hold in case she falls."

In the bathroom, Julia put Mrs Kehoe's hands on a rail and told me to keep her steady while she undressed her. Mrs Kehoe knew the routine and lifted each arm, then each leg, without being asked, so her clothes were whipped off with ease. Goosebumps prickled her skin and she shivered. It was the height of summer, but there was a chill in the room. I hoped they put the radiators on full blast in winter.

When the sink had filled with hot water, Julia lathered a flannel and set about scrubbing Mrs Kehoe, who winced when Julia cleaned her 'bits'. Was it sore, or the humiliation of me being there? My gran would be mortified if someone washed her, particularly in this manner. But Mrs Kehoe didn't say a word. At least, while the process was undertaken without love, it lasted just minutes. Julia finished by rubbing her down with a towel. When Mrs Kehoe lifted one arm after another to allow her flannelette nightie to be slipped over her head, we were finished. While the sink emptied, Mrs Kehoe was deposited on the toilet. A tinkle, a wipe and a hand wash (the latter for Julia), flannel and towel thrown in the basket, and we shuffled back to the room.

"Pull the covers back," Julia said.

Was Mrs Kehoe being put to bed at a quarter to seven? How odd. Without argument, she allowed us to sit her on the bed, lift her feet onto the sheet and help her to lie down. As I tucked the covers around her, she watched me with disquieting eyes while clutching the top sheet to her chest.

"Goodnight," I whispered, although it felt ridiculous saying so at this time in the evening.

As she drew the curtains, Julia said, "If we had more time, I'd train you to do this. But we don't."

We moved on to the other residents. I found it embarrassing to give the men personal care. Two residents were downstairs, the other two upstairs, their rooms reached via a staircase that sat behind what looked like another bedroom door. Until we reached Mr Trott, all were calm, and did as they were told.

"Where's my Lindy?" Mr Trott's wide eyes searched the room. His thick eyebrows reminded me of Denis Healey.

"She's dead, remember?" Julia said. She turned to me. "You have to keep reminding him all the time. Otherwise, he can become a handful."

"My little Lindy's dead? But she's just a wee bairn. How can this be?"

His eyes filled with tears. He had a gentle tone, with an accent that suggested he came from the north, but I couldn't tell where. There would be little point asking him. Unlike the lovely residents on my table, he was locked in another world – one in which he lost his Lindy time and time again.

When we reached the bathroom, he looked at me. Not

through me, but *at* me. I could see the intelligent, caring man he'd been before old age and – I presume – Alzheimer's had stolen his memories. He shook his head. "My poor, poor Lindy. Such a bonny lass."

"Who is Lindy?" I dared to ask Julia as we crept from his room. I didn't want to leave this man sobbing to himself in bed, but I had no choice.

"His daughter. She died of meningitis when she was eight."

"Isn't it easier to pretend she's still alive somewhere but not able to visit?"

She gave me a thin-lipped smile. "Lie to the residents? No, I don't think so. We should do all we can to maintain their minds, even if he'll forget what he's been told within ten minutes." She pulled a key from her pocket and locked the door, something she hadn't done to the others.

"Now go and fill the beakers with water. You'll find them on the side. Make sure you put the lids on tight." She sighed. "I really don't need a mishap like last week. Jackie and I will deal with Mrs Calam."

I was about to ask where I'd find the beakers, but she shooed me away. I hurried down the stairs and found them stacked beside the fridge in the little kitchen. After doing exactly as I was told, pressing each lid on firmly, I carried the laden tray back, and found Julia and Jackie in the bathroom with an agitated Mrs Calam.

"Leave them on the table at the end," Julia panted as she wrestled Mrs Calam's cardigan from her arm.

"Harold!" the woman squealed, her other hand clawing

the air, as if reaching for someone. "Haroooold!"

"Go and clean the downstairs bathroom. This one will be ready for you to do by the time you fin—" Her words were cut off by Mrs Calam's flailing hand striking her face. Julia dabbed her smarting eye with the heel of her hand and her jaw tightened. "Will you please behave, Mrs Calam? Jackie, for goodness' sake get a grip on her or someone will get hurt."

Then she spotted me in the doorway. I fled. I'd begun the day scrubbing toilets and I finished it the same way. But instead of thinking about Joe and TV, I thought about Mr Trott. Why wasn't it kinder to leave him thinking his Lindy was at work or even on holiday? Especially if he couldn't remember from one moment to the next. Instead, the fresh, crushing grief would batter him relentlessly. For him, death would be the only escape.

# Chapter 27

When I'd spoken to Joe earlier, he'd offered to pick me up, but I'd turned him down, knowing he'd had a busy day. Instead, I dwelled on Mr Trott and Lindy as the bus trundled along the lanes between Rocklington and home. At home, Mum looked alarmed when I announced that I wanted to go straight to bed. The next morning, I found her in the kitchen in her fluffy dressing gown and slippers. For some reason, she reminded me of the residents, even though most of them had thirty years on her. Without her usual foundation and mascara, she looked washed out. Grey smudged the skin beneath her eyes.

She stifled a yawn. "Got time for a cuppa, love?"

I shook my head. "Sorry. Did you have a bad night?"

"Just the change. It comes to us all."

I'd never thought of Mum getting old. Once Gran had told me that she still felt like a young woman inside, but her body insisted on proving her wrong.

"My mum used to tell me the same, but I couldn't believe it." Gran had tapped her head. "But, up here, I'm that young woman in the dance hall who thought Fred and Ginger had nothing on her. But one high kick now and I'd be laid up for weeks." She'd lifted her leg a few inches and groaned. "Make that a low kick."

Freda had said something similar. Did all older people feel the same frustration? My thoughts strayed back to Mr Trott and the previous night. He'd be waking to learn about his Lindy again, with no one to comfort him. It made me want to cuddle Mum. A hint of her favourite Youth Dew perfume clung to her skin.

"I love you," I said.

She pulled me away to examine my face. "Are you feeling okay, love? You look a bit peaky."

I chuckled. "Snap! I'm fine. Just a bit knackered. Thank goodness it's a half day." I picked up my bag. "Are you in this afternoon? Want to go to a café or something? I'm seeing Joe this evening."

"Sorry, no can do. I start work at one." She chuckled. "We're like ships in the night. How about seeing your gran? She'd like that."

I smiled. I'd like that too.

♦

That night I sat with Joe in his favourite pub, the Garden Gate, nursing my half a lager. While I didn't mind going there, it was one of those places where people went to compete. Even if you dressed down in jeans, you'd pair them with your best top and shoes – except for the odd few who didn't care for the dress code. Tonight, this comprised a gaggle of older men who sank pints by the bar and raised their voices over the music blaring from the speaker above them. It made me sympathise with my mum when she told me to turn that blasted racket down, especially as I wanted to spend time chatting with Joe before Charlotte and Dan arrived. I'd already given Joe a summary of the previous evening while driving here, but we'd spent most of the time talking about Mr Trott. Just thinking about his existence made me sad.

"I can't get over how little love was shown to those residents," I said.

"Maybe you can work out a way to make a difference."

"It was a one-off, though. I won't get asked back. Each time I go along the corridor, I'll know they're stuck on the other side of the door and there's not one flaming thing I can do about it."

He pulled me closer and kissed my head. I'd allowed Gran to take off my headscarf that afternoon and snip my fringe, so it didn't look quite so odd. But I'd dreaded Joe's reaction. I needn't have worried. He'd just said he was glad to see my hair growing back. I snuggled into him, making the most of our time alone before his friends arrived. He bent to kiss my lips, his stubble brushing my face.

"Ahem!" A man cleared his throat.

I glanced up to find Dan standing there, grinning. He'd arrived early. I'd been hoping for a bit longer alone, but I tried to look delighted to see him and politely shifted away from Joe.

"Where's Charlotte?" I asked.

"Chatting with a mate. Would you like a drink?"

Joe nodded, while I declined. I looked at him, my eyebrows raised. "Aren't you driving?" He grimaced. "I meant to ask you earlier, but when you got into the car you were upset about work. Then it went straight out of my mind. Would you mind if Charlotte drives you home? I've driven to Albridge for work, and I could really do with a night off. My car will be fine left here."

Albridge? That wasn't far from where I'd gone to polytechnic, so I could imagine how knackered he'd feel after driving that return trip. Poor Joe. He was always having to run me around. I really needed to start driving lessons, even if I couldn't afford a car.

"I can get a taxi back," I said. "It's not fair on Charlotte to go miles out of her way for me."

Dan waved me away. "Charlotte offered. She likes driving for some reason."

Charlotte stepped beside him. "Is everything okay?"

"I was just saying you were happy to drive," Dan said.

As Dan headed towards the bar, she slipped into the bench seat. "I am *never* drinking again. I got so drunk on Saturday, I made such a fool of myself." She covered her face with her hands. "I can't even think about it without dying inside. It was absolutely mortifying."

Joe laughed. "You didn't tell me this."

"Believe me, I'm not telling another soul. Dan's sworn to secrecy too, so don't bother asking him."

"She'll tell all later," Joe said. "I'll put a pound on it."

"Just a pound!" Charlotte's eyes sparkled with laughter. "Make it worthwhile. At least ten."

"No way! Unless..." His eyes narrowed. "We make it a fiver that you don't tell us in the next hour."

Charlotte hooted and held out her hand. "Show me the money and I'll tell all. It'll be worth it for that."

I couldn't believe it when he pushed a crisp five-pound note across the table. I'd have to work almost two hours for that.

Joe saw my expression and hissed, his words almost drowned out by the music, "I was going to give her petrol money. This'll cover it."

Charlotte didn't hear him. She snatched the fiver and stuffed it into her handbag. She was well off. Why did she need the money so badly?

Spotting my look of surprise, she laughed. "Joe knows me too well." She shrugged. "And he'd have given me it later anyway." She ran her fingers through her hair and gave her head a backwards shake, her glossy bob settling into shape perfectly. I wished mine would behave so well. If I dared to touch my hair, I risked it becoming a mass of frizz. When Dan reappeared, she moved to the other end of the bench to allow him to sit beside her. Only once he'd handed out the drinks did she start to tell the promised tale.

"Dan's heard this before. Anyhow, I went out with a few girlfriends to the Dog and Whistle. It was a bit of a wild night, with it being Cassie's birthday." She rolled her eyes. "The drinks kept coming. They were lined up on the table."

Dan yawned. "Not this again. Can't you make it shorter this time?"

For someone who was apparently too humiliated to speak, she'd obviously told this story a few times. How many fivers had she gained in doing so? I had to admire her. I'd blab without payment and, at the same time, give my listeners free heating, thanks to my burning cheeks.

Ignoring him, she ploughed on. "I needed the loo, but I was a tad unsteady on my feet. So I staggered off. I even had to sit on the loo seat to stop myself falling over, which is something I never do. When I came back, people started to laugh." She covered her face, peeking through her fingers. "Oh gosh, this is so embarrassing! I'd only tucked the back of my dress into my knickers. Worse! I'd become the Andrex puppy, with a trail of loo roll behind me."

She lowered her hands. "They should have dispensers, not loo rolls. That would have saved me."

"She wore bright red knickers. As red as her face." Dan grinned and turned to her, shrugging. "I thought I'd wind this along a bit."

Charlotte stuck her tongue out at him. "I wasn't going to tell them that part."

We moved on to chat about work, life and the terrible music – which the barman had turned up so we had to holler over the noise. When it became annoying, we decided to move to a quieter area of the bar, away from the speakers. As we wandered over, Dan and Joe were waylaid by a man they knew. Charlotte didn't wait for them, but nabbed a bar stool in the far corner. Then she promptly hopped off, begging to be excused to use the loo and promising to check she was respectable before she returned.

I hitched myself onto her stool and sipped my drink. The men I'd seen earlier had decamped to this section too, no doubt to get away from the music. One of them – a shabby man with lank hair – met my eye, so I glanced away, groaning when he appeared at my side.

"Do I know you from somewhere?"

He didn't ask in a lecherous way, so I kept my response civil. "I don't think so."

"You look familiar. Where do you come from?"

"Little Rocklington."

He slapped his thigh then pointed his finger at me, his thumb held upwards like a gun. "Pow! Got it!"

Pow? Who on earth made bullet noises at his age? He must be at least forty. He chuckled. "You're Mo's kid, aren't you? You're the spit of her."

When I gave him a nervous nod, his smile broadened. "I've seen you naked!"

"*What?*" Was he some sort of weirdo? I pulled a face to show my disgust, but he carried on. "My girlfriend used to babysit for your mum. I went with her sometimes. I've changed your nappy." He tapped his mate on the shoulder and pointed at me. "Hey! I've seen her naked!"

Their leers turned to cackles. Why me? I'd come to the chavviest pub in the area and met the dregs from Little Rocklington. Why didn't they stick to the spit-and-sawdust Rose and Crown? Joe came up beside me, his expression a mixture of concern and bewilderment. His arrival silenced the pack of hyenas, who shuffled back, leaving babysitter man gazing uncertainly at Joe.

"What's going on?" Joe said.

The man's friends regrouped, arcing around us, pints in hand, watchful. Nearby, one of the bar staff flapped her hand, calling for help. Were those men going to fight over this? How daft!

I rolled my eyes. "He apparently changed my nappy once, so he's telling all and sundry that he's seen me naked."

Charlotte stepped between us, firing the man an angry glare. "Pervert! Do you have a thing about babies?"

It was a typical comment I'd expect from Tracey but, unlike her, Charlotte had perfected a headmistress-like tone. It did the trick. Flushing, the man put his pint to his lips and swung around, trotting away with his gaggle back to the corner. Not a peep more came from them.

Charlotte nudged me. "I leave you for one minute and you're beating my loo roll episode, hands down. Did he really change your nappy, or is there something more salacious on offer?"

"Well…" I let her hang on my words. "Let's just say, I may have been naked, but I wasn't enticing him with a crimson nappy with toilet roll dangling. On embarrassing underwear stories, you still win."

# Chapter 28

The days rolled by until, for the second time in a week, Sally summoned me to Miss Young's room. The commode was empty but for a small tiddle, but the stench of poop hung in the air. I knew what was up. Last time, I'd tried to argue that it was Sally's job to clean the room, so anything outside the commode belonged to her, but she'd disagreed.

"You deal with commodes, you deal with … it."

Why Miss Young had taken to hiding her poop, I had no idea. I wished she wouldn't. It was bad enough cleaning the commodes, but this was a whole new level. Last time she'd tucked it between the divan and mattress. That had taken some scrubbing to remove it.

Alice surprised me by poking her head through the door, grimacing at the smell. What was she doing here? When she spotted Sally – who had her back to her – she put a finger to her lips and tiptoed away. If Sally hadn't been here, I would have followed Alice to find out what she was up to. But I wouldn't give Sally more ammunition to moan this morning. She disappeared to check on the new worker – I hadn't met her yet – leaving me to lift the mattress on my own. Nothing there. Miss Young had found another hiding place. A quick search revealed the offending item tucked away behind the curtain on the windowsill. As I reeled off a ream of toilet roll – I didn't want to touch it! – Alice appeared at the door. "Oh dear!"

She put her hand to her mouth. "Poor Mary. It'll be her turn next to go to the loony bin."

"You shouldn't be here!" I hissed. "If Sally catches you, she'll give you what for."

"I needed my glasses." She lifted the pair that hung on a chain around her neck. Then she sneaked away, leaving me frowning, certain she'd been wearing her glasses when I saw her minutes earlier.

Sally returned to find the parcel wrapped and dumped in the commode, ready to be taken away. She pointed towards the lift. "Was that Alice Swann I just saw?"

I shrugged. "I've been in here the whole time."

It was the truth.

She bit her lip. "Make sure you keep all the rooms closed between cleaning. We can't have her wandering around willy-nilly."

♦

At lunchtime, Alice raised the topic of Mary Young, leaning forward to whisper to the others that she feared for her future. Everyone on the table gazed at the frail woman, who sat at the other side of the room. Thankfully, she didn't seem to notice, but anyone watching would know that something was amiss.

I hushed Alice. "You mustn't gossip about other residents."

She folded her arms and gave me one of her looks. "It's not gossip when it's fact."

"If I were you, I wouldn't let Gloria hear. You weren't meant to be upstairs." Back in May, I wouldn't have dared to speak to Alice in this way, but it had to be said.

When she patted her glasses, I sighed, "I know! But still."

Freda frowned. "But you had them already. You were reading in the lounge."

"No, no, you're quite mistaken," Alice said. "Those were borrowed."

Her shifty expression, combined with Freda's puzzled one, suggested otherwise. But Freda let the matter drop, directing her next comment at me. "When are we next going out, duck? The weather looks lovely this weekend."

While I'd agreed that we would decide on a date for another picnic, I hadn't anticipated having one so soon. Anyhow, Joe's parents were away and he'd asked me to stay over.

"Let me check with Gloria and Joe," I said.

Ernest swallowed a mouthful of food, dabbing his mouth with the napkin. "Joe? It's not a woman-only event?"

Alice huffed. "Apparently, we need to be escorted by more than one person. It's utterly ridiculous."

"I like Joe," Freda said.

"Did I say I didn't?" Alice snapped. "But at our age we shouldn't be treated like children."

Freda gave me a sympathetic smile. "Don't mind her, duck. She's just letting off a bit of steam." She turned back to Alice. "While you might be a sprightly thing, sadly, I'm not."

I expected Alice to bite back, to tell her not to speak on her behalf or that I wasn't part of the bird family. But she didn't. Instead, she sagged in her chair. "Age is such a dastardly thing. Life too. Just when one is free to do as one pleases, the manacles return."

Had she been chained up in the mental hospital? Or was it a figure of speech? Either way, I felt for her. From the little Joe had told me, she'd only tasted freedom for a few years before coming here. But her true story was kept secret. My thoughts turned to Mr Trott upstairs, begging for his daughter. Had his life been generally happy? Or had the loss of his child destroyed him? He played on my mind. If only I'd never met him. Then I regretted that thought. If only I had the power to do something. But, like the residents – Alice, Freda, Mr Trott and everyone – I had no decision-making powers.

Ernest piped up. "This picnic, then. If men can come, can I?"

He looked so wistful.

Alice went to speak, but Freda broke in first. "Of course, duck. If Belinda is able to take you."

Peter beamed. "That sounds like a grand idea. What do you think, Wilf?"

Five people? "I'd need to ask Gloria. If she agrees…" I hesitated. I hated to admit it, but it was the truth. "I don't know if I can afford to buy everything."

"That's easily resolved," Alice said. "We'll club towards an outing kitty."

♦

Oddly, Joe didn't seem to mind spending yet another Saturday afternoon with a group of old folk. Gloria agreed to allow Ernest, Peter and Wilf to join in, on the understanding that I was to go no further than the park bench and I had to come straight back if we had any problems. Of course, she'd made a face when I asked her, but after thinking for a few minutes, she reasoned that at least Wilf was level-headed, stable on his feet and less likely to need assistance. That way, she figured, we'd tick the 'one person to two residents' ratio. Neither of us mentioned that Joe was no longer an employee. I had no idea if it mattered.

But first, I had more pressing matters in hand. I'd booked an appointment for the following afternoon at the family planning clinic. It seemed an odd name when I was planning anything but a family. The clinic was held at the rear of the cottage hospital, or so the woman told me when I booked the appointment. With a mixture of nerves and trepidation, I headed past the brick and flint Victorian building into the car park, where I spotted a squat wooden terrapin at the rear. As I reached the steps, I took a deep breath and tried to fight back my embarrassment. Fingers crossed I'd see a female doctor, nothing like my fusty old GP.

I'd expected the interior to be the size of the caravans we'd holidayed in years ago, but more modern. The last time I'd been in one, it had oil lamps and Mum had moaned about the smell. When we woke each morning to damp bedding, she swore never again. She said that about childbirth too, hence me being an only child. Mum was good at keeping her word. She'd also said she'd kill me if I got pregnant without a ring on my finger. Apparently, I would be the one to change our family history. For me, that meant going on the pill, while she'd rather I just kept my legs shut. But, although Joe and I had been good so far, I had an inkling that this might change. Especially with his parents away this weekend.

To my surprise, the terrapin was like a Tardis, with a spacious reception area and two rows of chairs. The receptionist took my details and asked me to take a seat. To distract myself, I pulled a magazine from the pile in the corner. *Cosmopolitan*. Soon I became engrossed in reading about female orgasms, learning more than I could have believed possible in the space of ten minutes. When my name was called, I sighed. Now I'd never learn about sex appeal and what 'knocked the socks off three men'.

If I'd gone in flushed with shyness, I came out a shade of crimson that would have matched Charlotte's knickers. In the reception area, someone sat, legs crossed, immersed in the magazine I'd been reading. I did a double take. Seriously? Of all the people in Rocklington, I had to bump into her here.

"Flaming Nora! You sly devil!" Tracey beamed in delight, reminding me of a cat who'd snared a mouse and was readying itself for fun.

Opposite us, a woman chuckled, taking delight in my

discomfort. Even the receptionist raised her hand to mask a smile.

Tracey patted the chair beside her. "Here, come and tell Auntie Trace all about it."

"There's nothing to tell. Well…" I shrugged. "Other than the obvious."

"Likewise. I'm here to change my pill. They put me on another one and it's causing havoc with my face." She pointed to her chin where, beneath her heavy foundation, mini volcanoes erupted. "But you…" Her eyes widened. "Kept this quiet. I take it you're still with Joe."

Just then the receptionist called her name, saving me, but Tracey jabbed her finger at me. "Don't move. We'll walk back together."

Before I could argue, she disappeared into the consulting room. At least it meant I could read more about men's views on sex appeal. I liked the idea of knocking Joe's socks off. What a shame it wouldn't be this weekend unless we used a condom. I'd been gutted to find it would take at least a week for the pill to work. If only I'd confided in Tracey before. She would have known.

# Chapter 29

Life was going too well. As usual, something happened to mess things up. Namely Sally, who thumped across the landing, making the floorboards shudder.

"Watch out, watch out, there's a Sally about," Tracey hissed as she loaded her cleaning bucket. "Did you see Gloria's mood earlier? She hoiked Sal—"

Sally appeared at the cleaning cupboard entrance, her mouth a grim line. "There's a meeting in Gloria's office at eleven forty, so get on with your work. No chitter-chatter."

Out of sight, Tracey and I rolled our eyes at each other. When she thundered away – no doubt to bark the same news at Elspeth and the others – Tracey grimaced. "Any idea what it's about?"

I shrugged. "Who knows? From the look on her face, maybe we're getting a pay rise and she's not." I took my container from the shelf. "I hope Miss Young doesn't want me to play hide and seek with her commode contents again, or I'll be late."

"Good luck!" Tracey called.

Thankfully, Miss Young's commode hadn't been used and there was no telling pungent smell in the air. After finishing the bedrooms, I headed into the lounge and zipped through the cleaning.

"Sorry, I can't stop to talk," I told Freda when she asked me to help her with a crossword clue. "I've been summoned to a meeting."

"I heard."

As she nibbled on her pen her eyes darted to where Alice sat on an outside seat, arms folded, back straight, gazing at a fuchsia bush. Alice didn't turn when I used the nozzle to vacuum the grit and crushed petals from the sill. Her clenched jaw belied her serene appearance.

"She's been like that all morning. Ever since Gloria had a word with her about something," another resident told me.

How odd. Gloria didn't usually chide residents in front of the others. Unless she hadn't, and the gossip had made its way from the reception area, where the nosier residents sat.

Slotting the hose back into the hoover, I said, "She'll have my guts for garters too if I don't get a move on." I whizzed away and finished hoovering the living area. I finished with a few minutes to spare, then shot off to Gloria's office, alternating between fanning my face and flapping my top to circulate air around my clammy body. I slowed down when I realised that, if we all arrived early, Gloria might think this time could be shaved off our cleaning duties and put to better use elsewhere in future. But after seeing Tracey and the others looking hot and bothered too, I didn't worry so much. We'd struggle to do this every day. I joined their sweaty huddle in the corner of the office, none of us wanting to get too close to Gloria's desk. Strangely, Sally wasn't among the group.

Gloria appeared, her expression grim, closing the door

behind her. She jumped right in. "It appears that one of our residents has been stealing from the others. But we need more evidence and a lead to this latest missing item and, hopefully, the others."

We all glanced at each other, looking puzzled. Then it hit me. Alice! That must be why Gloria had a word with her. After all, she'd 'borrowed' Wilf's pen, taken the butter knife and who knew what else. But would she stoop to stealing money and a watch? It didn't fit with the woman I knew. Trinkets – and hoovers – seemed more her style.

"What was taken?" Tracey asked.

"A jewellery box. Though Alice denies it, of course. Goodness only knows how she's hidden it."

"When was it taken?" I asked.

"It must have been Wednesday morning – that's when Sally spotted her snooping around upstairs during cleaning. The owner didn't notice until last night. It was secreted at the back of their wardrobe, under a pile of boxes." She sighed. "I keep telling them to put their valuables in the safe, but they won't listen."

"She stole all their jewellery?" Tracey gasped.

My mind whirred back. Alice *had* been upstairs then. While she'd lied about leaving her glasses in her bedroom – or so it seemed, as Freda had spotted her with them that morning – she'd been empty-handed. No way could she have tucked a jewellery box in her clothing, unless it was tiny.

"The box was empty," Gloria said. "But it was

Victorian. Rosewood, apparently. Quite unusual. And valuable."

She shaped her hands to show the size of the box. About the size of the one I'd had years ago with a clockwork dancing ballerina. Too big to be squirrelled away. I clenched my fists. If I spoke up, I'd be in trouble for not saying that I'd seen her, but I had no choice.

My face prickled with heat. "She couldn't have taken it that morning. I saw her!"

"You *saw* her?" Gloria snarled. "Where was this?"

I winced at her tone. "Upstairs. I was clearing up after Miss Young…" My voice trailed to a whisper, but I forced myself to speak up. "Alice went past when I was talking to Sally. Then a few minutes later she came back. When I told her she shouldn't be there, she said she'd come to collect her glasses."

Voices echoed outside, along with clatter from the kitchen.

"Hold on," Gloria said. She hurried outside and the door slammed in her wake.

"Flaming Nora! Now you're in for it, Bee," Tracey said. "I wouldn't have put myself on the line for that woman." But she gave my arm a squeeze. It didn't reassure me, especially when Gloria reappeared with Sally, who shot me a look of pure hate. I know I'd denied seeing Alice when she'd questioned me, but her anger seemed extreme.

"Everyone but Belinda can leave," Gloria said. "We need a private word."

Ominous. Tracey gave me a sympathetic smile and filed out with the others, leaving me to face Gloria and Sally.

The door hadn't closed when Sally spat, "You lied! Why?"

"I didn't lie." I knew that much, although I couldn't recall exactly what I'd told her. I tried to think back, but Sally didn't give me time. She jabbed her finger at me. "Yes, you did! You said you hadn't seen her."

Beside her, a stony-faced Gloria folded her arms, her eyes locked with mine. I found her coldness more unsettling than Sally's fury. What had I said? But try as I might, I couldn't recall my exact words. "Look, I didn't lie. But I'm sorry. I didn't tell the whole story either. I should have done. That way we would have known it couldn't have been Alice."

"How can you do both? It's either the truth or a lie!" Sally screeched. Her voice rebounded off the walls and, no doubt, into the reception area where the residents would be listening, ready to relay our conversation – or Sally's shouted part of it – on the grapevine.

Sally swung around to Gloria. "Listen to her!"

"Believe me, I am." Gloria's cool tone made me shiver. "So why didn't you tell Sally?"

I hesitated. "At the time, it didn't seem important. I was cleaning up in Miss Young's room, so I was a bit distracted. As I said, I told Alice she shouldn't be there and she left right away."

"Cleaning?" Gloria frowned.

Sally rounded on her. "For Pete's sake. That isn't the point!"

Gloria crossed to the window, rubbing her cheek as she gazed outside. I could feel Sally's eyes boring into me, but I refused to look at her. She huffed, but Gloria ignored her too. Outside, the laundry company van pulled up and the driver jumped out to open his van's rear doors. Still Gloria didn't move. She let out a deep sigh. "Alice said it wasn't her."

She turned back to watch the laundry man, who was hefting two orange bags out of the van.

"You know what Alice Swann's like," Sally bleated. "Always stealing stuff."

I gazed at her. Long and hard. I could imagine her bouncing up and down in the classroom, hand in the air, 'Miss, Miss! She took it.' Why was she so keen to pin the blame on Alice? It didn't make sense. We needed to find the culprit – the real one.

"Alice takes small things. Silly bits," I said. "I don't know why, but I can ask her."

Sally threw her arms in the air. "This is—"

"That's enough!" Gloria snapped. The doorbell tinkled. "Sally, go and get the bags then come back."

For a moment, I thought Sally might refuse but then she snorted, shook her head and stalked away.

"Will you speak to Alice after lunch?" Gloria said. "We need to get to the bottom of this."

♦

Alice refused to come to lunch, saying she wasn't hungry. Instead, she kept her vigil on the bench in the garden, where she huddled like a frail sparrow, rather than her namesake swan. Although it was a warm day, I worried about her getting a chill. In the dining room, her anxious table companions fixed their gazes on her empty chair.

Freda's lips quivered. "I tried to talk to her, but she sent me away. I don't understand. Do they think she stole Margaret's jewellery box?"

When Wilf cleared his throat, I winced. He'd remind them about his stolen pen and they'd pronounce Alice guilty. Instead, he surprised me. "I can't imagine she'd do that."

The grooves deepened between Ernest's eyebrows. "But—"

Wilf held his hand up. "I know what you're about to say. Yes, Alice took my pen. But she wouldn't steal money, or Margaret's jewellery box. And what about Freda's ring? With all these other items going missing, I can't believe it was carted off to the laundry. There's no way Alice would take Freda's ring."

"Why not?" Rather than challenging him, Ernest sounded curious.

"She thought my pen was a piece of tat. When she realised it meant something, she was upset. And..." He chuckled. "She apologised too. Since when does Alice say sorry?"

He'd hit the nail on the head. That made me feel happier about defending Alice, even though she'd lied about retrieving her glasses. What she'd really been up to was anyone's guess.

Rather than clearing up after lunch, Gloria packed me off to speak with Alice, handing me a tray with a cheese roll, a slice of chocolate cake and a teapot with two cups, a sugar bowl and a jug of milk. She'd gone out of her way to arrange this, as the residents had eaten shepherd's pie followed by my favourite pudding. I'd drooled over Freda's treacle sponge. The smell had wafted towards me in devilish waves, tempting me to reach for Alice's bowl (which Wilf later snaffled). But I didn't succumb. My reward would come later. According to the scales in the treatment room, I had a pound to go before I hit my target weight. That would be some celebration! Although not one to share here. The residents didn't like the new me – they moaned that I had to eat or else I'd fade away, but I loved the way my clothes fitted me now.

One of the residents shuffled ahead, blocking my path. My arms ached with the weight of the tray but I kept to his pace, unable to overtake until I reached the lounge, where I dashed past.

"Blimey!" He clutched his chest. "I've got a dicky ticker without your help."

Apologising, I rushed through the milling residents, who seemed to be playing musical chairs to the sound of the *Neighbours* theme tune. Whenever I got the chance I watched it, loving the chemistry between Scott and Charlene. One of the residents' children had been a ten-pound Pom and he'd once proudly told me that his son and grandchildren had sent him actual photos of the real-life Ramsay Street. I'd love to go to Australia one day. It looked amazing with its blue skies and gardens with swimming pools. I chuckled to myself. My own boyfriend had an outdoor pool, although it wasn't the same when we had the good old British weather to contend with. I was on his mum's side when it came to pool heating. A necessity in this country, although we'd been lucky to have a few warm days recently, especially after a wetter than usual July.

I stepped onto the patio and gazed up at the clouds. The weathermen had assured viewers that we were in for a hot spell, but I wasn't convinced. After placing the tray on a nearby table, I went over to Alice. She didn't look up as I sat down beside her. "I... er..." I clenched my fists, willing myself to find the words. "I ... I know you didn't take the jewellery box."

Her fingers pinched her dress and her lower lip trembled, even though I could see she was gritting her teeth. I longed to reach out and touch her, to show that I cared, but an invisible wall sat between us. I wasn't her friend, but a worker. We may have gone on a picnic two weeks before, but I'd chosen Freda first. Someone who was easier to talk to, to feel compassion for. Unlike the prickly Alice. Yet I did care for this woman.

Behind us, I heard someone hiss, "They're not talking yet."

Had we beaten *Neighbours* for entertainment value? It was hard enough doing this without an audience.

"Can we move over there?" I pointed to two chairs beside a table on the far side of the patio, out of the residents' earshot. It lay beneath the windows of the independent living area, but those residents wouldn't have a clue what was going on. Living in their self-contained units, able to come and go as they pleased, they had no reason to stray into the residential home.

Alice nodded and crossed over to the seat. I followed with the tray and poured us both a cup of tea. I knew what she liked – two sugars and a dash of milk. I'd made her a drink often enough.

I kept my tone gentle. "You didn't tell Gloria that I'd seen you upstairs. If you had, she would have known it wasn't you."

Her gaze alighted on a butterfly flitting in the air, until it melted into the distance. Then she watched a sparrow on the nearby stone bird bath. She didn't want to talk. Fine. But I couldn't sit here all day. Only I could. Ahead of me stretched a long three hours until my second shift. It was lovely outside too. With the building sheltering us from all but a hint of breeze, the sun prickled my skin. I'd brought sunscreen in case I went to the park, but I hadn't thought to put some on before coming outside. I picked up my cup – leaving the saucer behind, as it seemed such a palaver to hold it too – and shifted in my chair, trying to keep to a strip of shade. As I did, a drip of tea splashed my trousers, which I blotted with my thumb.

Alice frowned, raising one eyebrow to assess me with her beady eyes. "The saucer is not merely for decoration."

I shrugged and smiled, but I didn't pick it up, like I may have done months before. At least, my social faux pas meant we'd made eye contact. For my next trick, maybe I should steal a bit of her cake. I couldn't believe she'd let me do that without making a fuss – although she hadn't mentioned the food yet, or even glanced at it.

"About Gloria." Alice stiffened, but I pressed on. "Why didn't you tell her about me?"

She harrumphed to herself. "What? Get you into trouble too?"

"It was lovely of you. Really. But there was no need. I'm a big girl."

Again, her eyebrow lifted, but this time she chuckled. "You were. Not so much now."

I took it for the compliment it was and smiled. "I need to ask you something, though. It's important. I think Sally suspected you—"

"That Sally is the one you should be watching. Whereas I … I like shiny trinkets. Wilf called me a magpie. He was right." She sighed. "I don't know why I do it. I was upstairs because I'd found a teaspoon. All this over a teaspoon, for pity's sake!" She huffed. "And where precisely does Gloria think I'm going to hide a blasted jewellery box?"

I'd been in Alice's room. She kept it spartan, with not an item out of place. The little she owned was tucked in her bedside cabinet, and a few dresses hung in her wardrobe. Unlike the other residents, she didn't have enough clothes to fill the wardrobe. She was right about the jewellery box. It was impossible to hide in her bedroom. Eagle-eyed Sally had found the butter knife under her mattress, and no doubt would come across the teaspoon in time.

Sally! Alice was on to something, I felt sure. Tracey had said she needed money and the pay rise that her hoped-for promotion would bring. She'd also seen her come out of the pawn shop in Bilton.

Alice continued, not registering my shock. "I think it stems from my days in the men— institution." Her voice quavered and her eyes brimmed with tears. "I wasn't allowed anything there. Not a book, not my favourite hairbrush. Certainly not my mirror. It was silver, with a long handle, and decorated with a beautiful swirl like the ivy that used to climb outside my childhood home. When I found pretty objects, I used to secrete them away. But when they discovered them, I was punished. Once I found a beautiful knife with a mother-of-pearl handle." She stroked her lap as if the knife still sat there. "That got me into dire trouble. They thought I was planning murder, but I simply loved its beauty."

Her wistful expression darkened. "My father sent me there. Mother tried to fight him, but he wouldn't have it. I'd sullied my family's name, brought us into disrepute, even though it was him…" She shook her head. "No. I won't go back to then. He stole my life with his lies, but his death released me. Afterwards, my mother came to find me. By then I'd been moved to a different institution – still a prison, but a better one – and we spent a few years

226

at home together. She tried to make amends, but I found it too hard. I should be grateful that he died first, or I could still be incarcerated in that awful place." She clutched the arm of her chair and took a deep breath. "I never got the chance to live. I mean, really live. My friends saw the world, had families. Have you ever been on an aeroplane?"

I shook my head. "Not yet."

"You should." She lifted her head towards a vapour trail in the sky, her eyes sparkling in the sunlight. Not from joy, but unspilled tears. "Make the most of what you have. You never know when it will be taken from you."

She began to weep. Stunned, I searched for a napkin, but Gloria hadn't put one on the tray. But Alice reached into the sleeve of her dress and pulled out a clean handkerchief. What was it with older people, stuffing bits of rag into their clothing? She dabbed her eyes and folded her hanky into quarters before tucking it back into its hiding place. As she collected herself, it felt as if she was pulling together all the pieces of her life and closing the lid with a smile. The jumble was still there, but hidden from view.

I ached for her, wanted to know more. But I wouldn't intrude.

She craned her neck to look past me to where the closing strains of *Neighbours* filtered in the air. Her distress had been packaged. Only her red-rimmed eyes betrayed her earlier upset, but now they gleamed with mischief. "Pass me that cheese roll. If you have time, feel free to join me in planning retribution for Sally."

Startled, I said, "Oh, I don't know about that."

"Not for real." Her laugh tinkled. "I find it rather cathartic to plot imaginary vengeance. Sadly, one learns that those who do ill to others rarely get their comeuppance."

# Chapter 30

Everyone on my table except Alice pecked at their food. I had to stop her from diving in for a third helping of the apple pie and custard after the others asked for small slices. They didn't wish to miss out on this treat, but neither did they want to be too full for cream teas at the common. It was my fault. I should have asked the cook to make a smaller dish for my table. When I took back half the pie, she offered to pop it in a tin, so we could take it with us.

We congregated at two o'clock by the front door. The men itched to get a move on, but Alice insisted that we keep to Freda's pace, made slower when she insisted on talking to one of the three women in the reception area.

"We're going for cream teas, duck."

"Cream teas?" The woman's face fell. "How come you're going?"

"You'd have to ask your table server. Belinda here organised this for us."

The woman nudged her neighbour. "Did you hear that?"

I hurried – if it could be called that – Freda and her Zimmer frame out of the door to where Joe stood with the men. He'd brought a collapsible chair, which he'd slung over his shoulder. Wilf and Ernest had taken the bags – while Peter hugged a bulky coat – leaving Alice and me with Freda. Gone was the sullen woman of the previous morning. Alice's chirpy voice rang out as she regaled us with a tale about a resident who'd got confused and gone to bed in the wrong room.

She cupped her hand around her mouth. "I think she fancies Bert."

Freda hooted. "He's quite a catch."

They must be joking. Bert was stumpy, with bowed legs.

When we reached the common, the men rushed to nab the best bench. It could seat six of us, although I pitied the person squished beside Peter. My mum would say he had a beer belly, but he was broad all over. Alice did the honours, sliding along the seat and patting the end for Freda. I sat opposite them, away from Joe, who had a chair to himself at the end of the bench. For a moment, I envied him until he sat down and his chin was level with the table.

"What are you doing down there?"

He grimaced. "Next time I'll bring cushions too."

As before, the conversation was stilted at first, even though we knew each other well. When I asked Mr Brenner to pass a tub to Joe – I'd organised individual servings of everything – Alice scowled.

"What's your surname?"

Puzzled, I answered, "Swift."

"Either we agree to use our surnames or we all stick to Christian names. We're not in the fuddy-duddy home now."

After a vote, we settled on first names. While we chatted, Joe made a cushion out of Peter's coat. Why Peter had brought it on this hot day, I didn't know. When Joe sat back down, we shared a secretive smile. Later we'd be going to his parents' house. I wouldn't have to rush back to work in the morning either. Gloria had agreed to give me the day off. Our anticipation was broken by Ernest who asked about Joe's new job, leaving me to hug myself with excitement.

After we'd finished all the scones and Alice and Wilf had made short work of the leftover apple pie, I started to collect the empty boxes and tubs, putting rubbish in one bag and the rest in another bag to take back and wash up. As I turned to take some litter to the bin, Joe called me back.

"Bee, would you mind taking this too?"

"Bee Swift?" Alice looked thoughtful. Then she cackled. "Be swift, my dear, and hurry along."

I rolled my eyes. That's why I'd never let anyone other than Gran, Mum and Tracey call me Bee when I was younger and, even then, it was only when we were alone. No way did I want to give the kids another thing to mock me with.

"Bee Swift," Freda chuckled. "That reminds me of Dick Stain."

A flash of disapproval crossed Peter's face, easing when the others roared with laughter. I'd never thought that my name could be linked with Dick's but, grateful for the change of direction, I headed away to the litter bin. When I returned, I found them all in fits, laughing about a Wendy Miller who had a problem with flatulence. I sat for a while trying to work it out, but couldn't.

We headed back, the men in front, leaving Alice and me on either side of Freda at the rear.

Freda startled me when she said, "Have you been to the pawn shop yet, duck?"

"How do—"

"A little birdie told me." She paused to lift her hand from her Zimmer frame and tap her nose.

"You mean a great big swan?" I fired Alice a look of annoyance. I'd told her in confidence about Tracey spotting Sally there. Alice had rubbed her hands together, saying it might be the retribution we needed.

Alice jabbed her finger towards Freda and hissed, "She knows to keep quiet."

"Mum's the word," Freda said.

I sighed. Much as I liked and trusted Freda, the deal had been to tell no one other than Joe – not until we had the evidence we needed. For all I knew, Freda's ring could have gone off to the laundry, as everyone but my table occupants now believed. Even if Sally was the culprit, she might not have taken it to the pawn shop, or it could have been sold by now. I wouldn't be able to go to the pawn shop to find out until Monday at the earliest. When I'd suggested postponing our picnic, so I could go today, Alice wouldn't have it. Sally wouldn't be allowed to take something else from them. The picnic was far too important.

"Describe your ring, so Bee…" – Alice emphasised my name and chuckled. Her mischievous expression told me that she'd command me to 'be swift' at each dinner service for weeks to come – "will be able to spot it."

# Chapter 31

Joe sat outside in his car at eight o'clock, his car engine rumbling. The smell of fumes wafted into the warm night. After tossing my bags into the rear seat, I slid into the passenger seat and leaned over to give him a peck on the cheek. We couldn't do more, no matter how much I wanted to give him a full-blown snog. Not when the low sun glimmered through the trees, lighting the shadows – and us. Anyone could be watching us from behind the net curtains on the first floor, especially since many of the residents had made their way to their bedrooms. Anyhow, I couldn't wait to get away. We had a lovely night ahead of us and a whole day to relax tomorrow.

First, I had some news for him. "You won't believe it! Gloria's asked me to work with Julia's team next week. She didn't ask Sally or Tracey, for some reason. It's more hours but…" Then I slapped my hand to my mouth. "Flipping great!"

The pawn shop! How would I go there on Monday now? The return trip would take me an hour, without factoring in the bus timetable and having to walk through the shopping centre.

Joe stopped the car, pulling down the visor to shade the blinding sun. "What? Have you left something behind?"

"No, but I promised to do something. We'll have to go window shopping in Bilton tomorrow, if that's okay with you."

Because he'd worked late, I hadn't seen him the previous night, and we hadn't been able to chat alone at the picnic, so I gave him a rundown on what had happened with Alice, the missing spoon and the jewellery box.

"That does sound suspicious. I'm happy to go into Bilton before lunch. But…" His eyes gleamed. "A whole week with Julia? That should give you a pretty good idea if something is up."

We chatted for the rest of the journey about everything but our jobs. Joe wasn't keen on regurgitating the sordid details of his week's work – his words, not mine – and asked if I fancied renting a video or doing something else. I shrugged. Who cared what we did? Not when we had a night alone together. My only regret was not going to the family planning clinic a week earlier. But there were a whole lot of other things we could do in the comfort of his bed, with no steering wheel or gear stick to manoeuvre around, while hoping a passer-by wouldn't chance upon us. I worried about that. Especially if it happened to be someone I knew.

We ended up with two videos. Joe had seen *Lethal Weapon* at the cinema but he said it was worth watching again, while *Mannequin* was my choice. Perfect for a romantic evening. I couldn't wait!

First, I had to shower the grime away after a day spent cleaning toilets, and change into something more casual. I had a another set of clothes for Sunday lunch but tonight it would be jeans and a white top, with a belt pulled tight to accentuate my improved waistline. When Joe took me to his bedroom, I looked around in surprise. It wasn't luxurious: a double bed with a striped duvet cover, two bedside tables and a wardrobe. But, just like the guest room, he had his own shower room.

"How many toilets does this house have?" I asked.

Chuckling, he handed me a fluffy towel. "Not all the rooms are en suite, if that's what you mean."

After showing me where to find the hairdryer, shampoo and shower gel – he actually put his toiletries in the cabinet, rather than leaving them strewn around the shower tray – Joe left me to discover that he had a power shower, with a dozen settings. The massage one was my favourite until it started to hurt, so I switched to a gentler mode. Steam filled the bathroom, even though the extractor whirred overhead. When I wrenched myself out, I debated putting on a dressing gown and going downstairs to reveal all but, to be honest, it wasn't my style. My old inhibitions were never far from the surface. Our fumbles in the car were invariably in the darkness or dusk, meaning I didn't have to worry about Joe seeing my belly. Even this close to my target weight, I could still pinch more than an inch. Mum swore by the Green Goddess on breakfast TV each morning, but I was out of the house by the time she put in her first appearance.

Checking myself in the mirror, I was stunned to find that I looked good in my jeans, even if I had to breathe in to get a flat stomach. *Looked good*? Since when had I thought that about myself? Bursting with anticipation, I padded down the stairs in my socks – no shoes on the plush carpet – and into the spacious hallway. We'd get a Chinese, watch a video or two and then … the night was our own.

The kitchen door was ajar. I guessed Joe must be in there watching the TV. I sailed through, coming to an abrupt and disappointed halt when Charlotte and Dan swivelled around on their bar stools to greet me. What were they doing here, tonight of all nights? Fingers crossed they'd just popped by on their way to the pub.

Behind their backs, Joe lifted his hands and mouthed, 'Sorry.'

Charlotte grimaced. "We didn't realise you were having a cosy night in. We can go if you'd prefer."

"No! Don't be silly." I flapped her away, rearranging my features into what I hoped looked like genuine pleasure. "It's lovely to see you."

It must have worked, as Dan said, "I will have that lager then."

Great! I'd just given them the go-ahead to stay. But then I felt bad. What harm would one drink do? Soon they'd leave Joe and me alone to enjoy our night.

"Make mine an orange juice," Charlotte said. "I'm driving."

"Unless we get a taxi." Dan took the can from Joe and poured it into his pint glass. "You don't mind us leaving the car here, do you?"

Joe's eyebrows lifted, but he shrugged. "Be my guest."

"In that case, make it a white wine." Charlotte slid her car keys across the counter and slipped from the stool.

"Dan, can you get the bottle from the car while I go to the loo? You might as well move it too, so we're not blocking Joe in."

They left Joe and me standing in puzzled silence until I hissed at him, "Are they staying?"

He grimaced. "No idea. Do you want me to tell them it's just the one drink?"

"I don't know. They might think we're being rude."

Dan sauntered back into the kitchen, clutching two bottles of wine. "I didn't need to move the car," he said. "It's fine where it is." He plonked the bottles on the worktop. "I brought both as Charlotte's back on the booze."

An hour later the four of us sat in the kitchen eating a Chinese takeaway. Two hours later, we held a vote on which video to watch. When Charlotte suggested *Mannequin* first, *Lethal Weapon* later, I took it in my stride. They were great company. It just wasn't the night I'd longed for.

Finally, the credits rolled on *Mannequin* and Dan shook the dregs from the bottle of Asti Spumante into my glass. After making Joe promise that we'd replenish his mum's stock before she discovered the loss – I didn't want to end up in her bad books – I'd tried a bit. Delicious! Nothing like the Pomagne I won each year at the Spin the Bottle stall at our village fete, although the bottles looked similar.

When I mentioned it to Joe, he chuckled. "Pomagne! That's why Charlotte won't touch cider."

238

I'd frowned. What had cider got to do with Pomagne? Wasn't wine made with grapes? But I didn't get a chance to ask, as Charlotte gasped. "I'd forgotten about that. Oh gosh! Sweet sixteen and blotto at Bilton Fair. Do you remember carrying me home?"

Joe grinned. "The first of many times."

Dan came in clutching the second bottle of Asti, another bottle of white wine and two lagers. He put them on the table. But when he went to unwrap the foil from the bottle, Charlotte jumped up.

"Joe! Where's that schnapps? Let Belinda try some of it." Her voice had a blurred edge. Was she tipsy? I felt a bit warm and fuzzy too.

Joe opened the sideboard doors, revealing what looked like a pub in a cupboard. My mum had a decade-old sherry and a bottle of Baileys tucked beside the cereals – nothing on this scale. He reached past the clinking bottles, lifted one out and poured the liquid into two small glasses, not much bigger than thimbles.

Charlotte raised her little glass and chinked it against mine. The drink tasted peachy. When I said so, Charlotte burst out laughing and slapped the side of the armchair.

"You're so funny. Joe, have you got any Sambuca?"

"You're not going to come out of the loo trailing a whole roll behind you if I give you that stuff, are you?"

She slapped him away. "I thought Belinda might like to try it."

He frowned at me, but I nodded, so he swapped our glasses for new ones. This tasted like aniseed, a bit like

Pernod. I took another sip. Wow! Why hadn't I tried it before?

Belinda staggered to her feet and helped herself to the bottle, refilling both our glasses. "Down in one?" She stood, all wobbly, and tipped it back. Then she gasped and shook her head. I managed mine in two mouthfuls.

"Watch it, that stuff's a lethal weapon," Dan laughed. "Talking about that, let's get the movie on."

Joe sat beside me, pulling me into his chest. I could hear his heart beating. Or was that my ear? A strange feeling crept over me. The room tilted, like a ship in a storm. The last time I'd felt like this had been in the SU bar at poly. I shut my eyes, trying to stop the room from moving. Charlotte pointed at me with two fingers. When I shut one eye, her fingers merged.

"You'll have to come clubbing with us. It'll be brilliant."

The movie started. I could hear the sound, but there were three screens. Blimey. Make that four. In each, Mel Gibson had three eyes. That made twelve! I squinted, covering my right eye, then my left, but it didn't make things any better. Outside lights shone on two azure pools, which merged and separated. Joe's body pulsed heat. Too hot. I pushed myself upright. As the room spun, my stomach clenched. Oh, please, no! Why did I have those last drinks? I stumbled to my feet.

"Are you okay?" Joe's voice seemed to come from miles away.

I nodded, clutching the settee to keep my balance. An

acidic burp told me I needed to hurry, but my feet wouldn't go in the right direction. Or they did, but my body wouldn't follow. My shoulder smashed the door frame and I jolted backwards, landing against the wall. Who'd moved it? I pressed my hand to my mouth – just in case – and used my other hand to lever myself off the wall. Someone gripped my arm, guiding me towards the toilet. They snapped the light on, blinding me with heavenly whiteness. But I felt like hell.

I knelt in front of the bowl, clutching the lid. The blue figures danced below. Who on earth thought a decorated toilet was a good idea? Someone pulled my hair back and rubbed my shoulder.

"Feeling sick?" Joe's voice echoed.

"Ye—"

But I needn't have said that. He could see for himself.

# Chapter 32

The sun streamed through a chink in Joe's bedroom curtain. I blinked, then squeezed my eyes shut. Flipping heck, did I feel rough. My mouth tasted like … urgh! My head … ouch. I leaned on my elbows, then flopped back into the pillow. Whose idea had it been to drink so much? But I could only blame myself. No one had poured that stuff down my throat. Shame engulfed me. I'd let myself down, shown myself up in front of Joe and his friends. What would he think of me? A fuzzy image of the night before flashed into my mind.

"The room keeps spinning," I'd sobbed. "Make it stop."

Joe had sat on the edge of the mattress, caressing my face. Then he'd kissed my forehead, holding my hand until I passed out. Had he come to bed and missed the film? I cringed with humiliation. I'd ruined our night.

Beside me Joe lay asleep. He looked gorgeous. His strong jawline, the hint of stubble, his hair dishevelled. To think I could be snuggled into him, recalling wonderful memories of our first night alone. I cringed, remembering the reality. Would he forgive me?

I ran my fingers through my hair, wincing as I hit a tangle. I had to make myself look presentable. As I eased myself from the bed, my head pounded. My foot knocked against something and I gazed down in surprise. A bucket? Then the penny dropped. Empty, thank goodness.

A glass of water sat on the bedside table, so I gulped it down. Then I staggered across the room into the tiled bathroom, where I gazed at myself in the mirror. Talk about a horror show. My hair stuck up on end, mascara speckled the skin beneath my eyes – and what was that? I scraped something from my face and washed it away under the tap. Yuck!

Would Joe mind me having another shower? I needed one. First, I had to rid my mouth of this disgusting taste.

Ten minutes later I stepped out of the shower, feeling a little better. When I wandered back into the bedroom, I found Joe awake, lying in bed, his arms behind his head.

"I'm so sorry," I said. "About last night. I can't believe I did that."

Grinning, he held out his hand. "Come here." He brushed his finger down the side of my face. "I shouldn't have poured you all those drinks. I'm the one who should be apologising."

"You didn't make me drink them."

"No, but I could see you were already a bit tiddly after the fizz." He chuckled. "Your cheeks gave it away."

Now he had made me blush again. What was it with me and my cheeks? They were like a Belisha beacon signalling my emotions: shyness, embarrassment, heat and drunkenness.

He lifted the covers and shifted aside, patting the sheet.

"My hair's wet," I said.

But he shrugged and pulled me to him, untucking my towel so it slipped down. My cheeks flamed, this time with excitement and lust. Two more to add to the list.

♦

We spent the morning in bed, only getting up because Joe had booked a pub lunch and he didn't want to let them down. Thank goodness Joe's planning was better than mine – he'd bought his own precautions. I followed him to his car, basking in a warm glow. Then I spotted the space where Charlotte's car had been parked. What would they think of me?

I groaned and voiced my thoughts, but Joe gave me a cuddle. "Don't worry. You're not the only one. Charlotte's christened our downstairs loo before." He scratched his head. "Several times, now I think about it."

It wasn't much comfort, but I took the crumbs he offered and gave him a wan smile. "Never again!" I echoed what Charlotte had said in the pub just a week or so before.

Joe chuckled and opened the passenger door for me. "I've heard that somewhere before."

He slung his rucksack with his camera on the back seat. We'd need that later. We may have postponed our trip to the pawn shop until the afternoon, but I was determined to keep my promise to Freda and Alice.

Lunch was delicious and very filling. I didn't eat the pudding, but only because it wouldn't fit. My belly strained against my waistband and I promised myself that tomorrow I'd peck at my food. I would reach my target weight. Then I'd go back to the woman in the charity shop and show her the new me.

After leaving the pub, Joe parked in the multi-storey car park behind Bilton High Street. We chose the stairs rather than the stinky lift, but the stairs smelled no better. I had to put my arm to my nose to ward off the stench. After crossing the lane behind the shops, we headed down an alley, sidestepping piles of dogs' mess. As I only came to Bilton by bus, I hadn't realised how grotty it was away from the main shopping area.

When I told Joe this, he laughed and said, "Wait until Charlotte carries out her threat and takes us to Blinkers."

The nightclub! I'd been there, but not for ages. Just thinking about drink and dancing made me feel queasy, and this wasn't helped by the fried chicken and kebab shop we passed. A group of lads stood outside with greasy hands and mouths, tearing strips off chicken drumsticks. Usually, the smell would make my stomach rumble, but now it churned.

Although they were supposed to be closed on Sundays, a few shops were open. Not the bigger ones such as Marks & Sparks, though. We crossed over by Woolies, and Joe led me down a side road by BHS. Fewer blobs of chewing gum and cigarette ends littered the pavement here and the shops were smaller. Beside a bustling café, the door to a record shop stood open, revealing a long row of albums. The neighbouring hairdressers and pet shop were shut, though. Chances were the pawn shop would be too.

It was but, thankfully, it didn't have shutters so we

could see the array of jewellery, watches and other knick-knacks on display. There was no wooden jewellery box. Neither could I spot Freda's ring. She'd told me that the band widened at the top so the diamond was encased within a thick yellow gold. I'd assumed she meant 18-carat, but I should have asked. My knowledge of jewellery was limited to Princess Diana's ring and the few tiaras I'd seen on TV.

I sighed and leaned against the window frame. "I can't see it."

Joe scratched his head. "I don't know why, but I was convinced we'd find them. Probably not Freda's ring – that might have sold already – but the jewellery box or even the watch."

He cupped his hand to gaze past the closed sign hanging on the glazed door and into the darkened store. Then he clicked his fingers. "Of course! When you said Tracey spotted Sally here, I assumed she meant this pawn shop, but I reckon we're at the wrong one. There's another one near the cinema."

We hurried back along the high street, past the clock tower and the kids doing wheelies on their bikes in the empty market area. I regretted wearing kitten heels, especially when my ankle twisted on the cobbles. But when Joe slowed down for me, I waved him on. He turned into a street and my heart sank. Victorian terraced houses lined the road, with small gardens and walls that fronted the pavement. How much further? But then he swung into an alleyway, not so dirty as the previous one, which led to another road – a shortcut I never knew existed to the cinema car park. Finally, we reached Rick's Bits at the rear of the car park. Beneath the name plate was the slogan 'Flog your bits here'. How tacky! Had he confused pawn for porn? Orange and yellow luminous star shapes were price marked, each declaring 'only' or 'now just', with more exclamation marks than I could shake a stick at. A lopsided 'closed' sign hung at the door but, unlike most of the prestige jewellers in town, it didn't have shutters.

Beaming, Joe jabbed his finger towards the display. "Is that it?"

I pressed my palms and nose to the pane, then grimaced and wiped my hands down my trousers. The windows hadn't seen a cloth in years. From the number of dead flies on the windowsill, neither had the inside. Making sure I didn't touch anything, I gazed inside at where Joe pointed. I couldn't see a jewellery box. Instead, two dozen antique rings sat on silk mounts. One of them was exactly as Freda had described it. Although its diamond was larger than most, it seemed small in comparison to its neighbour, a huge diamond and sapphire thing. But the price tag for hers shocked me.

"Flipping heck! Two hundred quid! How can it be that much?"

Joe tugged his Polaroid camera from his rucksack and took a picture. Moments later, the camera whirred and a blank photo appeared. He shook it and we watched the image appear.

"You have this," he said. "Show it to Freda. I'll take

another, just in case."

This time he brought out a different camera, one with a large lens. How many cameras did one person need? But then he was a journalist. He'd need photos for proof.

"What do we do now?" I said, taking care not to touch the still-sticky picture. "I can't see Gloria thanking me for this."

"She won't at first," Joe said. "But she will later. If you're really worried, I'll speak to her. But you've done the legwork on this. You should get the credit."

# Chapter 33

In the end, we decided that Joe should speak to Gloria. When I'd asked if we should go straight to the police, Joe said we should leave it until the next day. We had to check that it was Freda's ring. Besides, the pawn shop was closed, so there was no urgency. If Gloria didn't call the police, Joe would. But he wouldn't tell her that. If I wanted to carry on working with Julia, we didn't want to upset Gloria. While the items meant a lot to Sally's victims, Julia's patients could be suffering in other, more upsetting, ways, and we wanted to help them too.

I wasn't looking forward to seeing Mr Trott again. His cries for his daughter, Lindy, had tugged at my thoughts, almost reducing me to tears when I spent too long dwelling on him. So it was with mixed feelings that I stepped through the door to Rockbeare Care Home the next morning, clutching Joe's Polaroid photograph, with our plan in place. While I was cleaning the toilets, I'd sneak over to Freda's room before breakfast. There were too many curious eyes in the dining room. Including Sally's.

Except each time I stepped out of one of the toilets, Sally was there, beside Tracey, knocking on doors and handing out the morning teas, always in sight of Freda's room. With my work on this corridor finished, I had no option but to move onto the other wing. I rushed through, making up for my earlier dawdling, hoping to catch Freda before she left her room to join the other residents for breakfast.

Finally, I finished. I tossed my cleaning materials into the cupboard and hurried along Freda's corridor. Tracey and Sally would be downstairs now, setting up for breakfast. As I should be. I tapped Freda's door. From inside came the sound of huffing. It took an age before she cracked the door open and peered out, looking puzzled to see me.

"Is everything all right, duck?"

I pulled the photograph from the pocket of my pinny and smoothed out the crumples. "Is this it? Your ring?"

She frowned. "Hold on, let me get my glasses."

I gazed heavenward. Gloria would kill me if I spent any longer upstairs. Freda shuffled back, balancing herself against the wall with her hand. She popped on her half-moon glasses and peered at the image.

"Yes!" She looked at me in delight. "Have you got it back?"

A thrill of excitement ran through me, which faded when I thought about my next steps. I had to get into Gloria's office to make a call to Joe. Maybe Freda could come up with an excuse? After all, residents could use Gloria's phone. But I shoved that idea aside. Too risky. What plausible explanation could she come up with, having no family? If she said she needed to speak to her doctor, Gloria might ask why.

"Not yet. But we will. Please remember what we said and don't say a word about this to anyone. Joe is going to deal with it this morning." I tapped my nose. "Don't mention my name to Gloria either."

She mirrored my action. "I won't, duck. You have my word."

I dashed downstairs and into the kitchen. Gloria narrowed her eyes and glanced at the clock, but didn't say a thing. Breakfast that day was a stressful experience. As soon as Alice winked at me, I knew Freda had told her. It wouldn't have been an issue, but Alice kept swinging around to aim angry stares at Sally, who returned her gaze with a puzzled expression.

If Freda hadn't been sitting between us, I could have nudged Alice. Instead, I hissed, "Stop it!"

"Stop what?" Wilf said.

I shrugged, unable to think of an excuse.

Alice smiled. "She wants the extra piece of toast I was just about to take." She picked up the metal toast rack and gave it to Freda. "Pass it down to Bee … linda. It's wonderful to see her appetite returning."

Cow! She knew the last thing I wanted was more toast. But I thought again. Perhaps she couldn't think of an excuse. This was Alice, and she'd given up the last slice. It was like giving me her last Rolo. Although, by the sly expression on her face as I laid the slice on my plate, she was enjoying my discomfort.

After breakfast I spoke to Gloria, who surprised me by saying that Julia had a staff member off on holiday, and another had left without giving notice. I'd be released from commode duty, which would have to be carried out at the same time as cleaning the rooms. Gloria combed her fingers through her hair. She must have had a bad night. From the front it looked fine, but if she turned away, the back of her head reminded me of a crop circle, except not so pristine. She'd put on her make-up in a hurry too – or so it seemed. A thick strip of foundation marked her jawline. With all the staff leaving, she must be doing the work of several people.

Then I realised I had the perfect excuse. "I forgot to tell my mum I'd be home a bit later. Can I borrow your phone before I go off to Julia?"

She nodded. "Be quick. I've got some calls to make."

I hadn't bargained on her watching me dial the number Joe had given me for his direct line. When he answered, I felt sure Gloria could hear his voice from where she'd moved to stand, arms folded, by the window.

"Hi Mike," I said, making up any old name. "Could you pass a message on to Mum for me?"

Joe hesitated, giving an uncertain, "Yes."

"Could you tell her I'll be home by nine thirty tonight, not the usual time. And…" How could I phrase this? "Let her know that she was right. That dog did belong to that woman."

There was a silence. Then he chuckled. "I get you. Okay. I'll pass that on."

I hung up. "I'll go across to Julia now."

Gloria gave me a weary smile. "Thank you. I know it's not easy working there. I'm going to put another advert in the paper today." She sighed. "We must be the

*Advertiser's* best customers."

I grimaced in sympathy but didn't relay my thoughts. Perhaps if they spent more money on wages, they wouldn't have this problem. The trustees justified the low pay by saying that they fed the staff three meals a day. I rubbed my full stomach. Believe me, I'd go without their food for better wages. I headed away, leaving Gloria to make the call to the paper. It's a shame she didn't wait. When Joe arrived, she'd have another vacancy to advertise. Or so I hoped. She couldn't possibly let Sally get away with this.

♦

That morning, I saw a different side to Julia. I wouldn't say she nurtured her patients in any sense other than keeping them clean, fed and aired (this involved opening the windows), but she made sure that everyone was attended to. Like Gloria, she'd changed the day's order to accommodate the lack of staff. As I switched my pinny for the more formal uniform, she told me that my first job would be to help dress each person. Usually this would be done earlier, but with a sigh she told me that, due to the staff constraints, the residents had breakfasted in their nightclothes.

We spent the morning cleaning the rooms, working around the residents, who sat in their armchairs watching us – or in the case of Mrs Calam, spent the time in numerous escape attempts, which made our job three times as hard. When we finished, Julia took me to the small kitchen area where someone had put a trolley laden with covered plates.

Sighing, she checked her watch. "I'll give you the easiest residents. Mr Trott should be able to feed himself, but keep an eye on him. The same with Mr George. But you'll have to help Mrs Kehoe. Gloria is expecting you in the dining room at twenty past twelve."

I frowned. While I looked forward to having more interesting company, I couldn't understand why the residents at my table couldn't serve themselves if someone brought their plates out.

Julia echoed my thoughts. "It's ridiculous when we're in such desperate need here. But she's doing me a favour by loaning you and Sally."

Sally? When would she be joining us? Being short of time, I didn't ask. Instead, I hefted a tray laden with three plates and cutlery and hurried away. With all the challenges of the new role that morning, I'd forgotten about Joe coming to speak with Gloria about Freda's ring. It gave me another reason to want to stay in this section. I could imagine Gloria's mood when she found out.

# Chapter 34

Freda bubbled with excitement, while the others on my table darted inquisitive glances in Gloria's direction. In fact, the whole dining room buzzed with intrigue.

"Gloria called the police," Freda whispered. "They interviewed me. And Margaret. They're hoping to find her jewellery box. We're not allowed to speculate about it, though. They made that very clear."

Alice twisted around in her chair to look at Sally. Then she folded her arms. "Well, we all know the culprit."

"Alice!" Freda hissed. "Don't! You'll get me into trouble."

Although she tried to change the subject, each of the men kept coming up with different questions. When Wilf asked how Joe knew it was Freda's ring – he'd been spotted going into Gloria's office by the women in the reception area – Freda couldn't help glancing at me. I'd shrugged. *Stick to our agreement and keep me out of this.*

"I gave a description." Freda refused to elaborate, pointing out that the police had said that gossip might help the guilty person to hide their tracks. I had no idea how they'd do that, but I couldn't ask in case she let slip about my involvement.

When we cleared the tables and Sally had disappeared into the kitchen, I went over to Tracey. She looked paler than usual, her eyeliner smudged.

"Heavy night?"

She flickered me a smile. "Something like that."

I touched her shoulder to let her know I cared. If she was having problems with Aiden again, she wouldn't thank me for pursuing it here. "I've got an hour's break at two. Do you want to go to the park for a chat?"

She bit her lip. "No can do," she said. "Sorry. I've got … er … an appointment."

She had a secret she didn't want to spill, otherwise she'd say. I didn't mind. We might be friends but, since she'd met Aiden and I'd met Joe, we'd grown apart. I picked up my tray and headed into the kitchen. Sally concentrated on filling the dishwasher, keeping her eyes downcast. And so she should. Without a word she took my tray from me – something she never did – and stacked the plates. She ignored my thanks, so I shrugged and went off to clear the rest of the table. When I returned, I found Sally helping the cook to empty the bins. They worked in silence. Everyone did. But only Sally had a reason to try to mask her guilt with good deeds.

Gloria was nowhere to be seen. Her office door was shut. When we finished at two o'clock, I was shocked to find that there were about twenty residents in the reception area. They blocked the entrance, forcing us to sidle through. Gloria would be on the warpath if she found them creating a fire hazard, as she put it. To my table's credit, they weren't among the bystanders, some of whom leaned on Zimmer frames, others on walking sticks, while a few grumbled about their weary bones. It didn't make them move back to the lounge, though. The anticipation of a hoped-for return visit from the police trumped *Neighbours* any day.

I made it outside, then turned to Tracey. "Anyone would think they had nothing better to do."

But she didn't hear me. Without saying goodbye, she hurried away.

♦

I went to the phone box, called Joe and gave him the number to call me back.

His words shocked me. "We've done a bit of digging. It seems it wasn't a woman who took the items in, but a young male."

I gasped. "How did you find out?"

He chuckled. "We're journalists. That's what we do."

He wouldn't give more details, even when pressed. With a sigh of dissatisfaction, I changed tack to ask if he thought Sally was still involved.

He paused. "I don't know. But I should do soon. Do me a favour and keep your car to the ground."

"I'm in Julia's section, remember," I said. "I'll only be in the main area for meals."

"How's that going? Have you seen anything odd yet?"

After telling him about my morning, I gave Mum a quick call to remind her that I would be back late and to ask if she could put my other work clothes in the wash, then I strolled back to the care home. An empty police car was parked outside Gloria's office window. Shadows moved inside her office. But I couldn't see any more. I was surprised to find the reception area empty. Instead, residents hung around in the lounge area, some in huddles, gazing down the corridor, ignoring one of the afternoon part-time staff who tried to chivvy them back to their seats with threats of what Gloria would do if she caught them.

Alice dashed over, leading me over to Freda who sat cocooned by her Zimmer frame.

"It *was* my ring," Freda said. "They have it but they won't give it back yet. They're going to interview all the staff, duck. I thought I'd warn you, as I didn't tell them about your part in all of this."

After thanking her, I rushed off to my next job where I put on my too-large uniform, then went in search of Julia, who gave me the rundown for that afternoon's work. I wouldn't have time to worry about the police. First the residents had to get some air. This involved taking them out two at a time – a maximum of four between two helpers in their own small courtyard garden. The first group would have thirty minutes outside before being taken back to their rooms so we could take out the others. Usually, the residents were taken out earlier so they had longer outside but, with the lack of staff, they'd cut back the time.

Getting to spend time in the sun with residents should have been fun, but it wasn't. Julia answered questions in her succinct manner, but I didn't like to ask too many. Neither did I understand my role here. Surely we should be doing more than perching the residents on benches. If they got up, Julia encouraged them to sit back down.

While Mr Trott didn't mention his daughter – Julia said he was having one of his better days – Mrs Calam agitated over something she'd misplaced, but she didn't know what. The needle on her record kept hopping back to the start, wearing my patience. Julia must have lost hers years before, as she snapped, "That's enough now!" at Mrs Calam. It worked for all of two minutes. In contrast, Mr George's delight in the goldfish darting around the small pond made me chuckle, although he wasn't allowed to kneel at the edge, but hovered on the lip of the bench to catch glimpses of orange.

When we returned from the garden and took the residents back to their rooms, I was surprised to find a platter in the small kitchen filled with sandwiches and cake. I glanced at the clock. Four thirty. Time had sped by.

We followed the same routine as the morning: I looked after the three easier residents, while Julia and another helper attended to the others. Then I shot off to the main area, where I found Gloria prowling around the kitchen, with everyone scurrying around her like mice, fearful of being picked on. Following their lead, I darted across to the serving area, keeping my head down.

"Just the person!" Gloria's angry voice cut the air.

I groaned as she charged towards me, eyes narrowed, jabbing her finger. She must have found out about my involvement with the missing ring. One day she'd realise that I'd done her a favour. But this was now. And the headache I'd given her was about to become mine.

"Have you seen Tracey?"

Shocked, I said, "N-not since we left at two."

"And she said nothing to you about where she was going?"

"Just that she had an appointment."

She ran her fingers through her hair, assessing me with tired eyes. "I've tried to call her landlady, but there's no answer. This isn't like Tracey at all." She clenched her fists. "Why this, today of all days?"

I hesitated. "She said she had an appointment. Maybe she's ill?"

"If she was unwell, she'd phone to let me know," Gloria snapped. "Now we've got her work to pick up on top of yours."

From the other side of the room, Sally gave me an angry glare and stormed away. The other staff followed her lead. Were they blaming me for working in Julia's area? It wasn't as if I had much choice. Or was it something else? When Gloria stalked off, I hurried out with my tray, narrowly missing colliding with Sally at the kitchen door.

"You cow!" she hissed. "I know what you did."

But she refused to elaborate. In fact, she refused to speak to me again that day.

# Chapter 35

Tracey came back the next day, full of apologies. She'd felt unwell, gone for a lie-down and slept through to ten o'clock that night, which made it too late to phone the care home. She didn't mention her appointment, I noticed. Whether Gloria wondered about it too, I had no idea. She wasn't in the mood to talk, other than to tell us that the police would be coming at two o'clock to speak to the staff. Tracey paled at that comment. In contrast, Sally flushed and glowered at me.

"Bugger it!" Tracey hissed, out of Gloria's earshot. "I've got an appointment later."

"Another one?" I said.

"Yes!" she snapped and waltzed off, leaving me to my toilet duties. Strange how no one had taken those off me.

At breakfast time, the room bubbled with excitement. A new princess had been born to the Duchess of York the previous day. I couldn't get worked up about it. Unlike the residents, my mum wasn't a royalist. But I listened to their chatter and I joined in the toast to the new baby with orange juice. Apart from that, my day followed the previous format, rushing between the two areas. Except I'd spend my hour off speaking to the police. I didn't have the courage to ask Gloria if I could go into town first to make a phone call. I wanted an update from Joe before I talked to them. Had he mentioned me going with him to the pawn shop? If I hadn't been so exhausted, I would have called him the previous night but, after nearly falling asleep on the bus, I'd staggered home and gone straight to bed.

Gloria saved me by saying that I could go out for some fresh air, as she'd arranged my appointment for two thirty. It gave me just enough time to sprint to the phone box. I prayed Joe would be at his desk. He was. I held the door ajar with my foot – someone had used the phone box as a toilet since yesterday – while he told me not to worry.

"You don't need to lie. They know we were both at the pawn shop. I didn't tell them how involved you were, though. I just said that Freda had told you about the ring on our outing to the common, and you'd told me."

I sighed. Gloria would know those facts too. No wonder she'd been so terse.

"I'll pick you up later," he said. "You can tell me how it goes."

"I might be too knackered to talk."

"Don't worry. It'll be lovely to see you, even if you fall asleep on me."

The interview went well, although Gloria insisted on sitting with the policeman in her office, scowling as I told him what had led Joe to seek out the ring. When the policeman asked about my movements on the days the money and items went missing, I gave him as much information as I could recall, although some of it had become hazy. As I got up to leave, Gloria surprised me by thanking me for my honesty.

I opened the door, surprised to see Sally outside. How

much had she heard? I strode past, ignoring her spiteful sneer, but when I crossed the reception area and walked past a stony-faced Tracey sitting beside Elspeth, Sally grabbed my arm. Stunned, I tried to shake her off, but her fingers dug deeper, making me wince.

"What the—"

"You told them about me in the betting shop," she snarled. "Somehow, they know about my visit to the pawn shop too. Did that come from you?"

"Get off me!" I hissed.

"Just because I go to a betting shop or need to sell something, it doesn't make me a thief."

Gloria appeared, her eyes widening when she spotted us. "What on earth is going on?"

"Nothing," Sally sounded like a smarmy teacher's pet. "I was just checking that Belinda had told them everything she knew."

Gloria's frown lines deepened. When she gestured for me to leave, I didn't need asking twice.

As I scarpered, I heard her say, "This is not on. We need a word in the kitchen. Now!"

♦

Later that evening, I all but fell into Joe's car. My feet ached and I stank of sweat and goodness knows what else after cleaning the toilets in Julia's block. The last thing I wanted to do was head to the pub, but Joe asked if I'd mind going for one drink.

I yawned. "I'll need coffee. Maybe something stronger. And I'll have to call Mum from the pub. I told her I'd be home by ten."

When he gave me an odd look, I added, "She doesn't mind what time I get in. It's just so she doesn't worry."

"I didn't care about that." Chuckling, he pulled down the sun visor and pointed to my face. I tilted my head to examine myself beneath the light. Something brown smeared my cheek. Yuck! Then I remembered Mrs Calam.

"I think it's chocolate from her mousse at tea. At least, I hope it is." I grimaced, not daring to touch it in case I was mistaken. "We had a bit of a to-do when we tried to wash her. Julia dealt with it really well."

Now I knew why older people kept hankies up their sleeves. One would come in handy right now.

Joe concentrated on the road, squinting as a car passed us with too-bright headlights. "You don't think Julia is capable of hurting any of her residents, then?"

I hesitated, needing time to think. "She's got a lot on her plate with them. I wouldn't want to be stuck there in my old age, but…" I sighed. "I don't think so."

After a trip to the ladies to wash my face and a call to Mum from the phone box in the porch, I sat down beside Joe, who nursed a pint of Coke. He'd chosen the table in the corner where we'd sat before, giving us a view through the archway between the bars to the snug on the other side. On the wall *The Crying Boy* shed his solitary tear. A group of lads wandered past, blocking it from view.

Joe nudged me and hissed, "Talk of the devil!"

Recognising Aiden, I frowned. We hadn't mentioned him.

"What's he done?" I asked.

But Joe was absorbed by Aiden, who pulled a tenner from his pocket and waved it at the barmaid. "Five Fosters, love. Two with tops."

They kept their backs to us, tribal in their behaviour and clothing, one hand slung in their jean pockets, cigarettes hanging in their other, a cloud of smoke pooling in the air. Gary's flat top with its pointy quiff rose above them. I grimaced. How could Tracey have thought I'd be interested in him?

The words 'tart', 'bird' and 'slapper' filtered over, interspersed with raucous laughter.

Joe jerked his head towards the snug. "Let's go through there."

Since when did we move because of Aiden and his crew? But I picked up my Coke, slid out of my chair and led the way into the snug. I chose one of two wing armchairs, which faced the road and across to the George and Dragon. Aiden's usual haunt.

Joe lifted his pint and chuckled. "We might have been safer going there."

As he spoke, Tracey tottered out of the George and Dragon, arm in arm with another woman. They stumbled sideways, crashing into a sign in the middle of the pavement that advertised the pub's happy hour, then collapsed into a squealing heap. With her hands planted on the pavement and her bum in the air, Tracey pushed herself to her feet. She held out her hand to help the other woman, who pulled her back down.

"At times like this, I wish I had my camera on me," Joe said.

"It's only been an hour since she left work," I said, in my mum's voice. "How did they get in that state? How can she afford it? I wish I could."

"Ah! That's what I wanted to speak to you about."

I flashed him a glance, but a drunken cry distracted me. Outside Tracey was sitting on the kerb, her elbows on her knees, her head in her hands. Clutching her stiletto shoe, her friend crawled across to her and gave her a hug.

"Tracey's upset," I murmured. I went to get up, but Joe put his hand on mine.

"That's what I want to talk about."

I hovered above my seat – split between the need to console my friend and to listen to what he needed to say. Seeing his concerned expression, I sat down.

He glanced around. The snug was empty. The barmaid's voice echoed from the other side of the bar, where she chatted to Aiden and his mates.

"It's about…" He pointed to the other bar and mouthed 'Aiden'.

Shocked, I hissed, "Aiden? Is he two-timing her?"

By the kerb, Tracey huddled over, her shoulders shaking. Poor thing. I should go over. Give her a cuddle. Be the friend I hadn't been since she'd started dating *him*.

"No idea. This isn't about their love life. Or…" Joe

shrugged. "Maybe it is, but in a roundabout way."

Jeers came from the other side of the bar. Furious, I clenched my fists. Outside my friend sat in a sobbing heap, while inside her boyfriend – or ex, I hoped – laughed and knocked back pints.

"What is it about, then?" I didn't mean to sound so curt, but I hated seeing Tracey like that.

He kept his voice low. "It's about the ring."

Anxiety prickled me. "Freda's ring?"

How did Aiden feature in this? I gazed out at Tracey and her friend. Tracey smeared away the tears with her arm and gave her friend a wobbly smile.

"The description the pawn shop owner gave the police wasn't a woman, but a man in his mid-twenties, with a flat top and blond-tipped hair." Joe paused to caress my hand. "So I showed the owner a photo of Aiden. He confirmed it was him."

I gasped. "Why's he in here and not locked up?"

Joe chuckled and gave my hand a squeeze. "The police haven't worked it out yet. I wanted to speak to you first, before I tell them." He nodded towards Tracey. "But she'll know. I bet you ten pounds her behaviour is connected to this."

I shook my head. Not Tracey. She wouldn't let Aiden steal from the care home. She'd get the sack if Gloria found out that she knew about it. But I couldn't see Aiden creeping about in the dead of night. Anyhow, the jewellery box had been hidden. How would he know where to look for it? You don't just come across something stashed under a pile of clothes. Not if you were in a hurry.

"How would he get in?"

Joe pursed his lips. "*He* didn't."

# Chapter 36

As the bus trundled towards Rocklington the next morning, I leaned my head against the window and sighed. Everything Joe had told me made sense when pieced together. I'd never felt so gutted in my life. Tracey, my childhood friend, was a common or garden thief. Why? It couldn't be the money. Or could it? My stomach churned. I couldn't bear the thought of facing her. Joe had told me not to say a word, to leave it to the police. Of course I would. But I wished there was something I could do. If only I'd been a better friend – not kept my distance because I didn't like her boyfriend – she might not have got so involved with him. But we hadn't been close for ages. Not since I'd left for poly.

A tear slipped down my face. I dabbed it with my sleeve. Beside me, the woman shifted in her seat, her finger hovering over the bell. My stop too.

"Are you all right?" she said.

"Fine, thank you." My voice sounded claggy. "Probably just hay fever."

Was that a thing in August? It must be as she gave me a sympathetic smile. "My sister suffers terribly."

She dinged the bell and we got up, along with a few others, clutching the pole as we made our way along the bus to stand at the front. As the bus pulled to a stop, I spotted Tracey in the distance. Usually I'd wait for her, but not today. I strode towards the care home, ignoring her faint cries of "Belinda!"

I rushed upstairs, grabbed my cleaning bucket and dashed into the first toilet before Tracey appeared. Before darting into the next, I peered outside to check her whereabouts. It was a frustrating addition to my schedule as, for some reason, she'd been given the corridor to do alone, which made it difficult to bypass her. Once she spotted me, giving me a wave as she handed Sir Bartholomew his tea. Her innocent smile made me feel worse, until I corrected myself. The only innocent thing about her was that she didn't realise I knew.

I couldn't hide from her in the kitchen, though. But I had excuses to hand. "Sorry." I shrugged. "Can't stop now. I've got to get on. I'm back with Julia after breakfast."

She looked exhausted. The bags beneath her eyes were grey and swollen, her eyes bloodshot, her lids raw. Had she been crying again? I felt torn in two. I longed to put the tray down and cuddle her, tell her she was my friend – and also a stupid, selfish woman who'd get her comeuppance soon enough.

"You poor thing," Tracey said. "Sally's working there today."

I'd forgotten about Julia's day off. It hadn't occurred to me to ask who'd be in charge in her place. Flaming Sally, of all people. If I thought today had started badly, it was about to get a whole lot worse.

♦

By teatime, I'd reached the end of my tether with Sally's barked orders. *Do this, do that. Don't do that! Not that way! Didn't Julia teach you anything?* I didn't like the way she handled the residents either. I'd been watching Julia, and I'd realised that she was firm, not rough. From an outsider's perspective she might look too forceful, but she was nothing like Sally. When I headed back to the main area to serve tea to my table, I hated the thought of leaving the residents alone with her. But my fears were allayed when I went into the area's kitchen to swap my uniform for my pinny and found Sally in the corner, dunking a Rich Tea biscuit into her tea, a plate of sandwiches untouched beside her.

She glanced at her watch. "Forty minutes. No more. I know what you're like with your chitter-chatter in the kitchen."

She had no worries on that score. With Tracey around, I wouldn't be hanging about in case she wanted to talk. When would the police catch up with her? By now, Joe would have told them what he knew. From what I'd gathered, he had a contact at the local station who was happy to share information. Then I grimaced. Would Joe print a story about it? I couldn't imagine it would be worthy of publication in his paper, but I couldn't say for sure.

My sandwich stuck to the back of my throat. Gloria would murder me if she found out that Joe and I had anything to do with the news leaking out. I glanced over to where she sat at Sally's table, chatting with the residents.

Thankfully, Freda, Alice and the others on my table hadn't seemed to notice that I wasn't joining in with their name game. Who cared what the new princess would be called? They spent the meal placing odds: Victoria, Elizabeth, Mary, in ranked order. Alice proposed her own name, saying she'd been named after one of Victoria's grandchildren.

"What about her mother's name too? Helena?" she added.

I pulled a piece of cucumber from my sandwich and dropped it onto my plate. Then I put the sandwich down. The smell of paste turned my stomach.

Freda turned to me. "What do you think, duck?"

I swallowed back the urge to toss a sarcastic Sharon, Jackie or Tina into the mix. Or some more trendy names: Kirsty, Tiffany, Kylie.

Instead, I shrugged. "I like Helena." Then, seeing Alice's face, "Alice is pretty too."

Gloria saved me by coming over. "Leave this lot and go back to Sally. We'll deal with clearing up."

After making my goodbyes, I headed back. Three more hours of torture, then I'd be home. I found Sally still in the kitchen, an empty plate beside her, crumbs strewn across the table. She scraped them onto the floor. Another job for me to do later.

"Apparently…" Her voice was laced with sarcasm, "Julia's already got you dealing with the harder ones."

I followed Sally out. "Last night I helped her with Mrs

Calam."

"I wouldn't let you within ten feet of her. But Julia's given me instructions. For some reason, she wants you to learn."

We passed a helper leading Mr Trott across the corridor. "Don't do him yet," Sally said to her. "We're sorting Mrs Calam first, so we need the bathroom. Go and deal with Mr George or someone."

The woman hesitated, then did an about-turn, leading Mr Trott back to his room. Why couldn't we go elsewhere? But, as usual, I didn't say anything. Sally cracked open the door to reveal Mrs Calam asleep in her wing chair, her mouth open, hands clasped in her lap. The radio played classical music. Julia had put the radio in her room after realising that music soothed Mrs Calam.

Sally shook Mrs Calam's shoulder. "Wakey, wakey," she said too loudly.

Mrs Calam jolted awake. We hitched our arms beneath her armpits and heaved her upright. She gazed about, confused.

"Come on!" Sally said to me. "We haven't got all day."

Without bothering to take Mrs Calam through to the bathroom, Sally told me to remove her clothing. Then she disappeared. Unlike some of the others, Mrs Calam was steady on her feet, but she kept trying to sidestep me. Finally, I corralled her in the corner, beside her bedroom sink, and set about unbuttoning her cardigan. Her arms flailed, making me flinch. But then she realised what I was doing and started buttoning the top buttons as quickly as I could unbutton the lower ones.

"No. Don't do that." I kept my voice firm, but she ignored me.

I tried levering my hands through hers, pushing them away, but she slipped them below mine. As I undid the top again, she rebuttoned the ones at the bottom.

I sighed. "Come on. I need to get you ready for bed."

Sally strode back in, clutching a towel. She gaped at us. "I said, get her undressed!"

She shoved me aside and took over unbuttoning the cardigan. Again, Mrs Calam started to work against her, but to my horror Sally slapped her hand away. The noise reverberated around the room. Squealing, the poor woman clutched her hand.

I jumped in. "Sal—"

"Don't you dare!" Sally jabbed her finger at me. "If you'd bloody well done as I asked, I wouldn't have had to do that."

"No, no!" Weeping, Mrs Calam twisted around, desperate to get away. But Sally thwarted her, grabbing her arm and hauling her back.

"Julia doesn't do—"

"Is Julia here?" Sally shouted. "I'm in charge and this woman needs to be in bed."

Pinned to the wall, Mrs Calam sobbed.

"Go and get Jackie. She'll help me. You're bloody useless."

I hovered in indecision. If Sally behaved like this in front of me, what would she do if I left her alone?

Looking furious, Sally screeched. "I said, go and bloody well get Jackie! *Now!*"

This time I did as I was told. Surely Jackie had heard the fuss, even from downstairs. But when I found her in the bathroom, she didn't ask what had happened. Instead, she handed me over to a poor, naked Mr George without a word. He gazed at me with wide eyes. He'd heard, though.

I smiled at him and kept my voice gentle, although it trembled. "Hello, Mr George. Let's get you dry, toileted and into bed."

He nodded. Most likely because he was too scared to do much else.

# Chapter 37

I didn't know who to speak to: Gloria or Julia? Neither would thank me for bringing up the subject, but I had to say something. Joe was away on business for his newspaper that evening, so I couldn't ask him. I sobbed all the way back on the bus, although I managed to get control of myself by taking a few deep breaths at the start of my road. When I walked through the front door, to be hit by the familiar smell of baking, my eyes began to water again. A tub of rock cakes sat on the side in the kitchen, ready to go to Gran. Imagine if my gran was in Mrs Calam's place and someone had slapped her? It would be awful.

Mum sat curled on the sofa, eyes glued to the TV. When she gave me a welcoming smile, I burst into tears.

"Oh love, what's happened?" she said. "Is it your fella?"

I shook my head and, in between sobs, told her the story. When I finished, she frowned. "You've no choice. You must say something."

"I know, but…" I told her about Tracey and Aiden and the stolen items. By the time I reached the end of the tale, her face had transformed from shock to utter disbelief.

"It's confidential, Mum. I know you like Tracey, but please don't say a word."

She scratched her head. "*Tracey?* Are you sure? I can't quite believe it."

Choked, I nodded. "I thought it was Sally, but it wasn't. If only it had been. She'd be arrested and this whole mess would be sorted."

"You said Joe was already looking into this funny business with the residents?"

"He was, but it all seemed fine. He didn't find anything suspicious. I've never seen Sally hit anyone before."

"But you said she usually works in the other section," Mum reasoned. "Who could be weaker and more vulnerable than someone with dementia? It's not so easy to hurt someone who has a voice, like the others." She gazed at me, her eyes filled with love. "But you've got one, Bee. Use it for them. Come what may."

"I know," I whispered.

But I couldn't help thinking, why me? When Joe had first mentioned the rumours of abuse, it had seemed so far away. Something that happened to people I didn't know. Now the responsibility had landed at my feet.

Then it hit me. Tracey had once mentioned that Sally used to work in Julia's area. That she'd only transferred to the main area because she was looking for promotion. Maybe she'd been there when Cyril Axe had died? I shuddered. Sally was a long-standing staff member at Rockbeare. Would anyone believe my word against hers?

"Do you think they'll take me seriously? That worker I told you about, Jackie, didn't seem to bat an eyelid about it."

"If they don't, you'll know your next steps." Mum gave me a cuddle. "But we'll cross that bridge when we come to it. For tonight, just forget it if you can. I'll make you an Ovaltine and we'll watch a bit of telly."

♦

The next day, I dreaded going to work. Once again, I stepped off the bus and spotted Tracey in the distance. Again, I hurried away, keen to get on with the toilets without bumping into her, but this time I had the added complication of not wanting to face Sally too. At least she wouldn't be working in Julia's area today. After I'd spent the night tossing and turning – the scene with Mrs Calam on an incessant loop in my mind – I hadn't decided whether to speak to Gloria or Julia. If only I could shove all my worries in a cupboard and barricade the door.

Today's breakfast conversation made me apprehensive in a different way. They were reminiscing about the songs of their youth and dancing in halls, which was fine until Freda gazed at me, her grey eyes sparkling.

"Perhaps we could get a record player and you could ask Gloria if we could have a dance in the lounge, duck."

No way would Gloria agree to anything like that. Not with everything else going on.

"If anyone could get her to agree, it would be you," Wilf added.

They gazed at me with hopeful expressions. They had no idea that I had something more important to tell Gloria.

I grimaced. "I think that's one for next week. Or maybe even later. Once the dust has settled."

"Of course." Wilf sat back in his chair, throwing a knowing glance towards Freda.

She patted my hand. "Things will be back to normal soon."

Alice harrumphed. "Normal? What is that? The everyday tedium, that's what."

I ached for normality. To go back to scrubbing toilets without worrying about the people on the other side of that blank door in the corridor. I put my untouched toast back on my plate.

"Are you okay, duck? You're looking a bit peaky," Freda said.

Behind her, Gloria tapped her watch. I pushed my chair back from the table. "I have to go. I'm still helping Julia."

Alice chuckled. "Going over to the dark side."

I couldn't return her smile.

As I headed past the table, Freda said, "Do you think she's coming down with something?"

"No," Alice's clipped voice cut through the hubbub. Her next words brought me to a halt. "Did you see Belinda's expression when she had to go? I think my comment hit the bullseye."

Gloria must have heard her name, as her hawk-like eyes focused on Alice. Then her gaze turned to me. She frowned. I hurried off down the corridor, past the sunny lounge and through the door to Julia's dimly lit area. Mrs Calam's plaintive cries echoed in my ears, making me recall Alice's words. She was right. I had moved across to the dark side, in more ways than one.

◆

I waited until the afternoon to speak to Julia. Cowardly, I know, but I needed to find the right time. I'd assumed Julia would come down to the garden, but Mrs Calam was in a fretful mood, and she decided to stay upstairs to keep an eye on her. Instead, she told another helper to assist me with the residents outside.

When we returned to collect the second group, I found Julia standing beside Mrs Calam in the corridor. Classical music filtered from her room.

"She wants to go out," Julia said. "I'll go with you this time, just in case."

Julia went ahead, while I escorted Mr Trott, who lived up to his name, and Mr George, who got confused and tried to go back to his room. Between the two of them, I felt like a pushmi-pullyu.

I enjoyed time in the garden: the birds singing, the trees rustling in the breeze, the fish darting beneath the lilies in the pond. It soothed away the cloying atmosphere of Julia's area. But not today. Nothing could calm my mind. I needed to have a word with Julia, but she was sitting with Mrs Calam on her favourite bench on the other side of the garden, while Mr Trott liked to be near the pond. Mr George whistled to himself as he perched on our bench, stretching to watch the fish.

A shriek made my stomach churn. Mrs Calam was batting Julia away, refusing to be touched. "No, no!" she squealed, slapping Julia's hand.

"Come on now," Julia murmured. A cabbage white butterfly fluttered past, so she tried to distract her. "Look at that."

When Mrs Calam shook her head, Julia sighed and gave me a shrug. Just one of those days, her face said. But it wasn't. For Mrs Calam – even if she couldn't remember the detail, I bet she could remember the fear – it was the day after Sally had hit her. But I couldn't tell Julia that yet. I couldn't leave the two men. I had to console myself that I'd tell her later. But would she listen to me? After all, when Joe and I had met her for the first time and had assumed that she was being too physical with Mrs Calam, she hadn't taken it well.

After we'd taken the residents back to their rooms and fed them, I went to switch my uniform for my pinny, ready for my serving duties in the dining room. Julia was scraping the leftovers into a pot and stacking the plates onto a trolley.

"Can you take this with you?" She continued to work as she spoke. "It'll save Jackie having to do it."

I nodded, then hesitated. "C-can I-I … er … have you … not now, as I have to go, but ... can we have a word later?"

She frowned. "Is it important?"

"Y-y…" My face burned as I whispered, "Yes."

She passed me the trolley and smoothed down her uniform. "Very well. Ask Gloria if you can leave the dining room five minutes earlier."

In the main area, I found the kitchen in a state of

disarray, with Gloria rushing around squawking, "Get a move on!" to everyone. I snatched handfuls of cutlery from the drawer, counted out the plates, cups and saucers and rushed into the dining room with my laden tray, to find none of the tables laid. Sally, whose back was to me, set Tracey's table. It must be Tracey's half day. At least I wouldn't have to face her.

Before we had finished setting up, the bell clanged and the residents wandered in, looking surprised to find their servers still dishing out the plates. Nothing would stop these residents from getting to their tea. As they sat down, I sidled back to the kitchen to fetch a platter of sandwiches and cakes. When I came out, I had to wait by the kitchen door while the residents filed through. Hands on hips, Gloria shuffled impatiently behind Freda and – strangely – Alice, who was usually first through the door.

As Gloria passed, I said, "Could I—"

"I haven't got time!"

Although I was used to Gloria being abrupt, her curtness stunned me. She had more than a minute spare since she couldn't get past Freda, who huffed and clonked along with her Zimmer frame. I sighed. Without Gloria's permission to leave the dining room early, I wouldn't be able to talk to Julia in private before we started the evening's work. Perhaps I'd try again when she sat down.

"Come on, ladies. Come on!" she chivvied them.

When I sat down in my chair, I flapped my top, surreptitiously sniffing to check my Impulse still masked the smell of a busy day.

Freda peered at me. "You look a bit warm, duckie."

"Warm? I'm sweating buckets!"

Alice frowned. "Horses sweat, men perspire, but women merely glow."

I chuckled. "I must be a horse, then."

She lifted her cup, pointing at me with her little finger. "You have your friend, Tracey, to thank for everyone being out of sorts."

Freda gave her a hard stare. "I thought we'd agreed not to be so direct?"

"You'd prefer me to beat around the bush? I'm sure Belinda would rather we told her than someone else."

Frowning, I said, "Told me what?"

Freda grasped my arm. "Your friend, duck. The police came for her."

I gasped. The police! They must have arrested Aiden and now they'd caught up with Tracey. Alice sipped her tea but her observant eyes assessed me above the rim of her cup. Well, she could look all she liked. She wouldn't find anything but shock in my expression.

"I'm sorry to be the bearer of bad news." Alice's tone suggested she meant it.

Her face blurred. Embarrassed – I mean, why was I crying? – I turned away to dab my tears. Of course Tracey must have been involved. As Joe had said, it was unlikely that Aiden had broken in. She had access to all the residents' rooms. Still, I was stunned. Across the room, a smirking Sally surveyed us. The cow! If only she'd been the thief. Her slap reverberated through my mind, followed by Mrs Calam's sobs. They'd haunted me in my dreams, pursued me through the day. I couldn't bear it any more. I had to do something.

"Please excuse me." I balled up my napkin and tossed it onto my empty plate. The residents were more than capable of serving themselves cake.

I crossed over to Gloria. This time I didn't ask permission. "I'll be back in fifteen minutes to clear up."

Without waiting for a response, I strode away.

# Chapter 38

Looking surprised by my early appearance, Julia agreed to give me ten minutes. I couldn't take any longer; I had to rush back to the dining room to clear up, then return to help Julia get the residents ready for bed.

She pointed to a chair opposite. "Do you want to sit?"

I shook my head and clenched my fists, allowed my anger to flow. If it started to ebb, I only had to think about Sally. She'd become my thermostat, keeping me at boiling point.

"It's about Sally."

There. I'd said it. Now I had to tell her the rest.

"She slapped Mrs Calam yesterday."

Julia's curious expression vanished. Her mouth became a thin line. "Can anyone else vouch for this?"

"Jackie must have heard. Sally sent me away and asked me to get her, but…" I shrugged, knowing what I'd say next would weaken my case. "While Jackie must have heard, I didn't get the impression she was shocked."

"Mrs Calam is particularly difficult." She let out a long sigh. "Not that it gives anyone the right to hit her. I'll speak to Jackie on Monday when she's back at work. In the meantime, rest assured that we don't condone physical abuse here. We have three new staff members starting in a fortnight, all trained to deal with dementia patients. Regardless of Jackie's version of events, Sally won't be needed to work here again."

Her tone said that she expected Jackie to stick up for Sally. It also told me that she believed what I'd said. But it was unlikely that Sally would be punished. Without evidence, it was my word against two more senior staff. Along with her assurance that Sally would no longer work in her area came the unspoken message: proof would be impossible to find.

◆

As I'd worked long hours all week, giving up my half day, Gloria gave me Sunday off, even though the care home would have too few staff. When I offered to work, she refused, saying we all needed at least one day off each week. She hadn't had one, though, and it showed. No amount of foundation would hide the bags beneath her eyes.

I couldn't help feeling relieved when she turned me down. I needed a day off. When I'd phoned Joe that afternoon with the news that Tracey had been arrested, he suggested a night out in Bilton. We'd meet Charlotte and Dan, but we wouldn't be stuck with them if I wanted time alone. He would book a hotel room rather than worrying about driving back. Buzzing with excitement, I'd agreed.

But now, as I left the care home at nine o'clock, my feet aching, my eyes stinging with tiredness, I regretted my decision. I stepped into his car, ready to beg him to spend the night in the hotel watching TV, but then I noticed his shirt – new? – and a stronger than usual smell of aftershave. He bent over to kiss my cheek. "Got everything?"

I tapped the bag by my feet. "Yep."

"I'm really looking forward to tonight. It's been a hectic week." He gave my hand a squeeze. "And a horrible one for you."

By the time I'd showered and changed into my new dress, I felt much better, especially when I looked at myself in the mirror. My necklace draped over a hint of collarbone – the perfect amount. I didn't want to become too bony, as it didn't suit me. I ran my hands over my stomach. It was flat. I fist-pumped the air. Yes! This week's hard work and my lack of appetite had done wonders. I'd been too busy to check the scales, but I must have hit my target weight. I lifted my dress above my waist – a polycotton mix, so I didn't need to worry about creasing it – and lay down on the bed.

Joe gave me a bemused look. "I thought we were going out?"

"We are. I'm just seeing if I can find my hip bones."

Sure enough, they jutted out – not as much as Tracey's, but I could feel them.

Grinning, he lay down beside me and pinged my suspender belt. I hadn't worn one in years, but he'd said he liked them. Then he brushed his fingers over my stomach, making me tingle with lust.

"You've always been gorgeous. But tonight … wow!"

Forty minutes later, we made it to the pub across the road from the hotel, to find Dan and a tipsy Charlotte waiting for us. I chose a vodka and diet Coke, which Charlotte insisted on making a double, then bought two drinks for us all as the barman rang the bell for last orders. I grimaced as I sipped my drink. Not enough Coke.

"Drink up." She chivvied me by tilting the glass up, so the liquid splashed my face. "We've got partying to do."

I wiped my mouth. "I'm not having another night like last week."

"Spoilsport." She grinned. But she left me to sip my drink until the bell rang for time. I surveyed my two glasses. Could I get away with leaving one? But Charlotte shook her finger at me. "No one goes to Blinkers sober. It's like a kebab. You wouldn't touch it if you weren't sloshed."

I could see her point. I'd been there a few times, but not for ages. Living in Little Rocklington made it an expensive taxi ride back home. Blinkers – known for being the local 'meat market' for one-night stands, but also the birthplace of some longer relationships – might be a mediocre nightclub, but it was the only one for miles around. It also offered an opportunity to drink after eleven o'clock. For me, it was a spot for special occasions: friends' birthdays; the weekend before I left for poly, when I'd been full of excitement about my future. That night I'd gone out with a bunch of friends. But I hadn't bothered with them since I'd returned. My confidence had been knocked by my experience at poly and I'd wanted to lay low. But I had no excuse now. When I'd bumped into a schoolfriend the week before, she'd insisted we should meet up. She'd even phoned the other day, leaving a message with Mum, but I'd been too knackered to call her back. I would, though. It would be lovely to reminisce about the old days.

My thoughts turned to Tracey. But I shook them away. I wouldn't think about her or work. Tonight was about having fun.

My eyes smarting, I knocked back my drinks and we left the pub. The cool air made my head feel fuzzy. But I giggled my way up the hill, although I didn't laugh so much when I spotted the long queue outside Blinkers. By the time we'd made it inside and had ordered more drinks, my tipsiness had faded.

Music pumped from the corner, where the DJ stood silhouetted behind the flashing lights. A glitterball dazzled in the centre of the small dance floor. Most people came here to drink, not dance. It wasn't a trendy place either. A line of older people – mostly men – lingered beside the bar in the lounge room. That's where we headed, finding a table in the corner, so we could chat without having to shout. But before Charlotte could sit down, she was accosted by two squealing women.

Dan hissed, "We've spent the night hiding from them. They're absolute nightmares."

When I asked why, he grimaced. "You'll see."

My bladder twinged. I sidled past Joe, through the laughing crowd and into the Ladies', where I jerked to a stop. Of all the people! My heart sank, but I plastered on a grin.

"Tracey! What are you doing here?"

Her glazed eyes told me she'd had a few too many. "I could ask the same thing. Out with your new posh crowd?" she slurred.

Before I could answer, a woman came out of the cubicle. Tracey stumbled past her into the loo and slammed the door. The woman shot her an odd look and gave me a bemused shrug, which I returned. When a neighbouring cubicle door opened, I went in, sidestepping a glistening patch on the floor, which was littered with soggy bits of tissue. Next to me the sound of shuffling filtered through, then the toilet roll being pulled from its holder. Tracey would be finished soon. She'd then escape without giving me a chance to speak to her. I wasn't sure whether that made me sad or relieved.

I came out to find Tracey leaning against the sink, her arms folded, stony-faced. "So, you've heard?"

"About the police?" I pumped soap into my hands and rinsed with too-hot water.

"What else? What are they saying?"

I flicked water from my hands and tugged at the roller towel to wipe them dry. "I've been with Julia—"

"I know. But you're back for meals, so surely you've heard something."

I turned to meet her gaze head-on. "They think you stole the stuff and passed it on to Aiden to sell. Did you?"

I'd expected her to deny it, to come up with an excuse, but she sighed. "Yes."

Stunned, I said, "Why?"

"I wanted to say no." She bit her lip. "I was going to speak to you about it, ask your advice, but you're more interested in your fancy crowd."

She was laying the blame on me! I wasn't the one who'd sneaked into residents' bedrooms and taken their precious items. And what about Arthur? She'd taken money from a dead man.

"That's no excuse!" I fired back. "And you didn't have to ask me to know you shouldn't steal things."

"I didn't want to! But I had no choice. After his grandad died, Aiden asked me to help him out. He's got massive debts. He'd been borrowing stuff from his grandad, money and the like, which kept him afloat but without that he'd go under. I couldn't let that happen."

Not wishing to discuss Aiden – or Gary – I hadn't bothered asking Tracey which of the residents was Aiden's grandad. He must have been Mr Saunders, the first person to die after I started work at Rockbeare.

"Why not?" I shrugged. "Just because it was his grandad, it didn't make it right to steal from him."

Tracey narrowed her eyes. "Since when did you get so hard-faced?" Her gaze travelled down my body and she sneered. "You've changed in more ways than one. You were much nicer before."

I shook my head. Unbelievable! Talk about pots and kettles. She'd changed too. The Tracey I knew would never have considered stealing. But some things never changed. She'd always expected me to go along with her plans, let her be first in the queue for blokes (she didn't need to try too hard), while I stood back, ensuring all the attention was focused on her. Now I had new friends, she didn't like it. Nor did she like it when I answered back.

I scoffed. "Why's that? Because everyone loves a pushover? Well, that's exactly what Aiden thinks of you. You're his fall guy. The gullible idiot who agreed to steal just to keep her man happy. And for what? To give him a few more quid to sink down the pub? Flipping heck, Tracey! What were you thinking?"

Tracey's expression tightened, blotches staining her cheeks. "Oh, it's all right for you, Mrs Flaming Posh Pants! Out with your toffs, you don't care about anyone else. You've no idea what it's been like for me. You've got your head in the clouds if you think that lot is interested in you. They probably laugh their heads off at you behind your back." She tugged at my sleeve. "Take a look at yourself in your cheapo dress."

I went to storm away, but she grabbed my arm. A woman sidled past, holding her hands up as if in surrender. I gazed at Tracey's hand – at her bitten nails, the torn cuticles. She'd done something stupid, something she regretted, and now she was lashing out in anger, made worse by drink. If we carried on like this, we'd only say more unforgivable things.

"Look, I'll speak to you another day. When we haven't been drinking."

Her voice dropped to a hiss. "No, you won't. I don't want to speak to you ever again." She released my arm and stormed out, smashing the door against the wall. It rebounded with a bang.

It took me a while to compose myself. I couldn't stop trembling. When I re-joined the others, Joe looked worried. "I wondered where you'd got to."

I shrugged. "I bumped into someone I knew."

He touched my cheek, his gaze full of concern. "You look upset."

Charlotte butted in. "Nothing a dance won't cure. Come on, knock your drink back and we'll have a boogie."

"Boogie?" Dan chuckled. "Have you been lusting over John Travolta again?"

She jumped to her feet, throwing her arm up and down as if she was in *Saturday Night Fever*, although the 'Theme from S'Express' thumped through the speakers. "Come on, Belinda. I like this song."

I hesitated, unable to shake off my gloom after my spat with Tracey. Would I bump into her on the dance floor? *They laugh their heads off at you …in your cheapo dress.* Her words oozed like sticky tar that I couldn't wash off, but I consoled myself with another thought. If Charlotte didn't want to spend time with me, she wouldn't ask me to dance. She knew loads of people here. Stuff it! I would dance. We'd come to have fun.

Charlotte outdid me on the dance floor, both in stamina and style. I didn't mind. While she threw herself around, shaking her head, lifting her legs, I shuffled my feet and swung my shoulders. When Dan and Joe joined us, I became self-conscious once again, but soon I didn't care.

Dan was a terrible dancer, with unintentional robotic movements that would have been perfect in an old Kraftwerk video.

Something knocked against my feet and I looked down. I was stunned to see one of Charlotte's friends sliding below us, doing a strange snake-like move on her belly, her friend following her.

Dan chuckled, shouting over the music, "I told you they were loopy!"

The sticky wooden floor sucked at my shoes. Its stickiness gleamed under the strobe lights, even though drinks weren't allowed on the dance floor. Neither were cigarettes, but a few butts littered my feet, transported on shoes.

"They'll get filthy!" I shouted back, which made him double over with laughter. Maybe I was getting too old for this lark.

The music changed to a smoochy song and Joe took my hand, drawing me close. He wrapped his arms around me and bent to kiss me. Then he pulled me into his arms. I could feel his heart thudding beneath his hot chest. As we moved in our own circle – something I'd found excruciating on the occasions I'd had a partner for slow dances – I didn't worry about my feet. Or what other people thought. Instead, I lived for the moment, refusing to let myself think about anything but Joe.

Too soon, the trio of love songs came to an end. The lights snapped on and the 'Smurf Song' blasted out. For the first time ever, I didn't care about my flushed face.

We staggered out – tired, not drunk – and joined the taxi queue. Joe and I didn't have far to go to our hotel, but we'd had enough exercise for one night. At least, until we headed back to our room.

My stiletto made an odd clacking sound against the tarmac so I pulled it off, groaning when I saw the metal spike. I'd need to get them re-heeled. Beside me, Joe frowned as he watched two women walking past to the end of the queue. Tracey and her friend. Tracey's arms were wrapped around her chest, hugging her jacket tight, and she was looking away from us.

"I didn't know she was here."

I ignored him. Looking puzzled, he gazed at my shoe. "You could kill someone with that."

I shrugged. "It's a good thing I didn't know about it when I bumped into Tracey in the toilet then."

# Chapter 39

Monday rolled around and I returned to work, relieved to be back to my usual routine. Gloria had already found a replacement for Tracey: a woman with a broad smile and an infectious laugh. She wouldn't need much training, as she'd previously worked in a care home, before giving it up to raise her five children. Imagine that! Coming from a long line of only children, I couldn't believe that anyone would want more than one. Two at a painful push. Believe me, my mum's horror story was the best contraception.

Still Gloria tested the woman's mettle by giving her toilet and commode duty, while I switched to the nicer tea run and room cleaning. Trundling along the corridor with my trolley, I couldn't help chuckling when I spotted Sally leaning against a door frame, offering hands-off advice to the woman on the best way to scrub a toilet.

My laughter faded when Gloria rushed past me to speak to Sally. Snippets of their conversation filtered over to me. Julia had fainted and had to go home, so Sally had to take over from Julia. But she couldn't! Julia had promised that Sally would never be allowed to work in her area again. Maybe she hadn't told Gloria about Sally's behaviour? If she hadn't, I had to.

Sally hurried away, leaving Gloria to speak to the new woman. When she had finished, I asked if I could have a word. She checked her watch. "It'll have to wait until after breakfast."

At breakfast, the residents had plans, which they told me with gleeful expressions. Apparently, Gloria had served them at the table the day before and when they'd mentioned their love of dancing and music, she'd smiled and nodded. They'd moved on to talk about a dance at the care home.

I couldn't hide my disbelief. "You're saying that Gloria was happy about having an afternoon dance in the lounge?"

"Yes, duck." Freda's eyes sparkled. "I'll leave the legwork to the others, but it would be wonderful to watch."

I had a dubious feeling that Gloria's mind must have been elsewhere – worrying about the lack of staff and other matters – and she had no idea what she'd agreed to.

"We just need a record player," Wilf said, as if I could snap my fingers and make one appear. "And a few records. Sadly, it seems that none of us had the foresight to bring our record collections with us."

"Not by choice. It would have cluttered up my poky room," Ernest said.

The residents' faces lit up as they threw names like confetti – Jack Hylton, Sam Browne, Roy Fox. I'd never heard of them. Even Alice buzzed with delight, admitting that while she'd had dancing lessons in her youth, she'd never been to a dance.

For a moment, her expression darkened, but she wiped it away with a smile. "I feel like Cinderella compared to all of you. But, like her, I shall go to the ball."

"Who'll be your prince?" Wilf guffawed and slapped Peter on the back. He blushed.

As we chatted, they made it all sound so simple. After all, Gloria had been there the day before when they'd talked about a dance – and she'd smiled and nodded. But they weren't the ones volunteering to remind Gloria about it. Nor did they have to tell her about Sally. I had no idea which I should mention first. Either way, with so much on her plate, she wouldn't be happy.

Before heading off to clean the rooms, I took a detour to Gloria's office. I could hear her typing but, from where I stood, I couldn't see her. Hesitantly, I knocked on the door.

"Come in," she called in a pleasant voice.

When I stepped inside, she wheeled her chair from the corner table to her main desk. She looked at me. "Thank you for your work last week with Julia."

Startled, I said, "I-I didn't mind helping. B-but…"

She'd given me a good way to start our conversation. I could hardly ask about the dance and then go back to talk about Sally. I balled my fists, took a deep breath and told her what had happened. The more I said, the thinner her lips became until they were blanched strips of skin. When I told her that Julia had assured me that she would be getting more staff and Sally wouldn't be returning to her area, Gloria sat back in her chair and clasped her hands together.

"Julia didn't speak to me." She sighed and turned to the window. "I've known Sally for years. She can get a bit stressed, but I've never seen her lift a hand to residents before. I'll have a word with Jackie and see what she says."

I shook my head. Jackie hadn't seemed bothered by Sally's behaviour. But Gloria misconstrued my worried expression. "Don't worry, I'll phrase it in such a way that it doesn't implicate you. I was going to ask if you could spend a few days doing extra hours in Julia's area. I can't see her coming back this week. I need to rearrange the rota, then I'll let you know."

"Of course. I'll do what I can to help," I said.

At least that way I could keep an eye on Sally. Looking pleased, Gloria smiled and sat back into her chair. Now was my chance.

"I have something to ask too. Do you remember agreeing to an afternoon dance in the lounge when you were serving at my table yesterday?"

She'd done little more than smile and nod, but what was a bit of exaggeration if it helped my cause?

Her frown returned. She didn't answer for a moment, but twiddled with her biro. Then she tapped it on the desk. "I can't say I did or I didn't. They were talking about quite a few things – they're one of the chattier bunches – but I had so much on my mind, I wasn't really listening. Oh dear! If I've given them that impression…" She winced. "I hate going back on my word, but it wouldn't be safe. What if one of the residents fell over?"

"What if I organise it? I'll run everything by you. It'll be just a few records. The ones who are steady on their feet can dance, and the rest can listen to the music and watch. Maybe Joe could help?"

At the mention of the magic word 'Joe', her expression relaxed. What was it with him? His name could open doors that I could hammer on with no success. But if he was my key to helping the residents, so be it. At least we'd be together. I chuckled to myself. Maybe we could have another smoochy dance, which would lead on to other things, like it had at the weekend.

Gloria brought me back to the world of work. "I'll agree, on the understanding that it's a sedate affair. I really don't need an ambulance carting the residents off with hip fractures and the like."

♦

After lunch, at which Freda had squealed with delight at the news, I hurried to the phone box to call Joe and ask him which weekends he was available, and about a record player. He said he could do it in a few weeks, and would either bring his stereo or the old record player stashed in his loft.

My next stop was the charity shop, where I hoped to see the woman who'd given me such wonderful advice about making the most of my looks. She hadn't been there when I'd strolled past the other day. This time, when I walked in, she stepped out from a doorway behind the till. She'd changed her hairstyle for a shorter cut, which suited her. That, and her gorgeous summer dress, made me hesitate. I'd come to ask about records and to present the new me, but I suddenly felt shy.

"Good afternoon." Her pleasant smile was replaced by a look of surprise. Her hand shot to her chest. "My word! What a transformation. You look absolutely beautiful."

Embarrassed, I flushed. "Thank you, but I wouldn't go that far." I tugged at my fringe. "For a start, this is still growing out after a brush with a gas cooker."

"I hardly recognised you," she said. "You're standing taller too. You look more confident. The first time I saw you, you seemed such a bashful little thing."

I grinned. "I still go red all the time, but I don't care so much now." Then I corrected myself. "Well, I do a bit. But I try to fight it."

"Baby steps." She gave me a warm smile. "Well, I must say, you've made my day."

I pulled a crumpled sheet from my bag. "Thank you. I'm hoping you can help me do the same for our residents. Do you have any records by these people?"

She took the list and scanned it, then laughed. "My late mother loved Sam Browne." She headed to the record display and flicked through it until she reached the back and sighed. "We don't have anything further back than the late 1950s, I'm afraid." Brightening, she picked up an LP and waved it from side to side, as if she was a glamorous assistant on a TV game show. The effect was ruined by the front of the album, which showed four old farmers standing in front of a sow and her piglets. "Perhaps they might like the Wurzels."

I giggled. "Far too modern for our residents' tastes."

"I wonder…" She trailed off. "Now, what did we do with them? Hold on." She headed around the till and through the door. I assumed she'd gone to look in the storeroom, until I heard her voice and realised she'd called someone. Within minutes, the conversation had moved from records to talk about a dress.

"Oh gosh! I'd forgotten that!" She laughed. "I looked such a frump."

Her a frump? I couldn't imagine that. Whereas me… Tracey's words came to mind. Her nasty sneer about my cheap dress still stung. I began to rifle through the rails of dresses. Some smelled musty and were a bit tatty, but others were hardly worn. One even had an original price tag that made me gasp. My gaze fell on a green dress. I brushed a finger down the silk fabric and unhooked the hanger from the rail, holding it against myself. Then I checked the label. Size ten. My heart sank. I was a twelve, which meant I'd need to go on another diet to fit into it. But that wouldn't happen. I was happy with my weight. While I might not be stick-thin like a model, I felt right.

The woman came out, raising her eyebrows when she saw me holding the dress. "The colour suits you."

"It's too small." I went to put the dress back.

"I don't think so." She checked the label. "A ten can be small for one brand and generous with another. Why don't you try it on?"

I hesitated. What harm would it do? I had hours to kill before my second shift. She pulled the changing room curtain open and ushered me inside. Unlike before, when I'd tussled with a pair of trousers and a too-small top, this dress slid over my hips. As I slipped my arms through the straps, the dress began to take shape. I buzzed with hope. *Please let it do up!* I eased myself through the curtain, presenting my back to her so she could zip me up. The dress felt a tad snug after a morning spent in my loose-fitting work clothes, but it zipped up easily.

She smiled. "Fabulous!"

I stepped back in front of the mirror, tiptoeing as if I wore heels. The ruched material gave me curves in all the right places, while the fabric transformed from jade to emerald as I turned beneath the spotlight. It was gorgeous. But where would I wear it? Not to the pub or to Blinkers. It was far too fancy. Sighing, I said as much to the woman, who shrugged.

"It's timeless, so it won't date. It would have cost a fortune new, but it's only marked as a pound. Imagine wearing this to a Christmas party or a special occasion. You'd be the centre of attention."

I'd hate that. But I did love the dress. I gave her a coy smile. "You've sold it."

She beamed. "I think the dress did that. Now, about those records. My sister has a pile of my mother's old LPs in her loft. If you come back in a few days, we'd be happy to donate them to your care home. They'd get more love there than sitting in a box."

# Chapter 40

When I returned, Gloria told me that I'd be working in Julia's area from three o'clock, starting Wednesday, to cover staff days off. As usual, I'd have to pop back to serve tea in the main area, which would make for a chaotic working life. I didn't mind, but if word had reached Sally about my complaint, I might be in for a bumpy ride. At least it would give me more chance to watch her. As I'd suspected, Jackie had denied any wrongdoing on Sally's part. Mrs Calam was a challenging woman and had been restrained in a sensitive but firm manner. I'd rolled my eyes when Gloria told me that – I'd heard the ongoing commotion and shouting after being sent to attend to Mr George – but there was no point arguing.

"I'll talk to Julia when she returns and we'll take it to the trustees, but without evidence…" She sighed. "You've seen for yourself that things can seem shocking to an onlooker, even when the appropriate restraint is being used." She was referring to the time Joe and I had seen Julia with Mrs Calam. But this wasn't the same. As I opened my mouth to tell her so, she held up her hand to forestall me. "I'm not saying this happened in this case. I'm just explaining why it will be difficult to prove."

She ran her fingers through her hair. "As I said, I'll speak with Julia. But in the meantime, don't worry. You won't have any comeback with Sally or Jackie. I told them that someone had heard the noise through the door linking the areas."

When Joe picked me up after work, I relayed my conversation with Gloria to him, ending with, "Sally has a day off on Wednesday, so I won't have to work with her until Thursday."

"Just two days then, to prove that she's using unreasonable force."

"She's got Jackie backing her up, saying it's all fine. But when Julia returns, she'll confirm that Sally shouldn't be allowed to work there. Anyhow, there'll be no need in future, as Julia's getting new, trained staff next week."

"Which means that Sally will get away with it. And perhaps this Jackie woman too. I wonder if Julia was away when the other incidents happened. That would explain a lot." His fingers drummed on the steering wheel. Then he grinned. "I have an idea. You won't like it, but it's the only way to prove what's happening."

♦

My first job on Wednesday would be to open the fire escape. Not the one Sir Bartholomew used, but the one at the end of the corridor in Julia's area. Then I'd send a signal from the garden to let Joe know the coast was clear. I prayed Mrs Calam wouldn't be in one of her moods where she refused to go outside. That wouldn't be our only issue. There was the other worker to contend with. The one who stayed behind to keep an eye on the remaining residents. I hoped she'd be tucked in the rooms downstairs, so she didn't spot Joe and his colleague tiptoeing about the first floor. When I'd asked Joe why he needed to bring another person, he'd said he needed someone with technical know-how.

I didn't like it. While I could see the sense in his plan, it felt intrusive. Possibly illegal. It also made me like Tracey, who'd been coerced into doing wrong by her boyfriend. But unlike her and Aiden, who'd stolen from the residents without a care, I hoped this would make Mrs Calam's quality of life – and that of the other residents – much better. I clung to that thought. But it didn't make me feel happier.

The two workers liked my idea of taking the residents from the first floor out together, so the ones on the ground floor were easier to keep an eye on. I had no idea why they didn't do that already. Some of the procedures they followed were inexplicable, even to them. Thankfully, Mrs Calam shuffled from her room without much fuss. Once she and the worker were out of sight, I pushed open the fire escape. The lever clanked, the noise echoing along the corridor. My heart pounded. I hadn't expected that. I held my breath and looked around. A woman's voice filtered from a neighbouring room, cajoling Mr Trott out, but she didn't come to investigate.

Joe appeared at the top of the metal steps, holding a brick, which he'd place against the door to stop it from banging open – just like Sir Bartholomew did with the other fire escape, except that one was on the ground floor and hidden from sight by a straggly hedge. He gave me a thumbs-up and I scarpered, my nerves jangling. Would someone notice that the door wasn't shut when we brought the other residents out? If they closed it, we'd be in trouble. Once I was in the garden, I'd be stuck there, unless one of the residents asked to use the toilet.

When we took the residents downstairs, I made sure to keep to the side by the fire escape door to block it from sight. It worked. We made it to the garden without a hitch, and I perched myself beside two of the residents on a bench.

"Are you going to see Mr George?" I asked my colleague.

She nodded. "After I have a cuppa. After the day I've had, it's a medical emergency."

Great. She'd be in the kitchen for a while before going along to Mr George on the ground floor. Even better, the first-floor rooms would be empty.

Now for part two. Joe would be on the other side of the wooden fence. Hopefully, he'd found a knot hole in one of the panels that he could peer through. Either way, I had to let him know the coast was clear.

In a too-loud voice that made me feel like a wally, I called across to the other worker, "Are you okay over there with Mrs Calam? I'm *all clear* to come over if you need a hand."

The worker frowned. "Eh?" Then she shook her head. "We're fine, thanks."

I gave her a thumbs-up. "Great," I called. "Glad you're *all clear* over there."

She gave me another odd look. I cringed. Flipping Joe! Couldn't he have used another code word rather than 'all clear'? I'd told him it would sound daft, but he'd assured me I'd find a way.

I was on tenterhooks while I sat there. My anxiety must have somehow transferred to Mrs Calam, who became jittery, leaping to her feet but then refusing to go inside when her carer asked if she'd had enough. Each time I gazed anxiously at her, crossing my fingers that she wouldn't say yes. Why on earth had I agreed to this? If they discovered Joe inside the home, I'd be in deep trouble. The best scenario would be me joining Tracey in the dole queue, without a reference. The worst? I didn't dare imagine.

By the time we headed back – I took the men ahead of Mrs Calam – my whole body was trembling. My legs felt weak, as if I hadn't eaten for ages. Which I hadn't. At lunch, I'd been unable to stomach more than a roast potato and a spoonful of peas. They'd clagged in my throat each time I remembered what I was about to do. The residents on my table shook their heads and muttered about faddy diets, not believing me when I said I'd lost my appetite. Then they'd moved on to talk about the dance, coercing me into making it a dressy affair. As Alice said, if I sent out invitations – more work for me! – with a dress code of sorts, the other residents would comply.

Comply? When Mrs Calam clutched the architrave on her room door and refused to budge, I wished she knew that word.

"Come on, dearie." The worker – I think her name was Angie, but I couldn't remember – tried to encourage her into the room. She looked at me. "I'll be fine here. You go and take the others outside."

I wanted to go inside, to see what Joe had done and to check it was safely hidden from view so it wouldn't be found when the room was cleaned. Instead, I nodded and went to spend another miserable stint in the garden, gazing at the goldfish in the pond with the second group, while my mind churned with worry. It had all been too easy. Something was bound to upset Joe's scheme.

# Chapter 41

Filled with trepidation, I headed into Julia's area the following day, certain that the camera would have been discovered when the rooms were cleaned. But clearly no one had thought to check behind the bags and boxes stashed on the top of Mrs Calam's wardrobe. I had no idea what the camera looked like. When I'd asked Joe if it was like Tracey's dad's unwieldy camcorder, he'd laughed and said he had much better technology than that. This was 1988. Anything was possible. Desktop computers, portable cellular phones, video game consoles – you name it, he could tell me about it. He even had a phone in his house with an aerial receiver, so he could walk around chatting, while I was tethered to the hallway and the phone stand, twirling my fingers around the coil lead. His favourite programme was *Tomorrow's World*, which Mum refused to watch because it was, in her view, a load of claptrap.

As well as the camera, he'd also hidden what he called a time-lapse video recorder. I'd switched both off at the plug the previous night, scared that the night carer would hear the noise when she turned off Mrs Calam's radio. Joe had sighed when I'd told him this, as it meant he had to come back to reset them. But he'd have to do that anyhow, as he needed to check the setup and tape. Did that mean it would run out or it might not record? I didn't ask, wanting to know as little as possible. I hated all this subterfuge. It was all too technical for me and worrying, especially with Sally back after her day off.

Today, she wouldn't agree to us taking the first-floor residents out in one bunch. We'd have to do it her way, with some left upstairs and others downstairs. I had some comfort – knowing her, she'd spend the afternoon tucked away in the small kitchen, having more than one cup of tea.

This time, I refused to call out to Joe, insisting that once I'd opened the fire escape door, he'd have to watch through the knothole in the fence. I'd give a thumbs-up or two to give him the green light. Nothing more.

When we brought the residents back, I found no sign that Joe had been in the room. I breathed a sigh of relief – until I spotted a wire hanging at the back of the wardrobe. I tucked it out of sight. Not wanting to risk anyone else spending too long in her room, I offered to give Mrs Calam her tea. To my surprise Sally agreed, although it was probably just because she was pleased that she didn't have to feed Mrs Calam the strange-smelling gloop she had to eat because she refused to wear dentures.

Like a baby, Mrs Calam shook her head, moaning, "No," before each mouthful. But I managed to get most of it inside her. That is, until we'd moved on to dessert, when Sally appeared at the door. Alarmed, Mrs Calam knocked a spoonful of ice cream from my hand. Sally stomped over to where I knelt.

"For pity's sake! Haven't I taught you anything?" She pointed to the carpet. "Clean that up and I'll deal with her." Her voice hardened. "Now, Mrs Calam, I told you the other day, we're not having this again."

As I hurried out to fetch a cloth, I prayed that the camera would do its job. Joe had directed it towards the corner of the room, where Sally had stood when she'd slapped Mrs Calam's hand away. Fingers crossed they'd be in the camera's line of vision. A crash sounded and Mrs Calam began to howl. I stopped dead by the stairs, but forced myself onwards, even though I hated doing so.

"That's enough!" Sally's voice echoed down the corridor. "For Pete's sake, anyone would think a bit of ice cream was going to kill you."

When I returned with the damp cloth, I found Mrs Calam sobbing in her chair and the bowl of ice cream upended on the carpet. I longed to give the poor lady a cuddle, but I dropped to my knees and started to scrub.

Sounding furious, Sally towered above me, huffing as she told Mrs Calam, "Now, that's enough!"

When I finished, Sally spoke to me through gritted teeth. "Take over from Jackie downstairs. Tell her we're putting Mrs Calam to bed." She jabbed a finger towards the radio on the bedside table. "And turn off that racket too!"

"Bed at four thirty?" I focused on more important matters – the radio was needed to mask the hum of the camcorder. "If we turn it off, she'll be a nightmare. Julia said we have to keep it on."

I thought Sally would contradict me by saying she was in charge now, not Julia, but she didn't. As I turned the sound down a little, hoping it was enough to pacify her, she planted her hands on her hips, her lips trembling. Why? Fear, upset or anger?

My answer came when she hissed at me, "I said, *get out!*"

♦

I couldn't speak when I served the residents their tea in the main area. If I did, I knew I'd cry. After I'd switched duties with Jackie, I'd heard the commotion upstairs. Mrs Calam's squeals, the raised voices. Beside me, Mr George had put his hands over his ears and groaned in distress. But I'd done nothing. I'd let it happen. Perhaps Mrs Calam was having a bad day rather than Sally being too rough. But I knew the truth. If, Angie, the lovely worker from the afternoon had still been here, she wouldn't have let this happen.

When Freda tapped my hand and asked if I was okay, I gave her my best attempt at a smile. Minutes later, Alice came round to me. She laid a warm hand on my back, something she'd never done before. "You're not well. You should be at home."

I fixed a smile. "I just had a bad night's sleep." It was true. I'd spent the night fretting about the camera and getting caught.

Alice stormed over to Gloria, who sat in Sally's usual seat. I covered my eyes in disbelief as her words echoed above the hubbub. "You're working her too hard."

It was strange that Alice didn't worry about my workload when it came to me organising their dance! But I bit back the thought. Of course they wanted an exciting afternoon. They had so little to look forward to.

Gloria came over, wearing a concerned expression. "If you're ill, you should go home."

I fought back tears as I met her eyes. "I'm not ill. I promise."

"If you're too tired to help Sally, I can get someone else to do it."

"No, please. I'm fine, honestly."

If she refused to let me go back, I couldn't keep an eye on Mrs Calam. Not that I'd be able to do much more than hope that the camera gave us the proof we needed. If it did, then all this would be worthwhile.

When Gloria returned to her table, Alice fired me a look of exasperation. "You'll be no good if you make yourself ill."

By nine o'clock I felt dreadful. My head pounded, my body ached. Maybe Alice had been right and I was coming down with something. My last job of the day was to creep into Mrs Calam's room to switch off her radio and the video equipment. She lay curled in a foetal position in bed, snoring. I hoped her dreams were better than mine. After hearing the earlier upset from his room across the corridor, Mr Trott had spent the rest of the evening crying for his daughter, Lindy, shredding everyone's nerves. I'd been worried about him too after Sally had growled that, at this rate, she wouldn't be blamed for her actions.

I hurried out of the building to find Joe's car idling on the driveway. Usually, I'd kiss him, but I couldn't do anything but slump into my seat, shaking.

"Bee!" He stroked my cheek. "What's happened?"

The tears came freely. I brushed them away as I relayed the day's events. When I finished, he squeezed my hand.

"You're done in, I know. But…" He grimaced. "We need to go back in and fetch the tape."

"We?" I shook my head. "You can't go in there. Not at this time of night. Tell me what to do."

Back inside, I found Gloria in the hallway talking to the night manager. They stood by the lift and main stairs. Sticking to our agreed ruse, I picked up speed, pinning a frustrated look to my face as I rushed past towards Julia's area.

"Belinda!" Gloria tapped her watch. "What—"

I swung around, walking backwards to show I didn't have time to stop. "I'm such an idiot. I've left my bag behind."

Knowing my luck, she would have seen me leaving with it ten minutes before. But she waved me away and resumed her conversation.

I slowed when I reached the doors to Julia's area and slipped through quietly. The corridor lights had been dimmed but a shaft of light from the kitchen brightened the gloom. There was the chink of a teaspoon. Someone was in there! I tiptoed to the doorway, holding my breath as I peeped inside. I could just make out the duty manager's back. She murmured to someone and I gave a silent prayer of thanks. With both workers in the kitchen, I should be safe to go upstairs. Unless one of them came up and found me. What excuse could I give then? Heart thudding, I darted past and sneaked down the corridor to the stairwell where I crept upstairs.

The corridor lay in the same faint light as the ground floor. Blank doors lined either side. I paused outside Mrs Calam's room, my heart pounding so hard, I felt sure someone would hear it. What if she woke? She'd screech the place down. Holding my breath, I eased the door handle. The door clicked. I paused. There was no rustle of bedsheets or shriek of alarm so I pushed the door ajar. It brushed against the carpet. I winced. Why had I agreed to do this? But then I remembered Mrs Calam's earlier cries and I knew exactly why.

Mrs Calam lay asleep in the same position I'd seen her earlier. I dropped to my knees and crawled across the floor to the plug sockets on the other side of the wardrobe. The switches snapped like gunfire in the silence and the machine began to whirr. I grimaced. Surely she'd wake up now? But she didn't move. A terrible thought hit me. What if she was dead? But I pushed it aside. I'd heard her snoring earlier.

I reached up to the boxes on top of the wardrobe. Joe had told me which one to move. When I did, a luminous blue light filtered through a chink he'd missed when taping up the display on the video recorder. At least it gave me a starting point to feel my way across the buttons. I pressed one and the light went out. Great! At this rate, I'd still be here when the night shift started their rounds, or whatever they did. I tapped the button again and the machine blinked back into life. This time I pushed the neighbouring button. My hand shot to my mouth as the machine whined and clacked, ejecting out a tape. Stupidly, I put my finger to my lips to shush it, but Mrs Calam didn't stir. I removed the tape, put the box back in place and flicked off the too-loud sockets. Then I tucked the video under my top and crept out. This time I left through the door in the corridor, pausing at the top of the main stairs to check for voices in case Gloria was still about. The care home was quiet but for the crack of pipes and the creak of the stairs when I tiptoed down them.

Once in the hallway, I was safe. If Gloria saw me now, she'd assume I'd been talking to the night workers, although she might wonder why I didn't have my bag.

I got into Joe's car and handed him the tape. "I am never, ever, *ever* doing that again. I'm not cut out for it. I nearly wet myself when the flipping tape shot out."

He leaned over and kissed me. "Hopefully this will show something and make it all worthwhile. Do you want to take a look at it?"

"To be honest, I'm shaking so much..." I held out my trembling hands to prove it. "I could do with a drink somewhere quiet to calm down."

Joe raised his eyebrows in disbelief. But I couldn't face seeing what I guessed would be on there. Not when I'd heard Mrs Calam's howls. He didn't argue, though. Instead, he gave my hand a squeeze and pushed the gear into first.

"I understand," he said. "Let's get a drink, then I'll take you home. Unless you want to come with me. I hope you don't mind, but I'm going to watch it tonight."

# Chapter 42

At the pub Joe ordered me a brandy for some reason, telling me that it was good for soothing nerves. But it didn't work. After I refused his offer to go to his office to review the tape, he took me home, giving me a kiss before driving away, promising to let me know what he discovered.

In a way, I regretted not going with him. But I didn't need a tape to see the imagined scenes reeling through my mind. Unlike his video recorder, I didn't have a stop button, so they played on and on until I fell into a restless sleep.

The next morning, Gloria took one look at me and offered to send me home. But I refused, once again telling her I wasn't ill. But it gave me the opportunity to beg the use of her phone, because I'd forgotten to pass on an important message to my mum.

Gloria hesitated. I hoped she wouldn't ask what the message was, because I had no idea what I'd say but, thankfully, she pursed her lips. "Just this once."

This time she wasn't in her office when I called Joe on his work line. He answered, his voice grim when he said we wouldn't need more proof that Sally was a nasty piece of work.

"Will you bring the video over to show Gloria?" I asked.

"I'm getting a few copies made first," he said. "I'll

meet you at lunch and you can decide what you want to do. I haven't told my boss about this yet. But as I asked Al to help, and his friend, Maurice, has a vested interest after what happened to his dad, my boss will want to be kept in the loop."

His boss? I hadn't thought this would involve other people outside the care home. But of course it would. Joe had come to work here on an assignment. His boss might want a scoop in return for the effort Joe had put in. Where did I fit into this? Would I become the fall girl like Tracey, set up to do other people's dirty work? What would happen to me? But I'd *wanted* to help Mrs Calam. While I hadn't seen the tape, I did want to see Sally punished if she'd hurt her.

My voice trembled. "I only get an hour before I have to go back to work with Sally. Please don't say anything until I see you."

"Of course," he said, his tone gentle. "Please don't worry."

But I couldn't help worrying. It was all I would do.

♦

Our heads down against the drizzle, Joe and I walked hand in hand into the care home. My insides churned. I took a deep breath and plastered on a confident expression. We'd agreed to do this together, but I could barely think, let alone talk.

We passed the ladies sitting in the reception area. One

greeted Joe with a friendly wave, while her companion hissed at her. "Who's he?"

"He used to work here, remember?"

"There's so many…"

Her voice faded as we rounded the corner to Gloria's office, the *clack-clack* of her typewriter keys reverberating through the open door.

Joe chuckled. "Still in the Stone Age here."

I ignored him, my mind on the meeting ahead. Joe knocked and we entered. Frowning, Gloria gazed at us, then at the package Joe held. Still seated, she rolled her chair to her desk.

"Yes?"

"We've got something to show you," Joe said. "Can I close the door?"

She nodded and waited until he'd done so before asking, "What's this about?"

"Sally," I said. Joe pulled out the stills he'd taken from the video footage, along with a copy of the video tape. He placed them on Gloria's desk, turning each image so Gloria could see them. They weren't the best pictures, but it was obvious what was happening.

Gloria's face blanched and she snatched the photos from the desk. "How did you get these?"

It wasn't the question I'd expected her to ask first, although I guessed it would come at some point.

"A camera," Joe said. "In Mrs Calam's room."

"I can see what room it is. But what was a camera doing there?"

I leapt in. "You didn't believe me. You know, when I told you about Sally."

Gloria's eyes burned into me. She held up the photos, crumpling their edges, her voice a low growl. "I never said I didn't believe you—"

"You said there was no evidence," I butted in. "I couldn't let Mrs Calam suffer like that while you and Julia did nothing." My voice rose. "That's why I was so upset at tea yesterday. It was awful hearing her crying. Sally hurt her and Jackie didn't care. As long as they got the job done."

Gloria opened her mouth but I couldn't stop myself. I hadn't watched the video, but Joe had told me what was on it. "Don't tell me that Mrs Calam is difficult. I know she is. But she doesn't deserve to be slapped like that."

Gloria slumped back in her chair. "We haven't got the staff to keep going. They're under a lot of pressure."

Joe shook his head. "That's not the point. Plus, you could pay staff more if you wanted better ones."

She sighed. "It's not up to me. You tell the trustees that."

"I will," I stunned myself by blurting out. Why had I done that? I hated speaking in front of people. I couldn't help but add a tentative, "Once this is sorted."

Gloria reached out and picked up the video. "So, what does this show? And you do realise that you've probably broken a dozen rules doing this?"

Joe crossed his arms. "Believe me, what we've done is nothing compared to the seriousness of letting abuse happen under your nose."

I flinched at his tone. I'd known this would be a difficult meeting, but now I doubted I'd be walking out of here still with my job. Then I checked myself. Before I'd agreed to go through with the recording, I'd known that this could end with me on the dole queue. Sadly, that would also mean that the residents wouldn't get their dance. And Mrs Calam? I just prayed she'd get kinder carers. Whatever else we did, that had to happen.

Gloria sat in front of us, her expression unreadable.

Joe continued, "I didn't tell you before, but I work for a newspaper."

Gloria's mouth fell open. She looked at me. I shook my head. No, I did this job because I needed the money. Strangely, I could put up with the toilet cleaning and commodes if I got to spend time with the residents. But I didn't tell her that. Instead, I let Joe speak.

"We won't run the piece yet, on the understanding that you don't just fire Sally but you prove that the care home is going to deal with the abuse, not sweep it under the carpet." Beads of perspiration dappled Joe's forehead. I hadn't thought he'd be nervous. Unlike mine, his voice didn't tremble when he spoke. "My boss's friend had a parent who died here – Cyril Axe – he had bruises when he died, but his family was told that they were from falls. He hadn't been told anything about these, so he asked us to investigate. More than anything else, he just wants to know what happened to his dad. We need to find out if Sally was working with the dementia patients at the time, or if this Jackie was too. That means involving the police."

Joe and I would be in trouble too. The police wouldn't be happy that I'd helped Joe break into the care home. My mum would go mad. But then I reassured myself. Hadn't she said that I had to look out for the residents? Be their voice?

I could do this.

"How about you take a look at the video?" Joe said. "Is there a room where you can view it?"

He hadn't mentioned the video recording equipment still in Mrs Calam's room. We'd have to retrieve it later.

"There's one in the guest lounge, but that's not possible." Gloria gazed out of the window, something she did when she needed to think. After what seemed like an age, she turned back. "We'll find another one. But I don't need to see it yet to know my next steps. The photos are bad enough."

Joe nodded towards the phone. "Then you know what you have to do."

I glanced at the clock above the typewriter. I was late for work. If I didn't go back, the residents wouldn't get to spend time in the garden. That's if they were allowed out on a miserable day like this.

"I'd better head back," I said. "If it's okay with you."

Gloria's stony gaze settled on me, but she nodded. The axe hadn't fallen on my job today. But it would.

As Gloria reached for the phone, Joe gave me a smile and mouthed 'Good luck'. He knew that I faced another ordeal. I dreaded seeing Sally. Fingers crossed she wouldn't be there for long.

♦

Within an hour of starting work, to my surprise and
Sally's consternation, the lovely worker, Angie, bustled
into the kitchen. Sally was sitting at the table sipping a cup
of tea, while I was on my knees. With the residents in their
rooms, unable to go out in the rain, there wasn't much to
do, so Sally had told me to scrub the cupboards.

When Angie hooked her rain-splattered coat over a
peg, Sally frowned. "What are you doing here?"

Angie shrugged, but I noticed that her gaze didn't meet
Sally's. "Gloria asked me."

"Has she lost the plot? We've already got enough
people." Sally looked at me. "Unless she wants you back
there."

Her chair screeched over the tiled floor as she pushed
it back. "Hold on. I'll go and see what she's up to."

As Sally stormed off, Angie sighed and shook her head.
I set about putting all the mugs back before starting on the
next cupboard.

She interrupted me. "Are the residents in their rooms?"

When I nodded, she gasped. "They can't be stuck in
there all day! It's not fair."

She dashed off, leaving me none the wiser. How much
did she know about Sally and the accusations? No doubt
I'd find out at teatime. The resident grapevine would have
done its job, with help from the three ladies listening to

our conversation from the other side of the wall. I should have kept my voice down, but I'd been too upset to care.

Sally didn't return. But Angie must have known that, as she set a new procedure in place: the residents could go into the kitchen area rather than being shut in their rooms. She asked me to bring in three spare chairs from the main dining room. I walked past a gaggle of nosey residents, then Gloria's office door. Not a sound filtered through. But Gloria must be inside. The residents wouldn't be there if they didn't expect more news.

Later, I glanced out of the small kitchen window to find that Joe's car had gone. A strange feeling of desolation swept over me. Joe would be back to pick me up at nine o'clock but, until then, I had to deal with my worries alone. At least I didn't have Sally to contend with. And neither did Mrs Calam.

Gloria stayed in her office at tea-time, so the other staff helped to set up the table she was overseeing. And Sally's. None of them mentioned what was taking place. At least, not in front of me. Their unusual silence suggested that they guessed I was somehow involved.

The residents streamed into the dining room in a buzz of excitement. A few curious gazes strayed my way, but I was left to deal with my table in peace. If it could be called that. Alice came in with Freda and helped her to store her Zimmer frame.

Rather than sit down, Alice bent beside me, her beady eyes glinting. "You did this," she whispered.

I frowned. Did what? Her comment made no sense.

"You put yourself on the line to help Elsie."

Elsie? I didn't know anyone by that name.

"Elsie Calam," she hissed, but she may well have used a megaphone. Around us, heads craned to listen. If Alice hoped no one would hear, she'd got it wrong. She would have attracted less attention by sitting down with the others and keeping to her usual strident tone.

Shocked, I couldn't help stammering, "H-how do you know?"

When she tapped her nose, I groaned. Those flaming women in the reception area. How much had they heard through the wall? If I lasted another day here, I'd advise Gloria to soundproof her office.

Alice laid her hand on my shoulder and gave me a warm smile. "You should be proud of yourself. We could all do with people willing to speak out, no matter the consequence."

It was a shame that Gloria didn't feel the same way. I whispered, "Thank you."

Not waiting for Alice to be seated, Ernest picked up a sandwich. Perhaps he thought he'd make a start while Alice was otherwise occupied. Her face fell. After giving me another pat on the shoulder, she hurried to her seat. While she'd become more caring about other people since her friendship with Freda had developed, when it came to food, the old Alice appeared, desperate to snaffle everything in sight.

Wilf had sat with his hands clasped, waiting for Alice. As her hand hovered over the sandwiches, he turned to me. "*And* you managed to get Freda's ring back – no thanks to your friend."

Alice fired him an angry look. "She didn't just get Freda's ring back. She probably also lost a friend by doing so. We're not here to make judgements on their friendship. As I said, she's done all this for other people, and at what cost to herself?"

Tears blinded me, but I smiled and murmured a choked, "Let's eat, shall we?"

Freda's gnarled hand reached out to mine. "Thank you," she said.

In the background, Wilf and Peter nodded.

"Yes." Ernest flushed and laid his half-eaten sandwich on his plate. "Thank you."

# Chapter 43

For some reason, Gloria had put me on the rota for all seven days next week. I hadn't pointed out her mistake earlier, hoping she'd realise it was too late to give me a midweek day off and she'd be forced to offer me one at the weekend again. But my plan backfired. With everything going on, she didn't notice. I wasn't going to ask her either. As far as I was concerned, this wasn't the time to put my head above the parapet. Not when it would bring attention to the fact that she hadn't disciplined me – or sacked me – for helping Joe to break into the care home.

The police took my statement. They didn't seem interested in what I'd done, but *why* I'd done it. The constable was affronted that anyone would raise a hand to an elderly person, telling me that her mother had dementia.

When Angie asked Gloria if I could continue to help her until Julia returned on Monday, Gloria agreed. With Sally off the scene and Angie watching Jackie, Mrs Calam seemed calmer, sitting quietly in the garden when we got a break between the rain showers.

Still not sure how long I would be there before Gloria gave me the chop, I kept my head down, doing whatever I was asked. When the next rota appeared, giving me the Thursday and Friday off (Gloria must have spotted her error, but not mentioned it), I guessed I had a reprieve.

The next Monday, I was back to my regular work in

the main care home. I was also back on toilet and commode duty, but I didn't mind. After lunch I headed out of the door, ready to spend three hours at the library until my second shift. As I stepped outside, flicking my brolly open, I spotted a huddled figure standing at the entrance to the driveway, her hands in the pockets of her rain mac. I hesitated. Did she want another argument? But I forced myself to go to her.

As I drew close, she gave me a wan smile. "Hi. Have you got a minute?"

A gust of wind blew through the trees, splatting us with raindrops. My umbrella shielded me, but Tracey took the brunt. She blinked and wiped her face. "That's the second time. You'd think I'd learn to stand somewhere else."

"Do you want to go to a café?" I asked, then wished I hadn't. While it might be warmer inside, it meant we faced a ten-minute walk making small talk.

I held the umbrella over us as we hurried towards town. I needn't have worried about what we'd say – most of our conversation related to the weather and grumbles about being splashed by passing cars. We entered the café, its windows steamed with condensation, where I ordered two hot chocolates while Tracey picked a table in the corner. When I put her drink on the table, she ripped open three sachets of sugar and shook them onto the froth.

I raised my eyebrows. "I thought you took one sugar?"

She gave me a half smile. "If they served whisky, I'd have that."

Her jokey tone reminded me of the Tracey I knew,

batting away worries with a quip. But she didn't look anything like my lively friend of old, more like an urchin rescued from the street. A musty smell wafted from her damp coat, while her sodden fringe stuck to her forehead and droplets of rain glistened on her eyebrows.

She'd come to talk, but a silence stretched between us. While she bit her lip, gazing down at her coffee, I sipped mine, deciding to leave her in peace for a moment. I shifted in the plastic chair, trying to get comfortable. We should have chosen the other café, even if it meant walking another two minutes in the rain. This was more of a greasy spoon. The smell of fat hung in the air and the sticky plastic tablecloth sucked at my elbows.

A draught blew across us, brought in by a man who shook his umbrella and told everyone what a miserable day it was. A lady in the corner agreed.

Their voices seemed to shake Tracey from her thoughts. "If only the weather was all I had to worry about." She let out a loud sigh. "Look, I'm sorry about the other night. I took it out on you, and I shouldn't have. You looked lovely, by the way. Ignore what I said. I was being a…" She shrugged. "Well, you know."

I smiled. Although I hadn't often been at the mercy of Tracey's tongue in our twenty-year friendship, I'd seen her in action with other people. Not usually one to instigate spiteful jibes, she more than held her own with sharp retorts that left her opponent floundering for a comeback. Having said that, I hadn't given her much opportunity to aim her knife at me. That had been jabbed at my bullies. At school we'd had an unspoken agreement – I hovered in her shadow and let her shine, taking comfort in her protection. But our childhood dynamics hadn't moved on, even though I had.

"You've always been a good friend. I've been thinking about a few things. Aiden and stuff…" Again, Tracey shrugged. "I understand why you didn't like him. You picked a good 'un in Joe. D'you know, Aiden lied about me. Said I did it off my own bat and he didn't know the items I took had been stolen."

I gasped, shocked. "What? Will he get off the hook?"

She shook her head. "Gary's girlfriend told the police that she heard Aiden bragging about where he got his money from. I gave it all to him, you know. Cos he needed it. The lying bastard."

A woman on the neighbouring table tutted and grumbled to her friend. Both gave us disgusted looks, which I ignored.

"What did Gary have to say about his girlfriend doing that?"

"He's in love." She chuckled. "He said, what sort of bloke would grass up his bird? If Aiden had done that to me, what's to stop him doing the same to Gary one day?"

I sat back in shock. So Gary, who'd ignored me at the pub, wasn't all bad. I thought back to that evening. Perhaps he hadn't realised he'd been lined up for me, or Aiden had corralled him into a blind date. Either way, I hadn't been his type. Nor he mine. If he'd liked me, I'd have been stuck with him all night. Instead, I'd ended up bumping into Joe.

"If I can do anything to help, let me know," I said.

"I just want my oldest friend back," she said. "You've changed, but I like it. You were such a softy. You used to tell me what you thought I wanted to hear. Now if I ask how I look or ask for your opinion on something, I know you'll give me it straight. And I respect that." She grinned. "And if I don't? Feel free to knock some sense into me. I could do with some of that."

# Chapter 44

Joe threw an irate glance to the group of men at the bar who jeered and held out their empty pints to their late-comer friend. Laughing, the man agreed to buy a round and pulled out a thick wallet. As he beckoned the bar maid over, his mates slapped his back to cries of "Good man!"

"Maybe this isn't the best place for a talk. Do you mind if we go over the road?" Joe downed the last dregs of his pint and pointed to my lager. "Leave that. I'll get you another one."

I took his outstretched hand. Hopefully the next pub would be quieter. I'd been waiting to find out what he wanted to say since he'd picked me up. Curious, I'd tried to wheedle a few clues from him, but he wouldn't blab. He seemed nervous, his fingers tapping the steering wheel and, later, the bar as we waited to order our drinks. Then the loud mob had arrived and put paid to any hope of conversation.

Our jackets pulled over our heads, we dashed through the rain into the cosy pub opposite, relieved to find it so quiet that we could hear the thud of darts hitting the board above the hum of chat. Joe bought the same drinks as before and took them to a booth at the rear of the pub. I slid onto the bench opposite him and gazed at him in expectation. Now would he tell me?

He cleared his throat. "I don't know if you'll like this, but hear me out."

My anticipation changed to dread. Was this to do with putting the camcorder in Mrs Calam's room? Were we going to be charged? Would I get the sack? Gloria hadn't said a lot to me recently, but her frostiness had thawed enough for her to smile when I'd helped the new worker to set her table earlier.

"I've been doing a bit of digging," Joe said. "About your lecturer."

I froze in shock. I'd forgotten that I'd told Joe about him. In fact, until he mentioned it tonight, I'd not thought about the lecturer for ages. My new life with Joe had allowed me to draw the curtains on that episode.

"Why?" I asked.

"Because of what he did. If he hadn't behaved so badly, you could still be at polytechnic, looking forward to getting a degree and a good job."

"But leaving poly meant I met you."

He smiled. "Something good came from it. But what about the others?"

"Others?" My mouth fell open. "He didn't pick on anyone else."

Joe shrugged. "Maybe he didn't always bully them as badly as he did you, but he definitely tried it on – and he succeeded with a number of students. When you told me he'd come on to you, I guessed it wasn't a one-off. Men like him are predators."

I sank into the back of the bench. "Oh."

I didn't know what else to say. I was sure that my lecturer hadn't seen me as anything special, just as an easy target to bully. I had no idea why he'd then asked me to sleep with him. It was an odd way to go about it. A young boy might tease a girl he liked by pulling her hair to gain his attention, but my lecturer had gone much further. He'd ripped my confidence to pieces and scattered it to the wind.

"What did the other women say?" I whispered.

Joe leaned forward and took my hands, stroking them with his thumb. I gazed at our entwined fingers, too shamefaced to meet his eyes. I'd done nothing wrong, but I didn't want to be reminded of those days, when I had been stupid, ugly, fat, frizzy, ginger. The words coiled around me, tightening their grip. I fought to free myself. My frizz had been tamed with my new hairstyle – no thanks to the gas cooker. Joe's mum had ginger hair, like mine, and a cuddly body, and she was lovely. I'd lost a bit of weight: I wasn't fat or skinny, just healthy. And I wasn't stupid, I knew that, even though I'd done some daft things in my time. That just left ugly.

Finally, I met Joe's concerned gaze. I couldn't look that bad. Not when this gorgeous man loved me.

"I'm sorry if I've upset you," he said.

"You haven't. I just needed a few minutes to get my head around it."

He squeezed my hands. "Before I say anything else, I want to assure you that your name won't be mentioned. I've got more than enough ex-students willing to speak out. One of them left five years ago, so your lecturer's been doing this a while."

"Y-you're running a piece on this?"

"It's the only way. I'll be honest, Bee. My boss agreed not to run anything on the abuse at the care home because of his friend. The theft was too small fry for us. But telling this story will do good. It's the only way. No one else will know what he did to you, but you'll see him get his comeuppance. It's not the greatest scoop for us – I mean, it's not like he's an MP or anything." He gave me a wry shrug. Honest as usual. "But I wanted to do this. He's wrecked more lives than yours."

I hesitated. "Tell me about the others."

He released my hand to take a sip of his pint. Then he told me about Jenny, who'd been flattered by the lecturer's attention. He'd taken her to candlelit dinners – and the rest … although during classes he had ignored her, telling her it was easier if other students thought they didn't get on. Sharon, who'd fallen for him, hook, line and sinker, to be discarded with the excuse that someone had seen them together, but he'd promised her kinder grades if she kept her mouth shut. This went hand in hand with the underlying threat of worse grades if she made a fuss. That made me prick up my ears. He was a senior lecturer. The polytechnic might have turned a blind eye to his slimeball shenanigans, but grade manipulation was another matter. Joe nodded when I made that point, then moved on to tell me about Alison, Coral and Paula.

"How many were there?" I gasped. "It's not like he was that good-looking."

"A lot. Most wouldn't give me permission to print their

337

stories, and some denied it, even though other victims had pointed me in their direction. But I have four who are happy to be quoted, and it's pretty damning." He hesitated. "The thing is, he picked on one of them, just like he did to you. She was shy too, like you. He'd asked her if she'd like him to show her around the local area, in particular this great pub. But she guessed his real intention and turned him down. That's when he started to bully her."

I frowned. "I don't think…"

Then an old memory filtered to my mind. I was looking at a poster on the SU board when the lecturer had peered over my shoulder, making me jump.

"Crimpleeen Queeens?" he'd chuckled. "If you go to see them, make sure to wad your ears with cotton wool. I know a place that has much better music. It'd be right up your street. That's if you have good taste."

I'd gazed at him. Were lecturers allowed to take students out? Anyway, I liked the sound of the Crimpleeen Queeens.

"I'll take my chances," I'd said. "But thanks anyway."

I gaped at Joe. "He did that with me, but I thought he was just asking a question! You know, being friendly. I mean, why me? It's not like I'm a looker. He made my life a misery … just because I turned him down? Then, when he saw I was drunk, he thought he'd try again, this time with a more obvious tactic, and then deny it all. What a…"

I'd been just about to say the word Tracey had used

about Aiden when we'd talked in the café, but I didn't, in case anyone overheard us. While there were benefits to a quiet pub, I couldn't swear in outrage. Not unless I wanted a roomful of tuts.

Joe gritted his teeth. "Believe me, he won't be doing it again. I'll show you the piece before it goes to press."

# Chapter 45

Gloria stormed into the kitchen, curling her finger to summon me. "Come to my office before you start the rooms. We need to talk."

Being called by Gloria into her office always made me anxious, but today it was worse than ever. Her words jangled through the kitchen like a town crier's bell. *Belinda's getting the sack. Belinda's getting the sack.* Finally, after more than a week, during which time Aiden and Tracey had both been charged with theft – I'd do all I could to support her as a friend, but there was little more I could do – and Jackie and Sally had been formally dismissed, now my judgement time had come. By the looks on my co-workers' faces, they thought so too.

After clearing up the kitchen, I wiped my hands down my pinny and headed for Gloria's office. I found her door open. Inside, she was twisting a pencil in the cog of a cassette. Its tape spooled onto the melamine desk.

"I taped this, for the dance," she said. "In case you couldn't find a record player. But the damn thing keeps getting jammed."

"I-I thought the dance wasn't going ahead."

She shot me a puzzled look. "Why would you think that? I said it could."

I shrugged, thanked her and breathed a sigh of relief. She couldn't be getting rid of me, not if she wanted the dance to go ahead. But it raised another issue. Now I'd have to bring in my cassette player to reward her efforts, and we didn't have much time to organise anything special. Thanks to the woman in the charity shop and Joe, we had records and a record player and we could stretch to buying a few drinks. Maybe we could borrow Joe's soda stream too. We could get busy with the fizzy and give the residents a choice of drinks.

Gloria pointed to a chair by the wall. "Shut the door and bring that over."

She rarely invited me to sit down, preferring brief meetings. While I brought the chair over, she pulled a file with my name on it from her in-tray. My heart sank. Maybe I'd got it wrong. This would be a written warning, a verbal warning or worse. She opened the flap and pulled out my CV.

She steepled her hands. "You're a tenacious one, I'll give you that."

I'd never been called that before. Was it a compliment?

"There are odd gaps in your CV, but Tracey assured me you'd be an asset." Then she muttered to herself, "Look how that went. Joe was a bit of a surprise too." She raked her hands through her hair and sighed. "When Tracey let slip about a few things, I thought that a bit of hard work would send you running back to your office job or your education."

I frowned. I had no idea she'd found out that. She'd never mentioned it.

Chuckling, she flicked the page over. "If someone made me clean toilets and commodes after I'd had a cushy office job, I'd be rushing back to the typewriter. But now I don't want you to."

I gaped at her. What did she mean?

"I did as you suggested. I've convinced the trustees to put more funding into pay. Hopefully, it'll mean we spend less on advertising. We've also agreed a small pot for entertainment for the residents."

I couldn't believe it. The trustees had listened to sense and agreed to give the residents something to do, other than rotting away in the care home. I couldn't wait to tell Freda, Alice and the rest. Gloria returned my smile. She seemed so much younger without her perpetual frown.

"Yes, it is good news. The residents will be pleased. But I have something to ask you, and I hope you'll accept."

She couldn't be giving me the sack.

"Although there are people who have worked here for longer, you've proved yourself in a way that no other staff member has. I've been thinking long and hard about this. I'm sorry I didn't listen to you about Sally and Jackie. I should have dealt with it earlier. Thanks to my ineptitude, residents have suffered."

I fought not to show my shock. Gloria apologising! Whatever next? I didn't dare to nod in agreement, though.

"The trustees and I have agreed that you should be offered a trainee position with a view to becoming my deputy warden. It would mean a pay rise and, perhaps, longer hours. But you've been doing those lately and we'll work around the bus timetable."

Of all the things she could have said, I hadn't expected this. Now I'd have more say – or so I hoped – in what happened in the care home. I could help the residents. I couldn't wait to tell Joe, Mum and Gran. They'd be over the moon.

She gazed at me, looking puzzled. "Do you need time to think about it?"

I shook myself. "*No!* I'd love to accept."

She sank back into her chair. "I can't tell you what a relief that is. I need trusted people on my team – those who are prepared to stand up for what is right. To tell me the truth, no matter the consequence to themselves."

Tracey had said something along the same lines. That she much preferred the upfront me, rather than someone who said what she thought others wanted to hear. Although, like Gloria, Tracey hadn't appreciated my honesty until she'd had time to absorb the message.

Gloria grimaced. "There will be no further need for cameras, though. Is that agreed?"

I smiled. "Agreed." I got up to leave. "I'll get on now. That's unless I need to do anything?"

She patted the file. "I'll get that sorted."

As I headed to the door, a thought sprang to my mind. I hesitated. "This dance. Could Julia's residents join in? They might prefer it to sitting in the kitchen area if it's wet."

Gloria bit her lip. "Let me have a word with Julia. It depends on what she says."

I nodded. Julia was cautious and might turn down the

invitation. But, within moments of Gloria congratulating me for being frank, I was working on a devious plan. The nice worker in Julia's team, Angie, would be up for it. If I had a word with her, she'd encourage Julia to give it a go.

♦

Saturday afternoon soon rolled around. The residents had asked for the dance to be a dressed-up affair so I'd plastered a few posters around the lounge and reception area asking everyone to wear their Sunday best. Joe arrived in jeans an hour before the start, not wanting to dirty his suit while carting in his record player and soda stream, along with a basketful of cakes that his mum had baked for us. Once we'd set up a table in the corner of the lounge, he left us to get on.

I'd brought something special to wear – the emerald dress I'd bought in the charity shop. I didn't show it to Joe. I couldn't explain why, but I felt a bit bashful wearing such a glamorous thing. Elspeth and two of the new workers had agreed to stay for the party and we all got changed in the treatment room, moaning about the lack of mirrors.

When I hooked my straps over my shoulders, Elspeth shrieked, "You look fantastic!"

I ran my fingers down the silky material. "I wondered when I'd get the chance to wear this. It cost a fortune." Then I grinned. "A whole quid at the charity shop."

She gazed at me in envy. "Blimey! You lucky bugger."

Then she reddened. "Sorry, boss. I mean, well done."

Chuckling, I slid my feet into my kitten heels. No three-inch stilettos for me – we had residents to look after. If this afternoon went well, it could become a regular fixture.

We took it in turns to borrow Elspeth's compact mirror to apply our make-up, then set off to round up the residents. Some had got dressed in their finery before lunch – we'd used three times the number of napkins than usual to protect their clothes – but they still wanted to go back to their room to have a refresh or to apply a bit of lippy. I hadn't seen this much crimson lipstick and rouge in years. One or two had modelled themselves on Aunt Sally in *Worzel Gummidge*, but most looked amazing. I adored the transformation in them: not just their looks, but their excitement and giggles as they admired each other's outfits. They sounded no different to us when we'd got ready in the treatment room.

Joe knelt by the record player, looking incredible in a dinner jacket. He'd hooked up speakers around the room, which buzzed with anticipation. We'd given Freda a prime position near the food, with a clear view of the dance floor. As the first strains of music sounded, her eyes lit up with delight and she clapped her hands.

Looking every inch to the manor born, Alice chivvied the more able residents onto the dance floor, pairing up ladies – we had more ladies than men. Dapper in his suit, Wilf waltzed past with one of the women who haunted the reception area. I beamed at him until Alice tapped my shoulder.

"What are you doing standing there? You should be on the dance floor with your beau."

"Bow?" I frowned.

She jerked her head towards Joe. "Your beau!" she repeated, sounding exasperated.

Then my attention was taken by a kerfuffle behind us. I turned to find Mr Trott and Mr George being led in by Angie.

"You made it!" I patted two free chairs for them, but Mr Trott pulled himself free and headed into the throng.

Leaving Angie to settle Mr George, I went to join my chosen beau. Mr Trott beamed with delight as I took his hand, and we did a slow turn of the dance floor. Alice spun into view – in Joe's arms.

"Well, you didn't want him," she said and twirled away.

Outside, rain splattered against the patio doors but indoors there was a cosy glow. When Mr Trott and I glided around on our second circuit, I spotted Julia standing beside a group of chairs on which Mrs Calam and two other residents sat, jigging in delight. I'd never seen such joy on her face, even though we knew how much she loved to hear music on her radio. I turned back to Mr Trott, who hummed to himself. It seemed as if he'd been transported to another time – perhaps one before his beloved Lindy had died. But whatever memory he was thinking of, it was wonderful to see the years falling from his face.

Alice grasped my hand, making it clear that I should switch places with Mr Trott.

"How lovely to see you again, Fred."

Mr Trott gave her an uncertain smile but allowed her to sashay off with him, leaving me with Joe. He pulled me close and kissed the top of my head. I moved closer, enjoying his warmth and the scent of his new aftershave. If we didn't have an audience, I'd be doing a bit more than nuzzling into him...

"You look beautiful," he breathed. "The belle of the ball."

I chuckled, mimicking Alice. "And you look quite the beau yourself."

Some things might have changed, but I thought I'd always be one to duck from compliments, even though I secretly liked them.

Joe ran his finger down the side of my face and gazed at me. I swam in the depths of his blue eyes. How had I managed to find such a wonderful man? He'd given so much to me, and to all these people.

He sounded hesitant. "I know we haven't been together long. But I can't imagine being with anyone else. You're so selfless and kind. I've never felt this way about anyone." His eyes sparkled. "I know I could wait months or a year to do this, but I know my feelings won't change." He took my hands in his. "I love you so much, Bee. I'm not usually one to rush things, and we don't have to – if you agree, we'll take it at your pace – but I want to show you how much you mean to me."

Flummoxed, I stood there as he strode over to the record player and turned down the volume. He came back, a strange expression on his face – nerves? – and reached into his jacket pocket. To my surprise, he got down on one knee. There were gasps as he opened the box to reveal a gorgeous sapphire and diamond ring.

"Belinda Swift. Would you do me the honour of becoming my wife?"

Tears shone in my eyes. Happy tears. "I would love to."

I couldn't believe it. He'd proposed to me in front of everyone. We wouldn't get married soon – not for a year, maybe more. We had a long road ahead of us. Just knowing that the man I adored would be part of my journey made me cry with happiness.

Around us, the residents clapped and cheered, while Freda gripped Gloria's hand. They beamed at me. Along with Joe, I had these people to thank for showing me the true meaning of life. None of them had cared much for their previous jobs. Instead, they spoke about their families, the opportunities they had missed to see each other more, to make the most of each other. Sometimes they spoke about the war and the impact it'd had. Of course they would. It was a huge deal for their generation. Many of them had lived through two wars, with some, like Peter, losing their whole family. To think, in a decade or two these people would be dust and their memories gone forever. But I'd never forget them and what they'd taught me, especially Freda and her wily friend, Alice, whose jubilant voice cut through my thoughts and the excited chatter. "Isn't his surname Good? No more Bee Swift!" Alice hooted with glee. I groaned.

She held up a plastic cup filled with ginger beer. "Let us all raise a toast to the future Mr and Mrs Good." She gave me a wink. "To our new deputy warden, who has worked so hard on our behalf and who can teach us oldies a thing or two."

Alice raised her cup in my direction and paused for effect. I glanced at Joe, who wore a wider grin than Alice's. He knew where this was heading.

I did too.

"Everyone…" Alice laughed. "The future Mrs Bee Good."

# Other books by Sharley Scott

**Maddie Meadows Series:**

The Two Lives of Maddie Meadows

The Gift of a Rose

**The Devon Seaside Guesthouse series:**

Bedlam & Breakfast at a
Devon seaside guesthouse

B&Bers Behaving Madly at a
Devon seaside guesthouse